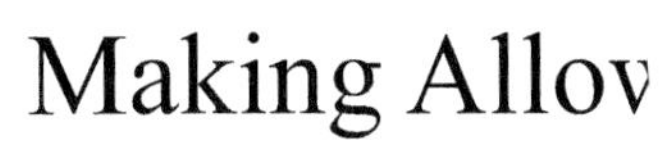

By

Charlie De Luca

This is a work of fiction and any similarity to any persons living or dead is entirely coincidental.

www.charliedeluca.co.uk
Edited by My Cup Of Tea

To my family with love x

Prologue

Finn was simmering with rage and indignation. Bloody Boothroyd was as mean as muck and twice as nasty. He continued to sweep the yard savagely, his frozen fingers grasping the wooden broom handle so tightly, he could feel the grain of the wood bite into his palm. The trouble was that Boothroyd had power over him, something the older man took great delight in rubbing in. As a seventeen year old conditional jockey, Finn had worked his way up from being a stable lad and thought he'd made it when the local trainer watched him ride out and said he'd be willing to take him on as a conditional.

But nothing had worked out so far. He lived in a dirty caravan in the back of the yard. His home was some six or so miles away and as he had no transport, it made sense to live in. His parents were angry about his choice of career and thought he should be an accountant like his father, but Finn knew he would shrivel and die working in an office and besides, he loathed and detested anything to do with maths. Instead, he loved to feel the wind in his hair with several tons of horse flesh beneath him, the smell of mud mingled with horse sweat, adrenalin pumping through him, as together, man and beast, they flew through the air over fence after fence. Besides, he was a good rider and could be an excellent jockey given half a chance. He had an affinity with horses, they instinctively trusted him and were eager to please.

He had just three stables to go and then he could go back to his damp caravan and sleep, a deep and dreamless sleep. Then he would be up at half five tomorrow and the work would start all over again. Mac, the Scottish Head lad would still be drunk and Darren, one of the other stable staff, would still be too stupid to know any better. And he would still be light years away from his dreams. One consolation was Rosy, a recent employee with a warm smile and a deep attachment to the horses, who looked warily at both Mac and Boothroyd and was at least an ally for Finn. But she would be gone in a couple of weeks, like all the rest, just as soon as she had worked out how Boothroyd operated.

Finn's shoulders were aching from the hours of physical graft; it was Rosy's day off, Mac was holed up with Boothroyd drinking and Darren was off sick. Finn recognised him as the type of lad who was, as his father would say, 'a sandwich short of a picnic', with a neglectful family. Just the sort of lad Boothroyd could bully and manipulate. Whereas Finn did have a decent family but was too proud to limp back home and admit defeat. It occurred to him that Boothroyd had probably sussed that out too, in the same way that he had realised that Darren had no one in his corner. He felt anger course through him as it dawned on him that he was doing the work of four stable hands and it wasn't the first time he had been forced to do it.

Worse in his book, he had only had two proper rides to date and the promise of a decent apprenticeship, with a view to becoming a professional jockey, seemed further away than ever today. Another problem was that Boothroyd was also supposed to pay him regularly, not that he had done so far or pay his expenses. He was owed three weeks wages and had yet to see a penny of the monies he had spent on new breeches, boots, a helmet and a body protector. He had asked Boothroyd several times, only to be fobbed off on each occasion.

He had to sort it out, the sooner the better otherwise he'd be destitute. He spread out the straw in the final stable and topped up the water bucket and moved Silas, the huge grey chaser, back into his clean box for the night. He patted the horse, removed his headcollar and glanced at the house. It was a huge grey, untidy place, where Boothroyd lived alone ever since his wife had turned tail and run. There was a light flickering in the kitchen window. Righteous anger coursed through him. The mean bastard! Not only was he withholding money, he worked Finn like a slave and refused to take his responsibilities as a guvnor seriously. He gave Silas one last pat, pulled up his collar against the cold and mentally rehearsed his speech, as he made his way up to the front door of the farmhouse.

He lifted the brass fox door knocker and released it. The sound echoed from within. He listened for any signs of life, felt relief and nearly walked away back to his caravan and the oblivion of sleep. But then he thought about how little money he had, of his aching muscles and the look of satisfaction on his father's face when he turned up back home, all his dreams of being a jockey having dissolved like a snowman in summer. He needed to sort this out **now**. Old Boothroyd would realise he meant business and was bound to stump up the money and whilst he was at it, he'd talk to him about the way he was treated. It was time to show Boothroyd he couldn't be pushed about. He'd get a few more rides and then be able to move on. The place was a joke anyway, all the owners were cronies of Boothroyd, and the horses were poor quality. He could do much better. He lifted the knocker again, higher this time and rapped the door five times in quick succession. This time he heard a distinct shuffling noise, the hall light came on and Boothroyd pulled open the door.

He was clutching a Scotch bottle and the alcohol fumes were enough to nearly floor Finn.

'Oh, it's you. What do you want? Have you finished those ruddy stables yet?' Boothroyd scowled into the darkness.

'Yes, Mr Boothroyd, I have.' Finn looked him in the eye. 'But I was wondering if I could have the money you owe me for my riding gear. I'm sick of being the only one who does any work around here, too. I came here to be a jockey not a stable lad.' Finn pushed out his chest. It was now or never. Some invisible force seemed to drive him on. 'And I think it's about time you treated me with a bit more respect…'

Boothroyd raised his eyebrows. 'Oh, you do, do you?'

'Yes, I do. I have done all the work today and it's not the first time. And what about the wages you owe me as well as expenses for travelling?'

Boothroyd glowered at him in disbelief, but once unleashed, Finn found that the words tumbled out of his mouth and he was unable to stop them. 'And if I don't receive the money, I'll have no alternative but to complain to the Authorities about you.'

Finn was about to continue when Boothroyd lunged at him. He was old and drunk, but he had been a boxer in his youth, and he had the element of surprise. Finn was seventeen, and although fit, he was very slim and was taken aback. He was floored by a left hook to his jaw.

'You useless, little, jumped up, good for nothing piece of shit… complain to the Authorities will yer? Yer worth nowt and you're nowt wi'out me, and don't yer forget it! You useless article!'

This was swiftly followed by several brutal kicks from the trainer's steel capped boots and finally Finn looked up to see Boothroyd lifting his arm which held the whiskey bottle, felt a sharp, searing pain and everything went black.

'God, Finn, what happened to you?' He felt like he was in a deep pool and swimming up to the surface then slipping back again to where the sounds were muffled, and the brightness dimmed. It was peaceful down there and part of him badly wanted to stay. But a sound kept intruding into his consciousness. He felt irritated at having his peace disrupted.

‘Finn, Finn open your bloody eyes. Who did this to you, bloody Boothroyd?’

Finn raised his eyelids and saw blue eyes set in a freckled face, framed with auburn hair. It was Rosy. Her face was creased with concern. His ribs were so painful, it was as though they had been through a garlic crusher, his head was pounding, and the cold had seeped into his bones. He had never been so pleased to see someone in his life as he was to see Rosy at that moment. Her freckled face was wreathed with kindness.

‘I only came back to get me things, good job I did. I’m calling the police, right now. Don’t worry, I’m off to work at Hollings, and they’re looking for a conditional. You can come too.’

She fished out her ‘phone. If Finn could have physically managed it, which he couldn’t, he would have kissed her. Instead, he sank back onto the frozen ground and waited as Rosie held his hand.

Chapter 1

It wasn't everyday he started a new job, especially one where he felt blisteringly envious of his clients, Finn McCarthy thought, but there it was. That was how he felt. *They* were starting out as jockeys, and *he* had just ended his career as one. They were full of anticipation, whereas he was going to be getting his kicks by living vicariously through them, guiding and mentoring them, like some desperate old has been. He picked up his running pace, hoping that the extra effort might rid himself of his gloomy thoughts. Finn was dressed in the standard uniform of a health conscious thirty something jogger, trainers, sweatpants and sweatshirt, which was darkened with perspiration. His hair was sable-black, curly and worn to his collar, his eyes were the deep colour of molten chocolate. Even this early in the morning, he cut a pleasing figure. His features were even and just saved from being too perfect by the hollow cheeks and the slight bend in his nose which was the result of a disagreement with a large grey gelding called Smugglers' Cove. He had lost the argument when his horse deposited him into a fence at Kempton, breaking his nose in the process. Still, it was a minor injury, considering the broken ribs, collarbones, legs and ankle he had sustained in his racing career.

National Hunt racing was a notoriously dangerous sport, but he still missed it like hell, the camaraderie, thrills, spills and the amazing high that winning generated. For a second, he felt utterly bereft, almost as though he'd had an arm amputated or become paralysed, when he thought about the life he'd had to leave behind. Then, he berated himself. He had a new career now and it was a fantastic opportunity to be a jockey coach. It was an important role. He knew from his own bitter experience how important it was to have a good guvnor and to be well supported as a conditional. It could either make or break a young jockey's career. For a second, he was transported back to a time where he was in such physical pain he almost passed out, from his injuries. Injuries inflicted by his boss. He was a man who promised him the earth and left him with serious wounds and, worse, profound psychological scars, which he still bore. He shook his head angrily, in an attempt to banish the memories. He vowed he would give his new role everything he had, so his lads and lasses had the right support, the support that he had so desperately needed when he was starting out. Right on cue, his mobile buzzed and he fished it out of his pocket. Finn stopped and caught his breath before answering.

'McCarthy.'

'Hi, it's Sam Foster. I have been assigned to you under the conditional jockey scheme. You left me a voicemail.'

The lad sounded young and slightly nervous, which fitted with the impression he had gained of him from his profile report.

'Yeah, that's right. We need to meet up and go through some paperwork. When are you free?'

The lad went through his engagements which were few and far between.

‘I’m racing at Wetherby on Wednesday, in the half past two race, if that’s any good, or you could see me at the guvnor’s? Whichever is easier.’

Finn hesitated then decided he didn't want to miss out on seeing the young man ride at the racecourse. Racing nerves could reveal deficits in the lad’s riding and give a more accurate picture than watching him ride at home.

‘Let’s meet up at Wetherby in the Owners’ and Trainers’ bar after your race at about four?’

Sam sounded a little uneasy, as though he hadn’t anticipated his mentor seeing him ride even before they had officially met. He hesitated but only for a second.

‘Yeah, OK. I’ll see you then.’

Finn grinned making a mental note to look up the race and Sam’s mount in some detail. Wetherby had been one of his favourite courses and it would be a great opportunity to study Sam’s riding and get a feel for the areas he would need to work on. He felt a sudden burst of optimism, his previous thoughts dispersed like the sun coming out from behind a cloud. It wasn’t as good as riding himself, but an afternoon at his favourite racecourse, immersed in the world of racing would be the next best thing.

Wetherby was nestled in West Yorkshire, a friendly racecourse and the scene of many of Finn’s victories. It was a cold, frosty day but there was a glimmer of sunshine which lit up the fiery reds and molten yellows of the trees, a reminder that autumn had not yet faded. He drank in the atmosphere, the clamour of voices, the pungent smell of distant cigars as the racegoers began to file in and felt it envelop him like a comfort blanket. He saw several familiar faces, stopped to chat with a couple of trainers he knew, and began to settle down in anticipation of a good day's racing. He had researched his conditional, Sam Foster, and was looking forward to meeting him later.

He drank in the sights and sounds of the meeting. There was a cluster of bookies, smart women wearing thick coats and gloves to combat the cold weather and the usual mix of punters, some slick young men in tight fitting, shiny suits and young women shivering in the cold. They mixed with older camel coated men wearing trilbies, carrying copies of the Racing Post under their arms with a look of experienced gamblers about them. He noticed the slim, stable staff and acknowledged some old hands he knew by sight. However, his eyes were drawn to an unusual sight. He noticed with wry amusement, that there was a group of school children, aged about nine or ten, who were dressed in racing colours. He was close enough to hear that they were having a short lesson on the rudiments of handicapping by an attractive woman. What would they think of next? Still, if it inspired the next generation's interest in racing, it had to be a good thing. The young woman had wavy auburn hair, held in place by a furry headband. She was wearing a long black coat adorned with a pink and red flower brooch made of felt. It gave her an arty, stylish look. Three of the boys were messing around circling and flogging their pretend horses with imaginary whips, their jockey silks glinting in the sunlight. They careered wildly about the place, almost falling into Finn.

'I'm so sorry,' the woman said. 'Now Kyle and Martin, mind where you're going. You nearly ran into that man.'

The taller of the two boys shouted, 'But, miss, I'm gonna be a jockey when I grow up, so I need to practice.'

Finn looked him up and down, but the boy was easily one and a half heads taller than his peers.

'I'm not sure you'll make a jockey. I think you're going to be a bit too tall.'

The effect was instantaneous. The boy frowned and hunched his shoulders as huge tears began to fall. 'It's not fair, I luuve horses…'

At least that was what Finn thought he said, it was actually quite hard to understand above the boy's wracking sobs. The other boy, Martin, continued to canter about oblivious.

The young woman was at the child's side in an instant, managing to both glower at Finn and soothe the youngster at the same time. Finn looked on, his throat full of remorse that he had no idea how to express. The woman's gaze was withering.

'I, er, look I never meant…' he managed.

'Listen, what weight do jockeys have to ride at?'

'Oh, ten or eleven stone for jumps and eight stone or less for the flat…'

The woman nodded. 'So, in theory, if he was tall but very slim, it would still be technically possible?'

'Yes, I suppose so…' Finn thought it would not be wise to explain that anorexic or bulimic jockeys were not likely to have much longevity in the sport. It seemed churlish to point this out whilst the child continued to sob and howl.

The woman squatted down to the child's height. 'Do you hear that, Kyle? As long as you're tall but very slim then there is no reason why you can't follow your dreams. You can be a jockey if you really want to be!'

The boy looked up, his eyes full of hope.

'Really?'

The woman silenced Finn with an icy stare.

'Yes, as long as you make the weights.' Kyle looked hopefully at Finn.

'How do you know?'

'Well, I used to be a jockey so that's how I know.'

The young woman studied him. 'Amazing. Isn't that interesting boys?'

He looked into the green eyes, the colour of fresh moss, which were bright with intelligence, but which were wary, like she was evaluating him and was undecided about the verdict.

'Did you ever ride in the Grand National?' asked a small girl in yellow and red colours that swamped her. 'Me dad and nan always have a bet on that.'

Finn thought about his particular experiences of that race. He had ridden in it three times, had a second place in one outing but it was still his last ride that stuck in his memory for all the wrong reasons, as it turned out.

'A few times actually…'

The young woman's expression softened slightly.

'Why aren't you riding today?' persisted the little girl.

'Well, I teach jockeys these days, instead…'

'Oh,' the girl replied.

The woman gave Finn a professional smile that didn't quite reach her eyes. She was obviously keen to get away. He felt about as welcome as a dose of influenza in a hospital ward.

'Now, that's enough now children. We'll let you enjoy the rest of your day.' She rounded up the children before turning back and nodding briefly.

Finn watched the colourful procession as they made their way down to watch the race, but his gaze was drawn by the vibrant young woman as her coat flapped in the breeze. God, what an idiot! He had only tried to be realistic with the lad about the likelihood of him becoming a jockey and he managed to cause a riot and crush a child's dreams, none of which was likely to endear him to the most attractive woman he had met in ages. Glumly, he recalled the woman's suspicious expression and realised that he was seriously out of practice at talking to the opposite sex.

Sometimes he did miss being in a relationship, but he hadn't made the effort recently to get out and meet people. He told himself that he wasn't yet ready, his wounds had not fully healed. Still, when your fiancée ran off with your best friend, it had the effect of making you very wary of the opposite sex and your ability to choose friends.

He studied his racecard and had a couple of small bets. This was a luxury in itself, as jockeys who have an active licence are not allowed to bet. The bookmaker, Thomas Dunn, squinted at Finn, his eyes widening in surprise.

'Now then, Finn. How are you doing? Long time, no see. How's retirement?'

Finn grinned back. 'Well, I work for the BHA now, mentoring conditional jockeys, in fact that's why I'm here. I'm working with Sam Foster who rides for Henry Teasdale.'

'Oh, great. I've heard of Henry, but not Sam. I'll keep my eye out for him, though.'

They exchanged pleasantries, Finn pocketed his slips and found a good spot to watch the next race from.

Sam was riding Saffron Sun for Henry Teasdale. Finn was surprised that the horse was the clear favourite, but heartened as this probably meant that Henry had a lot of faith in the lad. Still, as he had ridden under twenty winners, he could claim a weight allowance of up to ten pounds, which was probably enough to shorten the horse's odds to favourite, even considering the lad's inexperience. He was up against more seasoned lads such as Danny Doyle, someone that Finn had noticed was showing real promise, and the ex-champion jockey, Richard Egan. He watched the horse, a well-built dark bay, in the parade ring and saw Sam in the owner's blue and black colours. Sam was a slight, rather tall, young man who was baby faced, but at nineteen, that was hardly surprising. He recognised the tall patrician looking trainer, Henry Teasdale and recalled that he lived and worked locally and had a yard of about fifty or so horses. He had met Henry a few times and remembered he was rather posh and a bit distant. A bit of a cold fish, he had always thought. He wondered how Sam was finding working with him.

The race got underway and Finn trained his binoculars on the young man, watching his every move. With one circuit to go he was handily placed in about sixth in the pack and appeared to have carefully positioned his horse so that he had enough space to make a run in the final furlong. Apart from one fence, where the horse got slightly on top of the jump and should have been corrected by his rider, everything was going well. Coming up to the final three fences, Sam managed to find some space and moved his horse up the field, so that he landed over the second last in second place. The crowd started to roar, and were on their feet, as the jockeys stood poised and began positioning themselves and their mounts, raising their whips and rocking backwards and forwards, as in a blur of colour, mud and sweat, Saffron Sun edged forward, and Mulberry Bush pulled ahead into the lead. Sam and Saffron Sun began their final run. Finn was willing Sam to keep going and push to the finish post as the two horses fought it out. Mulberry Bush was beginning to tire, and Sam kept up the pressure, riding out strongly to win by a short head.

Finn felt a myriad of emotions, great envy and elation mixed with genuine admiration. It was a pretty good performance from the lad, and he looked forward to telling him so later. He had wondered whether or not he might need to do a course walk with Sam and explain how he should have ridden each fence, but that clearly wasn't needed. He followed the horses into the winner's enclosure. Sam looked delighted, the trainer barely raised a smile, but the owners, a middle aged couple with suntans and too much gold jewelry, scowled, especially at the jockey. Finn checked his racecard and noted that the owner's named was J. West. Jimmy West, was an owner Finn knew well, having ridden for him several times. He had aged since Finn had last seen him and gained a substantial amount of weight, was louder than Finn remembered him, and was wearing even more gold, a heavy bracelet, two sovereign rings, topped off by a rich brown sunbed tan. He was known for being a self-made millionaire, a native Yorkshireman, with a prospering international haulage business. The body language between the owner and jockey seemed rather tense, a little off key, Finn noticed. Perhaps, West had expected the horse to win by a larger margin and felt that Sam had almost left it too late? Still, a win was a win, after all.

Finn was amused to hear Sam being interviewed in the winner's enclosure by the course presenter and journalist, Tim Giles. Finn hoped the young man would be able to cope with this. Finn had not had the opportunity to discuss the do's and don'ts of dealing with the media.

'Congratulations Sam, well ridden. Talk us through your ride on Saffron Sun.' Tim had a well-modulated and fruity voice which was why he was asked to double as a racecourse presenter. Finn knew him slightly and the received wisdom was that Giles was a sound journalist, fair and well informed.

Sam hesitated a little and then said. 'Oh thanks, he gave me a great ride you know, kept going right to the end. He's a really game horse.'

'And I gather that Henry Teasdale has the winner's half-brother, Sun God, at his yard in Walton. How's that one shaping up? Is he likely to emulate his half sibling?'

There seemed to be a smile in Sam's voice. 'Oh, he's doing really well, working great at home, we're really hopeful about him too.'

'Right, we'll look out for him. Anyway, well done again, Sam.'

Not bad, thought Finn, breathing a sigh of relief. He had acquitted himself well.

Tim went on to interview Henry Teasdale and the loud and brash Jimmy West, the winning owner and trainer. Finn noticed that West appeared to have recovered his equanimity and was all smiles for the press.

Finn picked up some winnings, met lots of acquaintances and an old trainer friend Eddie Machin, and was so involved in talking about the 'old days' that he was almost late to meet Sam. He glanced at his watch, made his apologies and hurried off in the direction of the Owners' and Trainers' bar. It was tucked away, well behind one of the stands. The crowds were beginning to thin out as drizzle was falling and the last race approached. The light had faded very quickly. As he hurried, he saw a small huddle of racegoers peering at a figure slumped on the floor. He was about to walk straight past when he noticed that a woman in a black coat was bent over the figure. He recognised the curly, auburn hair immediately. It was the attractive woman with the school children, although her charges were being led away by a man, their heads in their jockey caps bobbing, as they craned their necks to look back at the scene.

Finn elbowed his way through and saw that the figure was wearing breeches and riding boots, topped off with a smart tweed jacket. Closer inspection revealed that the young man was bleeding heavily from his nose but judging by the way he was clutching his ribs, this was the least of his problems. Finn would know that face anywhere as he had studied it closely enough within the last couple of hours. It was Sam Foster.

The woman looked up and seemed relieved to see him. Finn took in Sam's bruised face.

'What the bloody hell happened, Sam? I was just on my way to meet you.'

The woman stood up. 'Look. Can you help me with him? He's been badly beaten up and is a bit dazed. I haven't been able to get any sense out of him actually.'

Finn grabbed one of the staff who was checking the badges for the enclosure. 'Can you get one of the medics or St John's ambulance staff right away? He's been hurt and needs to be checked over.'

The man took one look at the young jockey and hurried off.

Finn crouched down besides Sam. 'Can you move everything, is anything sore or broken?' The young man shook his head, began to make a strange gurgling noise in his throat and promptly vomited all over the tarmac.

Chapter 2

Once he'd been sick, the young jockey seemed to revive a little.

'Look, I don't want any fuss, no doctors, nothing…' The faint voice managed to sound resolute.

He struggled to his feet, chest bent over his torso, but Harriet still noticed how his pointed chin jutted out and she could sense his determination. However, he kept looking round him. Harriet knew a scared lad when she saw one.

The ex-jockey who she'd talked to earlier, gave her a look of entreaty. 'Listen, could you help me get him to my car? I can patch him up there and then find out what the hell happened.'

Harriet felt irritated that he was there after their earlier encounter. He clearly had absolutely no rapport with children but at least he had an air of authority about him, someone who people would listen to, who could command respect. He also looked vaguely familiar, she realised. And he was someone who made young children cry, she thought wryly.

'Yep, no problem. I'm Harriet Lucas by the way but everyone calls me Hattie. I work for the Racing to School Charity. You?'

'Finn McCarthy,' he said holding onto one of the jockey's arm and guiding him gently away. Hattie took his other arm and as they walked, fumbled for a hankie so the lad could hold it over his bleeding nose. Fortunately, the racegoers began to lose interest as the announcer ran through the runners and riders for the next race. Hattie called to her colleague, a sandy haired man who was hovering nearby, trying to keep the children amused.

'Can you help the teachers get the kids ready to go home Bob? The bus will be here to take them back to school in about five minutes.'

'Yeah, no problem.'

At a slow pace, Hattie and the stranger managed to escort the lad back across the path, along by the parade ring and out towards the exit and car park.

'Come on Sam, you're doing grand,' said Finn, every so often. Twice they had to stop whilst Sam got his breath and rest before hobbling further. Every so often Sam winced and made muffled cries of pain.

'You were with the kids in the racing colours, weren't you? Will the kids be OK without you?'

Hattie leaned forward to answer, feeling weird talking across the injured young man.

'Yeah. I arranged for my colleague Bob to sort everything. He's a good sort. Now where's your car?'

Hattie was glad that they were hardly noticed as most race goers were still at the course. Even the people who inspected the tickets had left their posts, so overall, they attracted very few curious glances despite their odd errand.

'Down there, silver Audi,' Finn told her.

They led Sam across the grass towards the car.

Finn clicked the key fob and they helped Sam, panting, into the passenger seat of what Hattie could see was a very swish, new car.

'Now lad,' said Finn, passing Sam a hip flask, 'have a tot of this before you tell me what happened.'

Hattie wondered if she should make her excuses and go back to help Bob, but both men seemed happy for her to stay for the time being. She was wary of Finn, but the young lad's situation had got to her and she was curious. She crouched down by him, like Finn and set about rummaging through her handbag for useful items, tissues, paracetamol and antiseptic wipes. It wasn't every day that an unusual event came her way. Hattie had noticed how the ex-jockey was well dressed but older than she had first thought, judging by the fine lines around his eyes. Quite good looking too, in a craggy sort of way.

Through shuddering breaths, Sam told his story. 'I was thrilled to get the win… really pleased...but then these two guys came up to me, said they wanted a word and then next minute they started hitting me. Must have put their money on another horse or something…'

Finn nodded towards the hip flask indicating that Sam should take another slug. Then he strode around to the driver's door, inserted the key and turned on the heater. Momentarily they all jumped as a blast of loud music, Pulp's Disco 2000, belted out.

'Crap music, mate,' said Sam with a grimace. 'You should get yourself something decent.'

Finn turned off the device which Hattie noticed allowed tracks from an MP3 player to be played. All mod cons she thought, not like her old beat up Polo. She slipped two painkillers out of the packet and offered them to him. Sam swallowed them, a tiny smile showing his thanks. Finn's expression was thoughtful.

'Hmm. I saw the race. You gave Saffron Sun a great ride, I was really impressed. More importantly, did you know either of the guys, would you recognise them again?'

Hattie leaned forward, keen to hear the next bit. She was naturally a curious person and she was very intrigued. It felt like the beginning of a Dick Francis novel. Sam took a deep breath and a look of hopelessness washed over him.

'No. They had caps on with the peaks pulled down, so I couldn't really see them.' He frowned as he tried to remember. 'Youngish, strong, big feet…' He shrugged and then winced in pain.

'I see.' Finn's face was expressionless, but Hattie saw a muscle twitching in his cheek. No one spoke for a minute or two.

'Did they say anything?'

Sam shook his head. His expression was guarded, and he wouldn't quite look Finn in the eye. Hattie thought they must have said something, surely? People didn't just assault someone for nothing, did they? They had to have had a reason for hurting him, even if it was a robbery, it just didn't make any sense otherwise. Finn turned to look at her.

'Surely you got a look at who did it?' he asked.

Harriet shrugged. 'Not really, they were all dressed in black hoodies, two of them, both white…' She thought back for a bit. She had noticed the men loitering, they seemed to be waiting for someone,

Sam, she now knew. Was there anything else unusual about them? She needed to think hard.

The effort of talking seemed to have exhausted Sam completely. At least with the warm blast from the heating, he had stopped shivering. The sun was obscured by cloud and the temperature had dropped dramatically.

Harriet surveyed the young jockey. He looked limp with pain.

'Do you want me to check him over? I am a first aider…'

Finn nodded and stepped back.

Hattie leaned over Sam, who was now resting back in the car seat with his eyes closed.

'Did you hit your head?' She ran her hand gently over Sam's scalp and he shook his head.

'He shouldn't be concussed so that's good.' She gently pulled apart the jockey's tweed jacket and gingerly lifted his polo neck jumper. There were several raised red marks and Hattie guessed there would be some nasty bruises tomorrow. Clearly Sam had been kicked and beaten mostly on his torso. She prodded a bump and Sam yelped and sprung up out of his seat like an arrow released from a strong bow.

'God, I'm sorry! At least one cracked rib I'd say, think the nose is all right, otherwise he's not too bad…

'You've done this before?' Finn offered her the hip flask and Hattie took a quick sip.

'Yeah. I've two brothers who played rugby. One still does. I've watched my mother patch them up as they were both too 'macho' to go to the hospital. So, what are you going to do now? Go to the police?'

Finn looked thoughtful. 'Not sure, get Sam to a private doctor friend, maybe take him back to mine and then try to find out what's going on...' Hattie could tell that Finn was not satisfied with Sam's answers. Something odd was going on. Why would two men beat up a young jockey just after he had won a race? Maybe they had backed the wrong horse, but even so it was pretty extreme to attack the jockey of the winning horse. Still, it was none of her business, but she could point Finn in the right direction.

She smiled. 'Look, you could ask around. You never know. The kids here today were from the local school, they might have seen something. In fact, I'm sure nothing much would get past some of them actually. I could give you the number of the if you like and you could give them a ring?'

Finn frowned as he considered the idea. 'I don't think that's a good idea actually. I can't just rock up at a school and ask the children awkward questions, can I?' He gave her an appraising look. 'But you could, couldn't you? You already know them and would have a legitimate reason to contact them again. Surely, the children will need to write something about their day at the races and you're bound to be involved in that, aren't you?' He shrugged. 'And besides, I don't want to cause a riot. You may have noticed that me and children don't mix well…'

Hattie nodded. 'You could say that. I've never seen Kyle so upset about anything! You certainly know how to trample on a child's dream.'

Finn flushed and looked suitably embarrassed. Hattie enjoyed her moment of triumph and she wasn't about to let him off the hook, which was why she didn't tell him that Kyle's class teacher had told her that Kyle was impressionable and hypersensitive. Last week he was desperate to be a fireman when the school had a talk from the Fire Brigade and a policeman when the local PCSO had come in to talk about road safety. She thought about his request.

'Anyway, what makes you think I'd do that?' Hattie was curious.

'Because you're that sort of person, because I reckon you are someone who cares about justice and think that Sam should be celebrating his win, not nursing injuries...'

She glanced at Sam who looked pale and very young and felt a pang of sympathy. Finn was right, she was the sort of person who championed the underdog and the young lad looked so solemn and sad.

Finn fished in his pocket and pulled out a card.

'Look, if you find anything out from the kids then give me a call. OK?'

Hattie nodded with no real conviction. After all, it was not likely that she would be passing the local school anytime soon and she was meeting her friends later. She glanced at her watch. She had to get back home, have a quick shower and find something smart but casual to wear.

'It might be worth taking pictures of the injuries, you never know, you could need photographic evidence. Look, I have to go.'

Finn laughed. 'Good idea. Listen, thanks for your help, by the way.'

Even Sam managed a smile.

'OK, any time… you take care,' she called to Sam.

She had been horrified at the sight of Sam's injuries but intrigued in a bizarre way too. Instinctively, she knew that there was more to this incident than Sam was letting on, but she really didn't want to get involved.

Hattie ran easily over the grassy car park back to the racecourse, and along to one of the spectators' boxes which had been set aside for the Racing to School initiative. This was a charity and consisted of sessions at all racecourses for local school children. Classes and their teachers were invited to come free of charge, usually one class at a time and through a series of lectures and practical challenges, children were taught about racing in a way which linked into the mainstream curriculum. Pupils were taught about weights, how horses were handicapped, told about colours, racecards, and about how jumps were constructed. There was even a mechanical horse, the Equiciser, which sometimes Hattie could persuade a jockey to use to demonstrate balance and so on. Hattie presently worked for the initiative for a few days per week at several local racecourses and had done for the last couple of months. The rest of the time, she was training to be a dietician at university. She had her last placement to complete, a few exams and that was it. It wasn't her first choice of career exactly. She had wanted to be an athlete.

For several years she had competed in the modern pentathlon. She had been successful too and had been in the GB Junior team. But her form had dipped badly following an injury which had never quite healed and so her funding was cut, and she had decided to study instead. Then there was the episode with Dale, her coach, a charismatic figure who she was in thrall to. The less said about him the better. She would not go there today. Missing out on her sporting career was a source of profound disappointment for her and she had struggled to adjust to being a mere 'civilian'. It caused her to be moody, gave her endless hours to fill and resulted in the sudden loss of friends, as many of them had been fellow competitors. She had found it hard to find her niche until her parents, fed up with her attitude, had come home with prospectuses from several local universities. Reluctantly, she had flicked through them and saw the dietician course and decided that was the one for her. And so, she had taken life by the scruff of the neck and decided to retrain, specialising in sports nutrition. Now in her third year, she enjoyed her course, was almost qualified and looking for jobs. But she still desperately missed the thrill of competing though, so the little escapade today had lit her imagination.

Seeing that her colleagues had already left, Hattie checked her emails. She was due to work at Market Rasen the day after tomorrow and had an email from Bob, her colleague, suggesting an outline programme for the afternoon. She emailed him back, thanking him for sorting the kids out and explaining that she had stayed to help the injured jockey, but everything was sorted now. Then she checked the details from the school visit today. The class were eleven year olds from All Saints' Primary School outside Wetherby. Still, she had no intention of going there. Finn would help Sam and there was absolutely no role for her. She pushed the whole incident out of her mind. She'd probably never get to know why Sam had been targeted and she was unlikely to run into Finn McCarthy again and frankly she didn't care. After all that happened with Dale, she had made a vow to herself to stay clear of any trouble and getting involved with the injured jockey's case was certainly that. Besides, she was an all or nothing sort of person and once she was involved then there would be no going back and that had not worked out well for her in the past. She would leave well alone. She set off home, full of anticipation of her evening out, the memory of Sam's pale face and Finn's inept handling of Kyle, receding like the tide going out.

Chapter 3

Finn had rung an old doctor friend of his and arranged for him to have a look at Sam. Dr Jamieson was retired, Scottish, rather brusque and old fashioned, but Finn trusted him with his life and actually had done exactly that on many occasions. In his late sixties, the white haired, tweed suited man was a reassuring presence. His advice on soft tissue injuries and minor fractures had helped Finn heal far more quickly than he would have done visiting the local GP.

'Och, well there's nothing too serious, there's a couple of fractured ribs, other than that just cuts and bruises. I'll pop some sutures in the cut above the left eye, don't want to ruin your beauty, young man.'

Jamieson was also quick to note that these injuries were not from a riding accident.

'So, what happened to you, Sam?'

He had told him about the attack but did not give any further information than he already had. Jamieson had nodded, asked if the police were involved and what had provoked the attack. Sam had said almost word for word what he had told Finn. He was adamant that his attackers were not known to him and that there was no reason for the assault. He was equally clear that he did not want to involve the police or the authorities. Jamieson had looked at Finn and merely raised an eyebrow. Painkillers were prescribed, together with ice and lots of rest. Finn had offered to drop Sam off at Teasdale's, and hoped to find out more about the lad, though he made a decision not to ask any more questions about the beating. Sam needed a good night's rest, first and foremost. He did not want to probe as he wanted to leave Sam in a positive mood, thinking about the future.

'So, you've had ten winners, so by my reckoning, you're on target to ride out your claim which is great. How are you finding things at Teasdale's? Good guvnor?'

'Yeah, he's OK.'

'How about the owner, Jimmy West? He didn't look too pleased.'

Sam shrugged and then winced in pain. 'He was only annoyed as he thought I'd left my run too late, that's all.'

Finn took this in. His words were positive, but his body language said exactly the opposite. It was as though the lad was speaking the words of a play, but his heart wasn't in it. His real thoughts had seeped through into his body language, but Finn resisted the urge to pry further.

'Any areas that you particularly want help with? I can help you with the media, insurance, diet, injuries, positive mental attitude and all that. Have a think and when we next meet, we can work on it.'

He spotted an almost imperceptible nod from the young man besides him, as they drove through to Walton where Teasdale's yard as situated. It was pitch black as he swept into the yard. Finn helped Sam out of the car.

'Do you want me to come and talk to Teasdale and explain about what happened?'

The boy waved him away with his hand. 'Nah, you've done more than enough. Thanks.' They arranged to meet in a few days.

'OK, just make sure you get plenty of sleep.'

Finn drove off deep in thought. It was hard to shake off his feelings of foreboding. Back home he made some notes, ate a quick omelette and decided to take his own advice about having an early night. He was pretty sure that all was not well with Sam, but on the other hand the beating could have been to do with lots of different things. He was dimly aware of feelings of disquiet, but whether it was from his encounter with Sam or from echoes of his own experiences, it was hard to tell. Teasdale was probably alright, if a bit remote. He didn't want to overthink things, but even so unease gnawed away at him.

Next morning, he was feeling more optimistic. He dismissed the incident yesterday. He had wondered if Sam had just been targeted by a random, angry punter or maybe he was beaten up for some other reason. Maybe the attack was the handiwork of a jealous love rival, perhaps? He was probably reading too much into things, he decided, acknowledging that young men often argued for no good reason, sometimes with their own shadows, so he didn't want to overreact. He had wondered about Harriet Lucas and wondered if she would make contact. She was young and attractive, far too young for him, of course, and his blunt manner of speaking to the tall boy which unleashed such anguish, was hardly likely to endear him to anyone. It was just that it was a common enough problem; young lads desperately keen to be jockeys but consigned to a life as a stable hand if they didn't widen their horizons and get some qualifications. He thought that straight talking was often lacking but admittedly he shouldn't have been so brusque with the youngster. He thought back to his failed relationship with Livvy. The fall out had been horrific, he had been devastated for months and had been unable to shake off the feelings of loss. He had been doubly hit because she had run off with his so called best friend, Nat Wilson, and he felt as though his heart had been ripped out because he had lost his girlfriend and best friend in one fell swoop. Finn had tried to carry on with his head held high but when his alcohol consumption increased, and his form dipped as a result, his misery was complete. Well, not quite because Nat had even ended up taking over from him as stable jockey for Michael Kelly when his boss had finally had enough of Finn's poor riding.

So, Livvy and Nat had walked off hand in hand into the sunset whilst he was left humiliated, without a regular income. In a matter of months, he had become someone people crossed the street to avoid talking to. He didn't blame them, he was miserable and self-pitying. So much so, sometimes he bored himself. After a vicious fall, which left him with a smashed leg, retirement swiftly followed. He found himself at a loose end when he was approached by an old mate, Tony Murphy from the British Horseracing Authority, who was setting up the conditional jockeys' coaching scheme. He had been lucky to get the job and he really wanted to give it his all and repay the faith Tony had showed in him. He winced when he remembered just how low he had sunk, but it didn't do to dwell on this. Life was a game of snakes and ladders and you just had to climb as high as you could when you had the chance, and now was a real opportunity. So, Finn had kicked the drink, got his head straight and just wanted to move on with his life. He needed to concentrate on his new job and had no time for any distractions.

Finn went through the list of jockeys that he coached and rang a couple who were conditionals at yards relatively nearby and arranged to meet. Harry Jarvis answered straight away, but he had to leave a message for the other lad. He arranged to meet Harry later that day. Harry was eighteen, tallish, fair haired, ruddy faced and upbeat even though he had been struggling with his weight lately. Finn watched him ride out and jump a few hurdles and chatted to the trainer, Melvin Pike, who seemed to rate the lad, which was encouraging.

He waited for Harry to untack his horse and decided to tackle him about his weight issues.

'Have you thought of getting in touch with the PJA for advice?'

Harry shrugged. 'Nah. I've just been sweating and going to the sauna, that's all.'

Finn nodded, feeling frustrated. The Professional Jockeys' Association gave some good advice regarding nutrition and he felt this could really help the lad.

'OK, but it's worth making the time to look at the PJA advice. They are great on nutrition in general. You must have sufficient proteins and carbohydrate to give you energy and there are lots of food groups that you can eat with very little weight gain, salad and fruit are the obvious ones, but also pasta, if you eat it with very simple sauces. The sauces are easy to cook and much healthier than shop bought ones. There's loads of recipes on the website too. Nowadays, there's no need to starve yourself to get down to your riding weight.'

Finn studied the young man before him, noting his slightly jittery appearance and small pupils with concern. Harry was still growing and sometimes lads could be tempted to take drugs, amphetamines being the most obvious choice, to make the weights. Often these lads had the skills but simply grew too tall to become professional jockeys. Finn studied Harry's pupils, thinking that they were pinprick small which was concerning. He wondered how to address this potential problem and decided to try a direct approach.

He continued. 'I don't need to tell you that taking any form of drugs, amphetamines or anything of that nature is strictly prohibited not to mention a short term answer. If you have been using them then stop. Get in touch with the PJA nutritionists instead. And if you must have alcohol make it a gin and tonic rather than a bloody beer. What weight are you making now?'

Harry looked shocked at the mention of drugs but didn't deny having tried them. 'About ten and a half,' he muttered.

They went on to discuss the races Harry was riding in and his strategies. Harry rode for a competent trainer, he should have the weight advantage to be offered some decent rides, so he could ride out his claim with the fixed seventy-five winners required. Conditionals had until they were aged twenty-six to do this, so in theory Harry had a good chance of making it, even though he had only ridden six winners to date. He only hoped that he wouldn't resort to illegal substances in order to keep his weight down. He could easily get caught out in random drug testing and then he would face a lengthy ban, not to mention lots of adverse publicity.

Harry showed him around the yard, and they spent a pleasant hour or so admiring beautiful horses. Finn helped his young charge muck out stables and fill hay nets. Sometimes it was good to go back to basics and he enjoyed the earthy, fresh grass smells of the stable yard and the hard, purposeful physical exercise. He left in better spirits, noticing that Harry seemed more settled and had chatted in a much more relaxed fashion as he worked alongside him. The twitching had almost ceased, so much so, he began to doubt his earlier concerns. Still, it would do no harm to speak plainly to the lad.

His next call was to a nearby yard to see Connor Moore. Connor worked for a small trainer, Vincent Hunt, who trained pretty much adjacent to Henry Teasdale. Connor hadn't rung back and wasn't picking up his mobile, so Finn decided to call in on spec. The yard was quiet as it was only about two o'clock, so he missed the opportunity to see Connor ride out. Several horses bobbed their heads over the stable doors, all eyes trained on the newcomer as they blinked in the autumn sunshine. The yard looked clean and tidy but entirely empty. He wandered around to see if anyone was there and when he found no one, tentatively knocked at the front door of the farmhouse. A dog barked in the distance. The farmhouse was built of mellow stone and a glance through the window revealed that the place had a lived in, homely look. A large collection of wellies and shoes were gathered in an untidy pile near the front door. Eventually a pale teenaged girl of about fourteen or fifteen, opened the door wearing jodhpurs and a colourful Joules fleece. She raked her hand through long blonde hair and looked at him warily.

'Hi there. I've come to see your conditional jockey, Connor. I'm Finn McCarthy from the BHA…'

She nodded and attempted a smile. 'Oh. Mum is at a friend's and Dad's at the hospital.' She frowned, clearly struggling how much to say.

'And Connor?' he prompted.

The girl chewed her fingernail. 'Well, he's the one who is in hospital. Got run over in a hit and run last night…'

Finn took this in. 'OK.' Alarm swirled in his stomach. 'Where is he? I mean which hospital. Is he badly hurt?'

The girl shook her head looking out of her depth. 'Sorry. I'm not too sure. Dad was a bit stressed, that's all I know. He's there now…' The girl bit her lip. 'I wanted to go with him, but he said to stay and keep an eye on the place.'

Finn nodded. 'Does your dad have a mobile?'

The girl grinned suddenly. 'Well, he does, but he like NEVER has it on…' She shrugged. 'He doesn't get computers and technology. He'd rather rely on carrier pigeons than email.'

Finn laughed. He knew the feeling; he had been something of a Luddite himself until Livvy had bought him an iPhone and now he was hooked. He reflected wryly that he had all the time in the world to check out his ex's wonderful life on Facebook and hear how happy and delighted she was with his ex-best friend, Nat Wilson. He felt a spasm of the familiar pain and told himself sternly to belt up. At times, it was very hard indeed to avoid going over the same old ground in an endless loop.

'OK. I'll call the hospital. Thanks for your help.'

Finn pondered about what to do next as he felt his stomach rumble alarmingly. He drove into the village and came across a whitewashed pub next to the picturesque village pond. *The Yew Tree.* He decided to call in as some of the lads might drink in there and he figured he would find out just what was going on just as quickly. He considered his experiences of his job to date. Sam Foster had been badly beaten up, Harry Jarvis *may* have taken amphetamines judging by the size of his pupils and now Connor Moore had been injured in a hit and run. Were these random incidents or were they connected in some way? He decided to check on Sam's progress, tried his mobile and left a voicemail as he walked up the steps to the pub. This would be the local for many of the lads and lasses. He decided to keep his eyes and ears open at all times; all he had to do was remain alert. He felt growing unease about the fate of his conditionals and needed time to think. He thought back to his own experience at Boothroyd's and shuddered. He knew he owed it to Sam, Connor and Harry to find out what the hell was going on.

Chapter 4

Hattie's mobile was going crazy the next morning. She had enjoyed several drinks with her friend Daisy and was feeling slightly groggy. She had to work on an essay later and was planning on lying in, but it was clear from the insistent buzzing from her 'phone, that someone had other ideas.
Reluctantly, she picked up her 'phone and read the messages. There were four from her colleague at Racing to School, Bob.

Hi Hattie. Can you help me out? Head from the school yesterday on the war path, keen to get missing medication and 'phones left at the racecourse yesterday. Have stuff here but, can't take it as looking after the baby and missus has the car!

Damn! She owed Bob from yesterday and she could appreciate his dilemma today. She wondered which children had left their medication and 'phones. Who even took 'phones to primary school these days? She felt bad about abandoning Bob, so she texted him back asking for his address and swung the duvet over her legs with a sigh.

A couple of hours later, Hattie pulled up outside All Saints' Primary School near Wetherby. She had 'phoned ahead and been assured by the secretary that she could pop into the classroom to personally hand over the medication and 'phones. She grabbed the bag with the items and a couple of photograph albums featuring old black and white photos of the racecourse. She remembered from her brief chat with the fresh faced young teacher, that the pupils were doing some sort of local history project. As she made her way to the main entrance, following the 'visitor' signs, Hattie heard her 'phone ping. It was a twitter post from a racing journalist which linked to an article outlining the assault on Sam and bemoaning the state of security at racecourses if a young jockey could be beaten up. They were probably fishing for a story, since she imagined that Sam had remained tight lipped about what had happened. The next part of the article she read with more interest, as it added that Sam's jockey coach was 'the ex-champion jockey Finn McCarthy who had struggled latterly in his career and had recently retired.' It hinted at some sort of scandal but also congratulated him on his new job as a jockey coach. She *knew* that she had recognised Finn from somewhere and was curious about the implied fall from grace. She recalled his face and slightly crooked nose and air of authority. She felt a frisson of interest about the incident which was why she was here in the first place. Something just wasn't right. Sam had been too keen to put the attack down to disgruntled punters. There *had* to be more to it.

As she was shown into the classroom by a very smiley and garrulous secretary, Hattie instantly spotted several children she recognised. There was Kyle and Martin, sitting on the same table, pouring over exercise books and chewing the ends of their pens. They looked rather different having swapped their bright silks for navy school sweatshirts and grey trousers, though Kyle still looked as though he belonged in a different class given his height.

Ms Simmons beamed as soon as she saw Hattie.

'Thank the Lord. Kyle's mother has been on the war path about his iPhone and so have the other parents,' she hissed. 'You're a life saver!'

Ms Simmons clapped her hands. 'Look who's here to see us children? Say good morning to Ms Lucas.'

'Good morning Ms Lucas,' came the sing song greeting.

'Ms Lucas has very kindly popped in with the stuff you left behind and we're writing about our visit to the racecourse, Ms Lucas. Why don't you wander around and have a look? Year 6, let's see if you can impress her with your writing. So, ten more minutes to break time and I want this done by then. OK?'

Hattie grinned at the sea of bright eyed children and spotted Martin, Kyle and the little girl, Ella, who had quizzed Finn about whether he had ridden in the Grand National. She placed the bag with the 'phone and medication on the teacher's desk, indicating what they were, and then walked over towards Kyle's table. She leaned over and looked at the page of scrawled writing and read it.

'Great,' she said, crouching down beside Kyle and scanning his work. 'So, Kyle, your favourite bit of the day was seeing someone being beaten up?' She rolled her eyes, the bloodthirsty little terror.

'You weren't meant to write about that,' said a girl who sat in between Kyle and Martin. 'Do you remember me Miss? I'm Ella. My favourite bit was walking the course and seeing how the fences were made and meeting the nice jockey man.'

Hattie raised her eyebrows at that remark and Kyle gave her a filthy look. He clearly hadn't forgiven Finn for casually trampling upon his dreams and she certainly hadn't. Hattie glanced at the children's writing. Most of them had written a few sentences and several had started with the attack on Sam. In spite of herself, she found her curiosity piqued.

'So, do any of you remember anything about the men who attacked the jockey,' she asked in a low voice. Kyle stopped writing and chewed his pen.

Ella shrugged. 'They had black caps and trousers.'

'Yep, you couldn't really see their faces…' Kyle said after a bit.

'Blue Nike trainers and skull,' said another boy, seated on the other side of Michael.

The boy looked at Hattie's shoulder but not at her face. His face was devoid of expression.

'That's Reggie,' Ella told her. 'He remembers everything. Where was the skull, Reggie? Who had the blue Nikes?' She asked the boy in a high voice like someone talking to a much younger child.

Reggie stared ahead but pointed to the side edge of his left hand.

'Was it the same man who had the blue trainers?' she asked. Reggie nodded gravely.

Hattie was intrigued but desperate not to attract attention to herself, she rose and wandered around the rest of the classroom, making positive remarks about the children's work and smiling.

'Right class. Pens down. Line up for break.'

Hattie watched Ms Simmons with awe. As the children lined up and the teacher nodded to indicate that they should leave, Hattie couldn't help saying.

'You make it all look so easy. How on earth do you manage it?'

Ms Simmons's freckled face reddened. 'Well, they are being good today, you should have seen them in September. It's taken weeks of training and hard work to knock them into shape.' She gave a quick smile. 'They're good kids though and I love teaching, so that helps. Listen, do you want to grab a coffee with me. It's the least I can do, Kyle's mum had been on and on about his bloody 'phone so I owe you.'

'I'm surprised he is allowed one in school.'

Ms Simmon's shrugged. 'His mum insisted. He has anxiety issues and it calms him down knowing he can ring his mum if it gets too much. She asked for special permission from the Head.' She rolled her eyes. 'The boy is always upset, he needs an extra layer of skin, I think.'

Over coffee in the staffroom, Hattie asked about Reggie. 'He seemed a bit...' she racked her brains, but her hunch was that he had some sort of special needs.

Ms Simmons came to her rescue. 'Yes, I saw him talking to you. He doesn't usually speak much. He's autistic, struggles with writing and imagination but has a memory like an elephant. Never ask him about the rail network,' the teacher rolled her eyes, 'or how to get to any station. Amazing really. He's never wrong about anything.'

Hattie grinned as she took this in.

'So, any information from him is likely to reliable, is it?'

'Absolutely. Spot on, yes.'

So, Harriet reckoned one of the assailants must have had a skull tattoo on the side of his hand for definite. That might help Sam find out who had attacked him.

'I've got some cool photos. They're in the office with the secretary, she's just checking out with the parents, which ones we can use in the school newsletter.'

When Hattie looked blank the teacher added. 'Some parents don't want any pictures of their children to be accessible, so we ask for permission and check before putting them out into the public domain… but I'll send you the ones we use if you like?'

'Great, thanks. I can use them for the Racing to School website,' Harriet replied. She wondered if the photos might have anything on them that could help identify the attackers.

On her way home that evening, Hattie considered what to do with the information she had been given. The description of the trainers and Reggie's memory of the tattoo of the skull might all prove useful. The school photos could also shed further light on the culprits.

She fished Finn's business card out of her purse and contemplated her next step. She was uneasy about getting involved. Finn seemed a dour, blunt sort of character and she sensed that Sam was troubled by something. She was intrigued but hesitant to contact Finn. Hattie turned up the radio and sang along to something by Adele. Bugger it, she should get over herself. They could do what they wanted with the information, it didn't mean that she had to get involved. She was a sucker for a hard luck story it had been her undoing before now. She would just send Finn a quick text and leave it at that.

She'd reached the age of twenty-six and after several relationships had no current boyfriend. In the end, she had always been too busy training, men came and went but there'd been nothing majorly significant since Dale. Some of her exes were fellow athletes and very focused on their careers to the exclusion of all else. Selfish and hard, her mother would say. Sam had been attacked and needed support and even Finn seemed to need a friend. Like her, he had been a professional athlete and was probably having a hard time adjusting from an all-consuming career. She could relate to the strangeness of having a normal job, with no endless training, goal setting and psyching oneself up for competitions. When such a passion was taken away abruptly from your life, it was hard to adapt. She had been so sure that she was going to make it in the world of athletics, her career nosedive had left her reeling. Maybe Finn had felt the same too? Still, one quick text was all that was needed. She drew into the drive at home and pulled out her 'phone and sent it.

Home was back with her parents for now, in Walton. It did seem odd to be living there again after all the travel and time spent at competitions but when her career ended, it made sense. Her parents were easy going. Her father was a retired detective inspector and her mother, a part time English teacher. Hattie's older brother, Will, had followed their father into the police and her younger brother Dominic, Nic, as he was known was still at Uni. Will lived with his girlfriend Nuala and Nic was back and forth so just now it was just her and Mum and Dad. It suited Hattie, now in her final year of her course to study from home and of course, it made economic sense too.

Hattie stepped onto the drive of the Edwardian villa. Mum's Golf was there and a black four by four which she recognised as belonging to Dr Christopher Pinkerton, the local GP and family friend. Brilliant, Mum said he was coming to supper, she thought, her mood lifting. Christopher was extrovert, good fun and very well liked. He always reminded her of an aging and fatter Charles Dance, complete with the beautifully cultured voice too. Hattie had a real soft spot for him. Inside she was greeted by barks from the family dog, Jasper, a border collie, and by the gorgeous smell of chicken and herbs.

Dr Pinkerton or Christopher, as she was urged to call him these days was sitting at the kitchen table chatting away to her mother.

'Hello Hattie,' he called in his deep, actorish voice, 'your Ma's taken pity on poor old me…' He stood up to hug her.

'Oh, hello love, help yourself to a glass of wine and pour one for your father, he'll be down in a mo.' Her mother, Philippa, looked distracted and flushed, hovering by the oven, stirring pots and testing the rice

Hattie took a sip of Sauvignon Blanc. 'So, where's Honor then?' It could, thought Hattie, be anywhere as Christopher's wife was often on jaunts, shopping in New York, visiting exhibitions in London, taking in a few shows or looking up old friends. Dad always said that she had expensive tastes and had never settled into her role as the wife of a country GP. Honor was much younger than him, very beautiful and Christopher completely adored her. The two had no children which might have been a disappointment to them, although this was never talked about openly, as far as Hattie knew.

'Health spa, trying that new one… just opened up in Harrogate...back tomorrow, no doubt reinvigorated,' a note of bitterness entered his tone, 'and leaving me much lighter of pocket. And it's her birthday coming up soon, so we'll have to have a party. You're all invited of course.'

'Great. We'll look forward to it,' added mum.

Just then Dad walked in, he wore green cords and a grey cable jumper. Hattie thought he looked so much better since he'd retired. Poor Dad, the life of a detective had been hard work, long hours and without the luxury of being able to discuss your work too much with your family. But now he looked rested and much younger. He flashed Christopher a sharp look, quickly disguised. Hattie sensed he didn't quite like the way Christopher let himself into their family home and settled himself down to be fed at Philippa's generous table quite so often. But the two men got on well enough usually. Hattie handed him a full glass of wine.

'Thanks, sweetheart, had a good day?

Before she could answer there was a flurry of activity as Mum served the food. Suddenly starving, Hattie took several bites of chicken and rice.

'Hmm, this is great, Mum.' She looked at her father and in between eating told him about her day. 'I've just popped into a school in Wetherby. The children came to Wetherby Racecourse and left some stuff on the coach.'

'Oh, wasn't that where the jockey was beaten up?' Her mother was trying to support her daughter in her role at Racing to School and had taken to reading the racing sections of the daily newspapers.

'Yes, that's right.'

Christopher put down his knife and fork, his eyes betraying interest. 'When was this Hattie?'

'Wetherby, yesterday.' She took another sip of wine and encouraged by Christopher's obvious interest, ploughed on. 'Well the jockey, Sam someone, was beaten up before four, I think. He'd been riding in the two thirty. Me and this other bloke, his mentor Finn McCarthy, found him around then anyway.'

Christopher took a deep breath and rolled his eyes.

'Bound to be about something stupid. Bloody fools, all of them. Honestly the things I could tell you about the jockeys and stable staff hereabouts...mostly a bunch of Irish tinkers if you ask me… mad as hatters the lot of them and they never do as they're told.

They ride when they're injured and risk their necks every day of the week and expect me to pick up the pieces…'

Harriet was taken aback by the vehemence of Christopher's tone. For a split second his expression changed to one of sheer malevolence, quite unlike his usual jocular self. There were about twenty racehorse trainers' yards in Walton and Christopher would get to see lots of staff who worked in the industry. It was also well known that the doctor liked a flutter on the horses every so often and sometimes Dad had hinted that it was more often than not. Christopher would probably know an awful lot about their injuries, struggles with weight, their addictions and so on. Hattie had her own issues with weight and injuries as an athlete and Christopher had always been unfailingly kind and helpful. She frowned, he seemed uncharacteristically irritable now. The GP must have had a bad day. Her father cut in,

'So, Christopher, how's your betting going these days? Backed any winners lately?'

'Huh, not as many as I should have, Bob. Damned jockeys not doing what they're supposed to do. That Sam wasn't supposed to win yesterday.' He speared a piece of chicken quite viciously with his fork and took a big slug of wine. Hattie watched him, transfixed. Seconds later he seemed to recover himself and gave a grim smile. 'Lost my shirt but you win some, you lose some. Anyway, I've got some great tips for next week.'

Weird thought Hattie, helping herself to more rice, you'd almost think that Christopher was annoyed with Sam too. What had he meant when he said Sam wasn't supposed to win today? Christopher must have placed his money on another horse and lost it. Still, gamblers were like that, she supposed. Perhaps he had more of a problem than any of them realised? The thought unsettled her. Maybe she didn't know Christopher as well as she thought?

After a pleasant meal, she settled down to watch some new detective series on the TV. Her 'phone pinged with a message and she scooped it up. It was from Finn.

Great. There's more stuff going on. I could really do with talking it through. Meet you at the Horse and Hounds in York, Friday at 8? Keep it to yourself though.

Hattie nearly dropped the 'phone in surprise. She was intrigued, flattered but then annoyed by his presumption that she would be willing to 'talk it through' with him. Of course, he could just be hitting on her, but then she hadn't got that impression from him at all. The attack on Sam wasn't anything to do with her, she told herself over and over again, but then, who was she kidding? She had been there, she now had key information about the attackers, had soothed and examined Sam and had helped Finn walk him back to the car. Despite her best intentions, she had to admit she was involved and was very curious about what Finn had to say. She spent the next ten minutes or so googling Finn McCarthy and found that there was loads of articles about him. There were photos of a youthful Finn grinning from ear to ear with a trainer called Reg Hollins having won several important races including some at the Cheltenham Festival and the Welsh Grand National.

She knew she had recognised him and was impressed with his record. There were several images of him with another handsome jockey, who was listed as Nathaniel Wilson. They were grinning at each other in their brightly coloured silks with easy camaraderie and were described as the best of mates. Later articles showed Finn scowling at the camera with the headlines, 'McCarthy parts company with leading trainer Michael Kelly' and she began to read on. There was further speculation about McCarthy fighting with someone in the weighing room just prior to the Grand National a couple of years ago. A jockey, the same handsome chap Finn has been so friendly with, was photographed with an absolute shiner of a black eye, said to have been caused by a fall in the race, although there was no shortage of speculation as to the real cause. It was Nat Wilson, who had gone on to be the Champion jockey several times and was very successful. She remembered the incident of course, as it had been widely reported at the time and read on with horror as there were further articles in which the unravelling of Finn's career was reported in some detail. It seemed to her that Sam was not the only one with secrets.

Chapter 5

The Yew Tree was a pleasant enough country pub with a wide stone fireplace, beams and horse brasses. Finn ordered a half of lager, as he didn't have to worry about his weight anymore. He rode out for a couple of local trainers from time to time but that was about it these days and they were more concerned with his expertise than size. The barman was in his fifties, greying with observant blue eyes. He towered above the bulk of his clientele who were clearly stable lads, all short and weather beaten and wearing the standard uniform of stable staff everywhere, boots, jeans or jodhpurs and thick coats. Finn thought he could even smell the faintest whiff of horse dung or perhaps he was imagining it?

'Are you working at one of the yards?' asked the barman taking in his obvious stable hand appearance.

Finn shook his head. 'No. I'm just passing through.' He had a feeling it might be better not to broadcast who he was.

The barman studied him. 'Ex-jockey?'

Finn shrugged as though it was fair cop. 'I did a bit of amateur riding a while ago.' It didn't do to give too much away. Finn nodded at the group of lads in the corner and at a pair playing pool. One of them was rather tall and wide for a stable lad and had a large face of such blandness it had the effect of making him instantly memorable.

'So, this lot are from the yards, I take it? Apart from the big lad.'

'Yeah. We get them in from all the yards before evening stables. That lot are from Johnson's, Teasdale's, Hunt's and McMahons. The big lad's mine, Patrick, though, he's known as Spud.'

That figures, thought Finn, he had a face as featureless as a potato.

A few more punters came in and the barman called Spud over to serve some drinks. He reluctantly put down his pool cue but not before he had handed something to one of the lads. As he came around the other side of the bar, he noticed that the bland faced young man had a small skull tattooed down the side of his left hand. Finn tuned into the lads' conversation, which all seemed to be about his young charge Connor Moore.

'Seems like he'll be fine, just a few cuts and bruises. He was walking back to the yard in the dark, silly sod.'

Finn was relieved to hear that he was alright. He made a mental note to contact Connor now he was out of danger and find out why he had decided to go walking in the dark. But there was still the issue about what had happened to Sam to consider. Maybe it was lads being lads? So early on his new job, he had to keep an open mind. His 'phone vibrated, and he picked it up. There was a message from Harriet Lucas. It read;

Hi. Have some info from the kids. One of the guys may have had a skull tattooed on his hand and blue nikes. Thought it might help? Hattie x

He looked at the screen for a while as her words sunk in. He felt a complex mixture of emotions, pleased that she had contacted him and surprise and alarm at the information she had sent. It matched the tattoo he had observed on the young man, though in themselves skull tattoos were probably fairly common, he decided. He finished his drink and asked for another, directing his request to Spud. He peered over the bar, noticing that Spud wore black trainers. Did that rule him out? Maybe he was the sort who had a whole wardrobe of the things?

Spud handed him his ice cool coke.

'So, do you go to the races much? You must get loads of tips with this lot around.'

Spud shrugged. 'Yeah sometimes.' His tone was non-committal.

'I was at Wetherby when a young conditional was beaten up the other day. Thought I saw you there.'

Spud mopped up some beer on the bar, his face flushing momentarily before he managed to compose himself.

'Nah, I was working for my dad. Heard about it though. Sam comes in here sometimes. He works for Teasdale. Probably pissed someone off, I reckon. Some punters just can't take losing money.'

Finn nodded, not at all convinced. Spud had the right build, that was for sure, to be a hired thug. Finn decided to up the ante.

'I'm sure that the police will find out who they were and what it was about.' Of course, it wasn't true. Sam had been adamant that he didn't want to involve the police, despite Finn's encouragement.

Spud nodded, his eyes were wary, though he feigned nonchalance as his fingers tightened around his cloth.

Finn drained his glass. 'Funny', he added. 'I never forget a face...'

He said his goodbyes and enjoyed Spud's momentary discomfort. He really needed to persuade Sam to talk to the police so that Spud could be questioned properly. Spud could easily be one of Sam's assailants.

Connor Moore's face was a mass of cuts, abrasions and livid bruises. Finn guessed that the lad had a face his own mother would say, 'had a map of Ireland across it,' which meant that somehow he looked very Irish. Now his entire right side was bruised and battered, and he had a broken collarbone and minor cuts and swellings. He groaned as he turned over to talk to Finn, his wine coloured bruising contrasting with the pure white, standard issue NHS bed sheets. Finn noticed a handful of 'Get Well' cards and a generous basket of fruit adorning his bedside table. Finn had spoken to Connor previously on the 'phone but hadn't yet met him.

'So, what happened, mate? What were you doing wandering around in the dark on a busy road?'

Connor shook his head ruefully, his Irish accent strong and hard to understand at times.

'Well, right enough it was a stupid thing to do, but to tell the truth I was short on cash, so I took a risk. Then this bloody car comes around the corner and nearly banjaxes me. Would have done much worse, but I saw it and jumped out of the way.'

Finn nodded. 'What sort of a vehicle was it?'

Connor thought for a bit. 'A big 4x4, but there's more than enough of them in the area. Black or dark grey, I'd say. Why do you ask, only I'm thinking it was me own stupid fault, no reason to go blaming someone else.'

'Maybe, but did they stop? If they didn't then that would be a criminal offence.'

Connor shook his head, his blue eyes sharp.

'No, they didn't. Probably thought I was a cat or a fox or something.'

Finn thought that was most unlikely. Even though Connor was wiry and slight, there would be no mistaking a collision with a human, surely?

'So, did you ring the police?'

Connor shook his head. 'The staff here did, and they have visited, but I told 'em the same as you.'

Finn cast around for something else to talk about. From his vantage point he could see the inscriptions in the cards. They were mainly from family, colleagues and Vince Hunt.

‘How is it going at Hunt’s overall? Is he a good guvnor would you say?’

The boy looked instantly wary. ‘Yes. He took me on, and he works us hard, but he gave me a chance, so what can I say?’

Finn was convinced that Connor was hiding something. There had been a flicker of watchfulness, even fear cross over his face, though he had been quick to hide it. Finn decided he should have a chat with Hunt. Conditionals were a vulnerable lot, as in order to make the grade, they had to work hard for little reward initially and they relied on their guvnor to pay their expenses and assist them. They would, Finn knew, put up with almost anything to follow their dream. Most guvnors were fair and saw the advantages of having a trainee who could claim up to a ten pound weight allowance for a horse ridden from their stables, but for some it was a way of ruthlessly exploiting vulnerable kids, using them mainly as stable staff and paying them as little as possible. He thought back to his conditional days. His second trainer had been the firm but fair Reg Hollings. A more decent man it was hard to imagine, but as for his first trainer, well, just the thought of him made Finn feel queasy. Only Rosy’s faith in him and Reg’s decency, had seen him through.

They discussed Connor’s recovery, about six weeks, he thought and likely rides when he was fully healed and arranged to meet. Connor was chatty and pleased that his coach had come to see him.

‘It’s no problem. Would have bought some chocolates, but I know you’ve probably got to watch the scales. So, next time you’re away from the yard and stuck for transport, what are you going to do?'

'Sure enough, I'll wear me hi viz jacket so there won't be a next time,' Connor assured him with a grin.

Finn went on his way, making a mental note to visit Vincent Hunt and follow up on Sam Foster's progress at the same time. Something bothered him about Connor's account that evening, too. Like Sam, he was *so* keen to come up with a plausible explanation. Sam thought he had been assaulted by angry punters and Connor was happy to take the blame, almost as though he didn't want anyone to probe further. There seemed to be a passivity about Connor that was odd. Most lads in his position would have been furious, he decided, and wondered why he didn't want to pursue the driver. So, what he was hiding?

Finn got out his 'phone and resisted the urge to search Livvy's Facebook page. That way madness lay, he told himself, sure that he was bound to find out something he didn't want to know. Instead, he texted Harriet and arranged to meet her in York the following evening for a drink and felt marginally better. He was interested to see what else she had found out and realised that despite the sticky start, he'd enjoyed her company the other afternoon. Then his 'phone chirruped into life. It was his boss Tony Murphy. Tony explained that he had been in the office answering 'phone calls when he had received one from Henry Teasdale, complaining that his young conditional had disappeared. Sam Foster had apparently spent a further day at Teasdale's following his win at Wetherby and then had simply vanished. Teasdale was angry but also expressed concern about his jockey.

Finn took the opportunity to run his own worries past his old friend. Tony listened patiently.

'So, you can see I'm quite worried about what is going on with these lads,' Finn added.

There was a silence whilst Tony took in the information.

'Well, it does sound a wee bit suspicious, but on the other hand there's lots of lads who don't make it. These three could just be eejits who are going to drop out and if that's the case the sooner they do that, the better. Still it will do no harm to have a closer look at them and I'll keep me ear to the ground too. Keep in touch and have a chat with this Teasdale fella will yer? Perhaps, Sam's a troublemaker, he may owe money or have annoyed someone so much that he had to do a runner.'

Finn agreed to make discreet inquiries and keep Tony informed. He thought about what Tony had said. Perhaps, he had misjudged Sam? But it simply didn't square with his gut feeling about the lad, he seemed steady enough, rode skillfully and had just had a really good win, for goodness sake, so why would he just leave his job when he had so much promise? It didn't make any sense. Finn toyed with the other possibilities. Perhaps, he hadn't walked out, had been made to leave or left to save his own skin. He began to feel uneasy, very uneasy indeed. What the hell was going on? He turned the car round and made his way to Teasdale's yard with a heavy heart.

The yard at first glance looked tidy and well ordered. It was only when he looked closer that he noticed that the place was a little shabby and in need of a good paint. He saw the farmhouse was in the same state as he was shown into the kitchen with a huge, scuffed pine table, old green Aga and stripped pine cupboards. The sink was full of dirty plates which were streaked with the bright orange of last night's curry, the smell of which hung in the air, stale yet pungent with overtones of some other chemicals. To one side was a sea of canvasses all of horses and dogs. They were beautifully executed. Teasdale noticed Finn's gaze.

'Penny, the wife is an artist, pets in the main.' He spooned coffee into two mugs and handed a chipped, china mug to Finn. 'Suppose you've come about my disappearing conditional, Sam, have you?'

Tall, patrician and with dark good looks, slightly going to seed, Teasdale was, Finn decided, like his house, struggling to keep up appearances. He had an air of someone who expected more out of life. His clothes were expensive, but much worn. He looked Finn up and down.

Finn cleared his throat. 'Yes, I'm his coach. I gather you rang Tony Murphy about him.'

Henry Teasdale explained that things had been going pretty well. Sam had a habit of spending too much time on his 'phone and he had to tell him to put it away several times when he was riding or in the yard but otherwise he worked hard, and showed promise, especially in his riding.

'Are you concerned for his welfare?'

Henry shrugged. 'Maybe. It's not normal to just disappear, is it? He'll be running away from something but I'm not sure what. He's a young man and he could be involved in anything I suppose, but I never got wind of anything. I don't mind telling you, it's bloody inconvenient because we need a conditional. Now even Hunt's lad has had an accident and is out of action. I don't know how you are recruiting these lads, but I think you ought to be more rigorous in your selection procedures.'

It was a criticism but delivered with a charming smile. Finn could understand Teasdale's annoyance.

'Did he ever say anything to anyone else, was he close to someone in the yard, do you know?'

'Hmm. He liked the new guy, Paddy, spoke to him a bit.'

'OK. Mind if I speak to him sometime?'

'Fine. He's not in today, but sure he may have said something that will help.'

'Great. I'll also contact his parents. I have their details so hopefully we'll find out what is going on.'

Henry nodded. 'Will you let me know the minute you find anything out? I do want to know that he's alright after all and he is owed some wages, so I could do with a forwarding address.'

Finn agreed to do so. He wasn't sure what to make of Henry Teasdale. He was definitely rather posh and well mannered, but he wasn't entirely sure he trusted him. There was something he wasn't saying, but at least Henry showed some concern and was decent enough to pay him his wages, which was something, he supposed.

As he was leaving a smart Jaguar pulled into the driveway and a thick set man with greying hair climbed out. He was smartly dressed in an expensive camel coat with heavy gold rings and bracelets adorning him. He reminded Finn of an indignant and overweight pug dog in a suit. Teasdale looked none too pleased to see the man. Jimmy West, Finn realised. Teasdale paused to introduce Finn.

'Jimmy West, Finn McCarthy. Jimmy has several horses here and Finn mentors Sam.'

Finn found himself appraised by a pair blue eyes and his hand being shaken by large powerful fingers.

Finn smiled. 'We've met. I rode for you a few years ago now. Nice to see you again.'

Jimmy frowned. 'Hmm. Oh yes, so you did.'

It was impossible to know if he had remembered Finn or not. 'If you're anything to do with that useless conditional then I'm not sure I can return the compliment. Lad has only gone and done a runner just when we need him and his bloody weight allowance too.' He jabbed a thick finger at Finn's chest. 'I'll tell you something for nothing. The trouble is the world's gone soft and the racing world is no exception. It's too bloody liberal. There's not enough discipline and hard work, if yer ask me! That Foster lad is no exception. Wants the glamour without putting in the effort, like most of 'em.'

Teasdale looked weary, as though he had heard rather too much of Jimmy's opinions.

Finn eyed Jimmy squarely. 'I'm sorry you feel that way. I happen to think that Sam Foster has what it takes to be a good jockey and I will certainly do my level best to find him.'

Jimmy looked rather surprised to be contradicted in this way. He surveyed Finn coldly.

'Well, make sure you do find 'im, if only so I can give 'im a piece of my mind, the bloody useless prat.'

Finn was about to reply when Teasdale intervened.

'Come on now Jimmy. Let's leave Mr McCarthy to his job. Come into the house for a drink.'

Jimmy glared at Finn and with a final hostile grimace made his way towards the house. Finn felt that he had made an enemy. He wondered why on earth Jimmy was so negative towards Sam? Could he have arranged to have him beaten up? It was entirely possible.

Back home his dark mood lifted. He was touched to find that his sister and mother had clubbed together to send him a 'Good Luck' card which had arrived together with a package. When he opened it, he was surprised to find that it was an iPad. A note fluttered to the floor from the packaging.

Thought it might come in handy in your new job as more portable than a laptop. X

He was thrilled and rang his mother who insisted he come around for Sunday lunch at the weekend and was pleased that his job was going well. He told her it was, but really with the problems his conditionals were giving him, he was beginning to wonder if it was beyond him after all.

He opened the iPad and thought it looked too complicated for someone of his limited IT abilities and decided to call in on his sister, Jenny, and thank her in person. She only lived a couple of miles outside York and he hoped she may be able to help him set it up. Jenny beamed as she opened the door. He caught the delicious smell of one of her spaghetti bolognaises, no doubt made from scratch, when she greeted him. It would definitely taste as good as it smelled, he knew from experience.

'You should have told me you were coming. Still, there's plenty to eat, come through. The girls will be delighted.'

Home was a small terrace made undeniably stylish yet still comfortable. As a mother to two girls of three and five, Jenny worked part time as a teacher and did the books for Drew, her husband, who had his own catering business. She was calm, efficient and always had his back. She was three years older than him and he looked up to her. She had bullied him into seeking help when he was drinking too much after everything happened with Livvy. She was the only person he had really listened to and he felt he owed her a great deal for her support and honesty.

'Thanks so much for the iPad. You really didn't have to do that, but I appreciate it.'

'It's no bother. Mum and I just wanted to give you a boost, it's a big thing starting a new job and especially after all the shit that happened.' Jenny put her dark bobbed hair behind her ears and surveyed him. 'We're very proud of you, that's all.'

On impulse she hugged him as his two nieces appeared. Thankfully they were not overly sensitive like Kyle and he was used to dealing with them.

'It's Uncle Finn,' Ava jumped up and down excitedly. 'We're having 'ghetti, do you want some?'

Before long Finn was eating a huge plate of spaghetti as three year old Lola got her dinner all over herself and Ava grilled him on his new job.

'Do you work in a school like Mummy?' she asked. 'Or do you work in a shop like Emily's mum?'

She seemed to think that these were the only two options.

'Not really but I teach people to ride horses.'

'Ponies. I luuve ponies. Do they have red or pink bows in their hair? You have to have pink, they're better.'

Finn wasn't sure how to answer that. 'Sometimes they have plaits but no ribbons.'

Ava lost interest after that and started to pull faces at Lola, who pulled them back. Finn wondered how on earth his sister managed at all, with Drew working all hours.

'No Drew?'

'Daddy's cooking food at a party,' Ava explained. 'There's even a chocolate fountain.'

'A wedding,' Jenny explained. 'The menu has changed about three times with interference from both the bride and groom's mothers and lots of arguments. Still, Drew smoothed everything over and now they love him and won't stop ringing.'

Drew was popular, and level headed, a winning combination in his line of work. He had worked with Young Offenders before starting his catering business, so would no doubt have gained a lot of people skills.

'Oh well, at least business is booming, I suppose.'

Jenny grinned. 'How is your job? Are you enjoying it?'

'Yes, it's fine apart from some problems with the jockeys.' Finn went on to explain about Sam, Harry and Connor.

Jenny looked thoughtful.

'Kids, how about chocolate mousse for pudding and then you two can watch a little bit of 'Frozen' before bedtime. I need to chat to Uncle Finn and sort out his iPad. OK?'

Both children screamed in delight. Finn was bemused at their reaction.

'What on earth is 'Frozen'? I've never heard of it,' Finn asked, having to shout above the children's voices.

'Hey girls. Uncle Finn has never heard of Frozen!'

Ava gasped in disbelief which set off Lola. They began to sing 'Let it Go' at the top of their voices. The noise was absolutely deafening. He sat and watched a little of the dilemmas of Anna, Elsa and the snowman Olaf before Jenny bathed the girls and he read them a story and settled them down.

'Now a glass of wine and you can tell me all about your conditionals. I'm desperate for some adult conversation.' Suddenly she pulled a face. 'Sorry, are you alright about drinking nowadays? I don't want to make you feel awkward.'

Finn thought back to those dark days after Livvy when he had completely fallen apart, and alcohol had seemed like his only friend. Thank God Jenny had made him seek help.

'No, I'm fine. So, what do you think about my jockeys?' He went on to explain about Sam, Connor and Harry.

Jenny listened intently. 'Hmm. Either, they're just a rubbish bunch of lads who're not going to make it or…'

'There's something serious going on?'

Jenny nodded. 'Trust your instincts is my advice. You won't go far wrong.' She studied him. 'So, what are they telling you?'

Finn was surprised at his own words. 'I do think something serious is going on and I owe those lads to find out what.'

'Hmm. I'm sure you'll get to the bottom of it, Finn. But promise me you'll take care, won't you?'

He realised that she was serious.

'Of course. Don't you worry about me.' But he knew that she did. He found the thought warmed him.

He drove home amused about his nieces' antics and with a greater clarity of purpose after his conversation with Jenny. She had also set his iPad up for him and he thought it would be really useful. The BHA had an IT system to record all his contacts and the work he had completed with jockeys upon and he needed to get to grips with it.

When he arrived home, he found another package had been delivered and was waiting ready in the communal hallway. It contained the form he had asked Sam for, neatly filled in with spiky handwriting. The package also contained a small metal mini MP3 player. He searched the form for any sort of clue, found none and decided that Sam was making a point about his musical tastes. Presumably it had been posted before he disappeared? He filed the form away and pocketed the MP3 player thinking he would try it out at some point. At least, if Sam was having a go about his music, he was unlikely to have come to any harm, which reassured him. He squinted at the parcel trying to see what the postmark said, but it was blurred and impossible to read. Damn. He tossed the MP3 player aside, making a mental note to play it later. It was odd though, because Sam sending the parcel with the jockey coaching form enclosed, meant that he was intending to continue to work as a jockey. So, what had happened since, to change his mind?

Chapter 6

Hattie replied to Finn's text with care. It had been a while since she'd been for a drink with a man and even though it wasn't a date, it felt good to be going out with an interesting companion. She was intrigued by Sam's story and increasingly with Finn. After the incident with Dale, it might be good to befriend someone with whom she was not romantically involved, have a male friend. She was perturbed by Finn asking her to keep the information to herself, although she had mentioned the incident to her friend Daisy in passing when they went out, but thankfully her friend had moved swiftly on to trying to fix her up with some lad that was paying them a lot of attention, but maybe Finn was right to be cautious. So, as she drove to her friend Daisy's house she resolved not to mention Finn, or anything further about beaten up jockeys, after all you never knew who was listening. She thought Sam could have been attacked for any number of reasons, but she sensed that he was scared and that he wasn't quite telling the truth. He definitely knew more than he was letting on.

Daisy Hunt was a showjumper. The daughter of a racehorse trainer, Vince Hunt, Daisy had helped Hattie with the showjumping part of the modern pentathlon which initially she had really struggled with. Having grown up around horses, Daisy was utterly comfortable with them and knowledgeable too. She thought nothing of vaulting onto an unknown horse and jumping a course of fences, the very thing which was required in the sport. So, she had helped school Hattie with characteristic generosity, so that eventually the showjumping element was something that she did rather well in. They became good friends, bonding over the horses and Daisy, in her own right was now rising steadily through the showjumping ranks and loving it. And she had easily persuaded Hattie to keep riding, to even compete in the odd showjumping class at local shows. A big factor for Hattie in this was the draw of riding her beloved Kasper. Bertoni Prince Kasper, as he was known in the ring. The horse had been destined for the top flight as a showjumper when a dodgy tendon had stopped his progress. Now demoted to an also ran, Hattie loved him and was happy to ride him. The owners kept him at Hunts' yard as they had no land themselves, they paid livery and were happy for Hattie and others to exercise him. It was a fluid, undemanding relationship and Hattie suspected that the owners were very well heeled, so that keeping the odd horse at livery here or there was nothing much to them. Hattie liked to pay her way and paid Daisy for lessons on him. After all, she and Kasper had a great deal in common she told herself, both invalided out of their sports and tinkering around at the edges of other ones for fun. Daisy also worked for the Racing to School scheme and sometimes she and Hattie worked together. She also bought and sold young horses which she schooled and somehow managed to make a living, but it was rather hand to mouth as far as Hattie could tell. Hattie pulled into Vince Hunt's yard and grabbing her hat and whip, made her way to the stables to find Daisy. The yard was relatively small, with around twenty horses and as common in Walton, not much land. But there were shared gallops and other facilities which trainers could use. Vince Hunt had also built an indoor school and that was where Hattie headed.

Daisy was schooling a huge bay and started to pull up when she saw Hattie. The horse was one of her youngsters and a good prospect, but Hattie forgot his posh name and only knew the gelding as Ears because he liked having his ears pulled.

'Hey, whoa,' Daisy reined in the horse and then jumped off and unfastened her hat. 'Hi Hats, Kasper's out in the paddock. The cheeky horse banged the door down this morning, so I let him out for a bit.'

Kasper was one of those horses who made his needs known very loudly. Hattie knew he would not reckon much to being in the stable on a fresh autumn morning.

'So, what are you going to do with him today? Schooling?'

Hattie had been going to do that but suddenly the lure of the sunshine on what might after all be the last sunny day for months, was too much. It felt thought Hattie, like a 'glad to be alive' sort of a day, far too lovely to spend indoors.

'I think I'll go for a hack.'

Daisy tossed her blonde plait over her shoulder and grinned. 'Great, I'll come with you on Monty, we can talk on the way!'

Monty was Daisy's sister's horse, and Daisy often exercised him when Alice was at school. Ten minutes later the two women set off, riding side by side, chattering. As they passed through the yard, Hattie noticed the usual array of busy people, stable lads, work riders and Vince Hunt in his tweed cap and quilted jacket. He gave her a wave of acknowledgement and then turned back to watch a horse being trotted up. Daisy paused, stopping the grey gelding Monty, and turned to yell at another man who was consulting a clipboard.

'You can use the school Andy, we're finished with it.'

Hattie was fascinated by the busy life at the Hunts'. She never understood how the yard survived though as there were many similar such establishments and good racehorses were, she knew, like good owners, very hard to find. Hattie guessed, although this was never acknowledged, that the money she paid for lessons was very welcome, even needed.

'So, how's the racing going so far this season?'

Daisy shrugged. 'OK, the horses seem to have got over the virus. We had a winner a couple of days ago, Angel Delight. Did you hear about Connor?'

Hattie said she hadn't. Her friend explained about the accident, alluding to the hit and run which the conditional jockey had been the victim of, and which had put him in hospital. Something pinged in Hattie's brain at the news that another conditional jockey had had some bad luck. Maybe that was what Finn was eluding to?

'He's coming out later today I think, so it's not too bad, he was lucky, I suppose. He rode Angel.'

Or unlucky thought Hattie, who like many people liked a good conspiracy theory. 'So, what's he like this Connor?'

Daisy urged Monty into a trot as they hurried to a passing place to let a horsebox pass. 'Nice, I think Alice fancies him, she goes all red and tongue tied around him. He's a bit steadier than some of them, you know what these young jocks can be like, a bit mad, all stars in their eyes, think they're going to be the next Tony McCoy until they realise how hard it is… But he is a sweetie. Poor Alice.'

Hattie grinned. 'Bless her. We were like that once.'

Alice, Daisy's sister, at fifteen was horse mad and just noticing boys. Daisy grinned back.

'I know, I think he's got a girlfriend back home in Ireland. He gets mail that look like love letters. So romantic, all I get is texts from my other half.'

Hattie laughed. 'And how is Neil?'

'Oh overworked, underpaid, always riding, you know.' Neil was Daisy's boyfriend, a fellow showjumper. 'Come on, let's go on the gallops, they're empty now, and I promised Alice I'd help keep Monty fit, he's such a greedy horse, worse than Kasper…'

They hacked down the bridle path along to where several gallops started. There was an array of shared facilities for the yards to use, an all-weather half mile track, a poly plastic gallop together with sets of starting stalls and hurdles with a few bigger fences thrown in. By eleven, they were largely clear, as the twenty or so trainers in and around Walton would have been up since dawn, and most horses would have been exercised and would now be safely back in their stables. They set off up the hill which was dotted with trees and small coppices.

'Hopefully all the spotters have cleared off by now too,' Daisy explained.

Hattie knew that some punters employed people to watch the strings of elegant horses at exercise trying to find out which animals showed promise, although how they could tell the difference between the mostly bay horses at that distance was, incomprehensible to her. They enjoyed a bracing ride travelling at a hack canter, laughing and joking as Monty tried to overtake the much bigger and faster Kasper. As they rode home after the canter, along a meandering bridle path and back to the yard, they passed another set of stables.

'Is that Teasdale's yard?' Hattie had noticed from her race card that the beaten up jockey, Sam, worked there.

'Yep, now *he's* a strange man. Sort of posh but cold if you know what I mean. I can't say I like him. Weird thing is, he and Dad, they are like this these days.' Daisy held up two touching fingers. 'Dad used to moan about the bloke too. But ever since last Cheltenham they're been quite friendly. Henry came over the other day, they were closeted away in Dad's study like a pair of bookends. Anyway, you off to Uttoxeter tomorrow with Bob?'

Their colleague Bob had helped them both settle into their roles at Racing to School.

Hattie rolled her eyes. 'Yes. Wish you were coming. I'll see you at Market Rasen, though.'

Back at home in the outskirts of Walton, Hattie declined the offer of food, even though her older brother Will had called in. He had a house with Nuala in York. Her sister-in-law was pleasant in a stylish, cool sort of a way and Hattie felt slightly intimidated by her. How on earth she coped with her rather uncool brother, was a complete mystery. He was currently devouring thick sandwiches in the kitchen before the lasagne, which she could smell was nearly ready.

'I'm just going to get ready. I'm off out to see a friend,' she announced.

'Great, more for me,' he told her with his mouth full of bread and cheese.

Hattie had a quick shower, dried her hair and then fretted over what to wear for her meeting with Finn. Black jeans, a purple top, boots and her leather jacket she decided, going for a casual yet cool look she hoped. She dried her auburn curls, slapped on a touch of mascara, a slash of maroon lipstick, a squirt of 'La Vie Est Belle' and she was ready.

'So, who's the friend?' teased Will, helping himself to seconds of lasagne when she went into the kitchen to say goodbye. Her parents also looked curious but knew better than to ask. 'Male or female?' Will gave her a searching look, as did her father.

'God, it's such a pain having two detectives in the family,' said Hattie, 'and it's a couple of friends from work actually,' she fibbed.

'Is it right,' said Will, sipping wine, 'introducing children to racing? I mean all that gambling and misery you might awaken, sis…' His voice was light, playing devil's advocate as usual, Hattie realised.

'Leave her alone Will,' said Mum, 'it seems like a lovely job.'

'You know full well she's only filling in, before finishing her degree and becoming a dietician…' Dad had great respect for degrees and was, she knew very proud of her. He also had more faith in education than in sport, and had not been sorry when she'd left the competitive world of the pentathlon.

'Hey sis, when you're on the racecourses listen out for any gossip will you? There's suspicions about some sort of drug network operating in the area, supplying amphetamines mostly.' Will looked at his father. 'Jockeys use them to keep the weight down,' he explained.

Hattie was about to quip that despite his misgivings about her job, he was happy enough to try to use her role to gain inside information. He looked deadly serious, though, and it occurred to her that his connections in the police might be useful in helping find out what was going on with Sam and potentially Connor too. Was it something to do with drugs?

'I will. Good job you don't have to make ten stone, with your appetite. See you later, I won't be late, off to Uttoxeter tomorrow. I'll keep my ear to the ground though.'

The bar of The Horse and Hounds in York was quite full. Hattie arrived a little late and was a little breathless as she frantically looked round for Finn. There he was over by the corner sipping a half of something or other. She waved at him and made her way over. Finn looked, she noticed, relaxed in dark jeans, a green shirt and a distressed looking Barbour jacket.

'Hi, it's great to see you.' The warm smile which reached those dark eyes lifted her spirits. She lost her nerves, asked him if he wanted another drink and went to the bar.

She plonked another half in front of him. 'So, you saw my text about one of the attackers having a skull tattoo on their hand? One of the kids from Wetherby told me, apparently he has an amazing memory and notices all sorts of things.'

Finn grinned. 'Better still, I think I might have met him in The Yew Tree in Walton.' He frowned. 'Works in the bar, he said he wasn't at Wetherby that day, but then he would say that, wouldn't he? I suppose lots of people might have similar tattoos though. Anyway, there's more.'

Finn went on to explain about Sam's disappearance and another lad being a victim in a hit and run.

Hattie's eyes were wide. 'I heard about the car accident. And what do you think has happened to Sam? Where has he gone?'

'Well, I went to Henry Teasdale's yard and he was as confused as we are. Things appeared to be going well, so it's all a bit of a mystery actually.'

Hattie thought for a minute. 'He seemed quite steady, surely not the sort to run off?'

'I agree. And watching his ride on Saffron Sun, I'd say he had a promising future.' Finn shook his head. 'I wasn't too sure about Teasdale though. He seemed to say the right things but chiefly he's worried about the inconvenience to him I think.' He moved his head from side to side, weighing up this judgement. 'Well, perhaps that's not fair because he did want a forwarding address, so he could give Sam his wages, but still there was something not quite right, almost as if he had an ulterior motive.'

'Hmm. My friend Daisy doesn't like him either.'

'Who?'

Hattie went on to explain about her friendship with Vince Hunt's daughter, Daisy.

'Course, that's the yard where their conditional was involved in a hit and run incident,' Finn explained.

'Yes. Daisy mentioned him. What's his name? Connor?'

'Yes. I saw him in hospital, but he claims not to know who ran into him, but he was just a bit too laid back about it and blamed himself for the incident…'

'Hmm. Almost as though he didn't want anyone to ask further questions.'

Finn looked at her in surprise. 'Yes, that's exactly it. How did you guess?'

'Comes from having two cops in the family.' Hattie thought she best get this information out of the way, she'd often felt that potential friends needed to know what her family was like. Instead of looking intimidated Finn looked impressed.

'Hey, that might come in handy. I bet they know all sorts of useful things.'

Hattie found she'd finished her drink and Finn got her another glass of wine. Then she told him what Will had said about the possible drug network in Walton.

'So, Hattie,' said Finn, counting the facts on his hand, 'we've got two, frankly dodgy, injuries to a couple of conditional jockeys, a beating, a hit and run and now a disappearance plus the info about the drugs. What do you think is going on?'

Hattie thought for a minute.

'Well, your conditionals are either very unlucky or being deliberately harmed. It could be drug related. Perhaps, they owe money to a dealer.' She frowned.

Finn nodded and lowered his voice. 'I'm pretty sure that the incidents are not accidental, but one possible theory could be drugs or even race fixing. Mind you there is supposed to be a drug culture in Newmarket so perhaps the same is true for Walton?' Finn waited for Hattie to take this in.

'Hmm.' She thought for a moment, cold fingers of alarm trickling down her spine. 'Well, that was certainly what my brother mentioned so I suppose he would know. What sort of drugs do you think?'

Finn nodded. 'Could be speed, cocaine, even illegal highs but I wouldn't mention anything to anyone else just yet. Let's just keep this amongst ourselves, after all we don't know who we're dealing with exactly.'

Hattie shuddered and wondered about her friend Daisy's father and, of course, Dr Pinkerton. He had had a rather extreme reaction to Sam's win. What was it he'd said, *he wasn't meant to win.*

She explained this to Finn who listened intently. 'Hmm. Sounds just like a serious gambler. Well, best keep our ears to the ground. So, what's the plan?'

Hattie wasn't sure about the way he said 'our' and had to stop herself from protesting, but it was intriguing to say the least. She remembered her own experiences of competing, how vulnerable she felt and how desperately she had needed someone to look out for her, just as Finn was doing with his young conditionals. She decided to articulate a decision that she knew she had made subconsciously a long time ago.

'Look, I do want to help. I suppose we need to find Sam Foster and ask him. It's quite something to just disappear, so it suggests he was running away from something scary.'

He flashed her a grin, as if acknowledging her decision.

'Well, it just so happens that I have his family details and I agree. I have a duty of care to the lad and would like to help him. We can start by visiting his parents.'

'Where do they live?'

'Parents are separated but his mum lives in a village. It's in Lincolnshire, not a million miles away from Market Rasen, so we can call in after the races on Saturday.'

She raised her glass and toasted him to seal their arrangement. So much for staying out of anything that might prove contentious. She knew she had to do this for Sam's sake.

'Great. It's a date!' Then she blushed furiously when she realised what she had just said, because Finn was just a friend and that was all.

Chapter 7

Finn still rode out once a week for a local trainer and friend, Seamus Ryan who had stables just outside of York on the road out to Walton in a village called Barton Vale. Seamus was an ex-jockey who had ridden when Finn was riding but retired because of persistent problems making the weights. He was ten years older than Finn and upon retirement had rented a yard with his wife, Rosy. Finn had met Rosy at Boothroyd's place and it was fair to say that she had saved him when Boothroyd had beaten him up and left him for dead. They had moved to Hollins' place together. Finn had vowed to help her husband Seamus when he set up as a small trainer. So far, Seamus had had some success with the dozen or so horses and the stable was expanding nicely. As Finn pulled into the driveway of the mellow stone farmhouse, he could see that there was another stable block in construction.

'Aye, it's going pretty well. We've ten more horses this year, so things are on the up,' explained Seamus. 'Now I'd like you to ride one of me new four year olds. He's called Jack the Lad. He's a bit of form in Ireland point to pointing and I reckon he could do well hurdling, in fact, he'd make a great chaser later too.'

Finn enjoyed riding the huge bay. He loved the physicality of getting back in the saddle, the scent of horse sweat, the feeling of the muscular power underneath him and the sheer exhilaration of feeling the wind in his hair. It was great to see that he could still ride, the old instincts and skills always came rushing back, a muscle memory which was ingrained in him. Seamus had him jumping some of the hurdles he had fixed up. The horse flew over them with no problem whatsoever. He showed great skill and had a handy turn of speed.

'So, what do you think?'

Finn stroked the velvety nose of the horse and laughed. 'I reckon you've got a good one here. He's got great pace and scope. If all goes well, he could be top class.'

Seamus grinned. 'My thoughts exactly. Are you coming in for a drink? We want to hear all about your new job. Rosy was after ringing you, but I told her you'd be in touch in good time.'

Rosy hugged Finn and looked him up and down.

'You are looking well, it's great to see you. Your new job must be suiting you! I want to hear all about it!' She made them both bacon sandwiches and they listened as Finn explained what had happened to his conditionals. They were a kindly couple and they were shocked that someone could just disappear, and no one had any idea why.

'So, as you can see there are some real challenges. Do you have any ideas?'

Seamus shook his head. 'I don't know what to make of it. I had been following that lad, Sam Foster. He has the makings of a good rider. Even thought, I might give him a ride or two. He can't have just disappeared, it makes no sense, for sure. These lads, they need decent support. Well, you know that, better than anyone, so you do. You must find him, Finn, you must.'

He was faced with a two pronged attack.

'God, Finn, you have to. Lads just don't vanish into thin air, like that. Whatever is behind it, it must be bad.' Rosy added. 'I mean look what happened to you…'

Finn looked at their serious faces.

'The trouble is I don't really know where to start apart from contacting his parents.'

Rosy looked thoughtful. 'Well, they always say cherchez la femme, find the girl, don't they? Is there a girlfriend on the scene?'

Maybe he had a girlfriend and decided to go off somewhere with her? That was certainly plausible.

'Yes, I think there is.'

Rosy beamed. 'Well, that's your first port of call then. If it's not that, he may have had some sort of a mental breakdown or something. Either way you need to find out what is going on.'

Finn felt two pairs of eyes bore into him expectantly. He agreed with their sentiments entirely, but it was easier said than done.

Finn spent some time looking at the files of Sam Foster, Connor Moore and Harry Jarvis. There was nothing much remarkable in any of the information he held on the lads. He went through the references that had been provided for each of them and their medical information. Both Harry and Sam had been to the Northern Racing College in Doncaster, whereas Connor had been riding in Ireland for years, started working for a trainer and then passed his riding assessment. Sam was described in complimentary terms by the racing college as 'hardworking with natural balance.' Harry was more confident, a little too confident by all accounts. All of them seemed to make the weights without too much difficulty, though Finn thought that Harry had probably grown recently, so that might not be the case now. It was always hard to predict a lad's height, even if you knew their parents' size, sometimes a rogue gene would prove you wrong. There were countless conditionals who were forced to give up their dream or face a lifetime of saunas and starvation to keep their weights down. Some lads were drawn to drugs to achieve this which was certain to land them in hot water one way or another.

His mind wandered off. His thoughts turned to Hattie Lucas. He liked her fresh, honest approach and the way she just said whatever came into her head. She was young, intelligent but forthright and open, which was no bad thing. She had been helpful so far and the information she had given him from her brother might prove very useful. His thoughts turned back to the task in hand. He may have been tempted to dismiss the misfortunes of his conditionals, except for the fact that Sam had now disappeared. He realised that Hattie was right; the only option was to find him. Otherwise, everything was pure conjecture and he knew the police wouldn't bother with more than a cursory investigation as Sam was over eighteen years of age and not considered vulnerable. But he was in a way, he had been beaten up and was struggling to find his way in a highly competitive world, but he knew the police wouldn't see it like that.

He rang another conditional, Callum Jones, who was based in North Yorkshire and was racing in the three o'clock which improved his mood as he drove there, taking in the rural sights. Market Rasen was a charming racecourse, set amongst the glorious Lincolnshire Wolds and near to a pleasant village. The countryside was gently undulating and the colours of the trees, red, mustard and yellow reminded Finn of the range of colours in a spice rack. Chilli, paprika, turmeric and garam masala. The course was small, quaint yet very friendly. He remembered that he'd had some good times at Market Rasen and felt a sharp stab of envy when he saw the jockeys arriving swinging their kit bags. He also felt a pang of apprehension when he realised that his former guvnor, Michael Kelly, had some runners here today and that also meant that his ex-best friend Nat Wilson was likely to be riding. His mood plummeted even more when he realised that he would no doubt be accompanied by Finn's ex, Livvy Jordan. Still, he had done nothing wrong and all he had to do was hold his head up high, he told himself. When he had been unceremoniously sacked by Michael, he'd had no need to attend the races and that had been fine with him, but in his new role, of course he had to face everyone and that included Livvy and Nat, first and foremost and then Michael. Still, he was damned if he was going to let them spoil his day. He had a perfect right to be at the races and he didn't see why he should skulk away when he had done nothing wrong.

He bought a racecard, ordered a sandwich and a cup of tea in the bar and studied form. Nat was riding three horses for Michael Kelly, and they all looked like quality animals who each had a good chance of winning. He felt a spasm of pain, sparked with anger. Yet, there was no point dwelling on what might have been. He examined the prospects of Callum Jones, his conditional, who was riding Juniper Berry in the fourth race. He applied himself to examining the opposition so that he might advise him on tactics.

As he was wandering round he heard a booming voice and recognised the Northern tones of the owner, Jimmy West. He was with another well-dressed middle aged man, wearing typical racing clothing with a large, blonde woman dressed in a leopard skin coat and a black Russian style hat, who he assumed was Jimmy's wife.

'Well, you do run a Continental Haulage business love, so the least I can expect is a proper sit down meal to go with all that lovely bubbly.' She nudged the other woman who looked like she would rather be anywhere else other than there at this moment in time. 'Come on, me and Carol are bloody starving, aren't we love?'

Jimmy's gaze suddenly fell upon Finn.

'Well, if it isn't Finn McCarthy.' His statement was neither friendly nor hostile. It seemed to Finn that Jimmy had seized upon his presence as a diversion from the vexing topic of lunch and he wouldn't have even acknowledged Finn's presence otherwise. But his wife immediately stuck out her hand for him to shake.

'Oh, Mr McCarthy, you wouldn't believe the winners I've had backing you. Delighted to meet you. I'm Audrey, Jimmy's wife. 'Her face lit up with real warmth. 'Jimmy told me all about your new job with these young jockeys. You've got your work cut out with some of them from what I hear.'

'Yes, some of them are proving a little troublesome. Do you and your husband have any runners here today?'

Jimmy answered with a sneer on his face. 'Queen of Sheba in the third. Teasdale's conditional was supposed to be riding, so at least we would have had ten pounds off the weight but now he's disappeared, and we have Danny Green and no weight allowance. Even Hunt's conditional is bloody injured.' He put his arm around his wife. 'Now we need to be getting on, we've got to meet Ted.'

As he moved off Finn couldn't resist adding, 'Good luck anyway.' Audrey smiled and waved whilst Jimmy merely have him a curt nod, and then Finn saw the man who they were meeting and felt his knees buckle. He felt as if ice cubes had been dropped inside the back of his shirt collar, such was the shock. The man had aged dramatically, his hair was almost white and his face much thinner, but Finn would know that steely gaze and long nose anywhere. Ted Boothroyd, his old guvnor. Finn felt momentarily light headed and slightly sick. Boothroyd must have seen him, but looked straight past him and gave nothing away. He had been warned off after his behaviour to Finn, and other jockeys revealed what he had done to them. As far as he knew he hadn't gone back into training when his ban ended, so what the hell was he was doing here? Then he realised that just like anyone else, Boothroyd was free to enjoy the races. He took a deep breath and set his shoulders back. What harm could he possibly do him now? Finn modulated his breathing as he had been taught to do to avoid a full blown panic attack. Breathe in for the count of seven, out for eleven, he told himself. Eventually, he felt much better and flicked through his racecard. It was clearly a day of surprises, but he was not going to let anyone wreck his day.

Finn made a mental note to keep a look out for Jimmy West's horse. Jimmy was certainly dissatisfied about the conditionals. Of course, he was only too happy to let them ride so he could make use of their weight allowances, but at the same time was he disgruntled enough to cause Sam to do a runner? Certainly, the conditionals would never please him whatever they did. He was a deeply unpleasant man and a real bully but was there something else going on too? He believed that any alliance that Jimmy had forged with Ted Boothroyd could only spell trouble. Boothroyd had ruthlessly exploited Finn as a conditional. Perhaps he and Jimmy had joined forces to do the same to others?

The racecourse was filling up. Finn started to feel much better. He saw several familiar faces, ex owners, trainers and stable staff. He finished the simple yet tasty ham and cheese toasted sandwich, sipped his tea and tuned into the noises around him. He heard Michael Kelly before he saw him, his soft Irish lilt and charm, belied a trainer of deep ambitions and a ruthless need to win. Someone had asked him about his horses' chances. Michael responded in such a casual manner that Finn knew that he had high hopes for his horses. He heard his softly spoken female companion and was assailed by the rich smell of Chanel perfume as it reached his nostrils. The deep wave of emotion it elicited made him struggle to breathe. Livvy was with him. At the same time Finn was aware that from his position at the front of the bar, that he had no choice but to face them as he could not leave unseen. So, he tried to ignore his quickening pulse, plastered a smile on his face and made his way through the bar.

Michael's sharp blue eyes spotted him first and he smiled a little uncertainly. Finn smiled briefly just as Livvy turned around, flushed, looked away and then turned back to him.

'Hello Finn. How are you? What brings you to Market Rasen?' she purred, recovering her equilibrium. She was wearing her flared red coat, a long black woollen dress and shiny black boots, and looked undeniably stylish. Her shoulder length dark hair shimmered and the waves of Chanel No 5 he used to buy for her, made him think back to much happier times. Never had she looked lovelier.

He felt his mouth go dry. 'Hello *Olivia.* I work for the BHA these days, so I'm here on business.' She looked momentarily surprised and then irritated when she registered his use of her full name, which he knew she disliked intensely.

Michael nodded. 'Aye, you look well, so you do. Would you like a drink?'

Finn declined as Michael made his way to the bar. Livvy asked after his parents and he responded. It was rather awkward, so Finn muttered his excuses and was about to leave, when Livvy clutched at his arm.

'Actually, Finn, I'm glad to see you.' She swished her hair and pouted. 'We never had the chance to talk about things, did we? Nat and I, well, we didn't plan to fall in love, it just happened.' She tailed off. 'Anyway,' her face clouded, 'I have a favour to ask you actually.'

Finn could hardly believe his ears but was perplexed by Livvy's expression. She looked genuinely worried and upset. Still, why should he care?

'I'm not sure…'

'Look, I know it sounds like a bloody cheek after what happened, but you are, were, Nat's oldest friend and he just seems so stressed these days and he won't tell me why. Something is really worrying him…' She looked, he surprised himself at the thought, almost scared. 'So, would you mind talking to him?'

Finn gaped at her. 'You were right, first time, it *is* a bloody cheek. Surely, you can't expect me to drop everything after what you did, I mean, what do you take me for?'

Livvy looked shocked and then almost tearful. Finn fought back the urge to explode and looked into the middle distance, where Michael was coming back with two gin and tonics. Livvy hurriedly fished into her bag for a pen and scribbled something down and thrust it into his hands.

'Here, this is his new number. Have a think about it, please, for me, because I am really concerned about him and I don't know what else to do. Just meet him for a drink or something, can't you? It's time to let bygones be bygones anyway and once you've broken the ice, he might confide in you. You're my only hope. You could meet him after he's finished up here? Please…'

Finn shook his head in disbelief, not trusting himself to speak. First Boothroyd and now Michael and Livvy. He stuffed the piece of paper into his pocket and turned on his heel, leaving Livvy looking after him, her eyes shining with tears. But it was clear that the tears were for Nat, not him, he thought bitterly.

Finn was glad to be outside watching the races and mingling. He loved the crowds and the drama at the racecourse, and it was a welcome change from thinking about Livvy and her strange request. It was true, that they hadn't had a chance to discuss everything but that was only because he had come home to find Livvy had gone, and the hangers were still swinging in her empty wardrobe. She had simply left a brief note to say that she had moved in with Nat. Still, to think that he would put himself out to help them was ridiculous. She had abandoned him without a thought and having gone from someone who would walk over hot coals to help her, he couldn't care less. How like Livvy to brush her betrayal off and expect him to 'let bygones be bygones' as she put it. He had to admit that he felt a tiny bit pleased that everything wasn't exactly perfect for them, but also curious. What could be causing Nat such angst? After all he had the girl and the job, so from where Finn was standing, he had nothing to complain about.

Outside, he turned up his collar against the cold and strode through the crowds to go to the parade ring. When he spotted the tall, slim figure of Hattie dressed in the same long, black coat with her flower brooch, he felt his spirits lift, noticing the bright colours the children wore as they trailed behind her. It was great to see a friendly face. He caught her eye and smiled. He briefly chatted to his conditional Callum Jones and watched, as he gave a creditable performance to finish fourth out of a field of ten. He had timed his run just a little late and became blocked between two horses at one point, so Finn made a note to talk through positioning with him. Queen of Sheba was running in the same race and came in second behind an outsider. He noticed Jimmy's furious expression as he talked to Danny Green and thought that he would not like to be in the young jockey's position.

In the next race, he could not avoid seeing the rangy figure of Nat Wilson, striding out of the weighing room into the saddling enclosure. Nat was charming, good looking and something of a ladies' man, so much so, that Livvy initially disliked him and had been critical of his 'love them and leave them escapades' until, ironically, she had fallen for him herself. Finn positioned himself behind a row of young men in suits and studied his rival. Nat looked tired and strained which made him even more intrigued about what might be upsetting him. Extravert and something of a practical joker, Nat was usually untroubled by life's up and downs, so it must be something serious, he decided. Instead of feeling pleased he found his curiosity was piqued.

He watched the last couple of races and noted that despite Nat's alleged worries, his race riding seemed unaffected and he managed two winners and a third place. Finn caught up with Callum Jones, arranged to visit him at his guvnor's yard and as the last race approached, he went to find Hattie. She was in the process of getting the children to line up and file out to their coach. The same homely looking man he had seen her with at Wetherby, was there to assist. Harriet saw Finn, spoke to her companion and then joined him.

'Hi there. Have you had a good day?'

Finn smiled back. 'Not bad at all. Are you ready to go?'

Hattie nodded. 'Can I just get something to eat? I haven't had anything all day.'

'OK. Sam's parents live about twenty minutes away, so we've plenty of time.'

How great to meet a girl who actually eats, Finn decided. He would have found it annoying when he was riding, but now it didn't matter. There were some advantages to not competing and he was discovering this more and more. They went into the bar and chatted about their day over a cup of tea and sandwich for Hattie.

'Right, time to go,' said Finn standing up. 'We'll have a think what we're going to say on the way there.'

Hattie got to her feet. 'OK, no problem. I have a few ideas actually.'

Finn bent down to listen to her. As he walked out, Finn felt the warmth of someone's gaze upon him, and realised with satisfaction, that Livvy was watching them.

Chapter 8

'So where will we start?' asked Hattie. She'd opted to let Finn drive and leave her car at the racecourse. They'd checked with the staff on leaving the course that the car park would be open for several hours after racing had finished.

Finn moved the car along slowly in the queue to leave the racecourse.

'I suppose I've got an 'in'. I can ask naive questions because of my jockey coach role.' He glanced at Harriet trying to gauge her mood. 'Listen, are you sure about getting involved in this? I can handle things on my own, but thought that two heads were better than one and as you will no doubt have noticed, I'm not the most tactful of men…'

Hattie laughed. 'Yeah, I remember, trampling all over Kyle's dreams and making him cry.'

Finn suddenly felt the need to explain. 'It's just that I've seen too many lads grow too tall and suddenly have to rethink their career options, that's all. I'm just trying to look out for them, it's hard when you're starting out.'

Hattie grinned impishly. 'Yep, I agree that youngsters need support so that's why I want to help Sam. Anyway, I was going to explain that he had offered to demonstrate riding 'The Beast' for the Racing to School if his parents were suspicious.'

'The what?'

'It's a new Equiciser, you know the mechanical horse. We get jockeys to talk the kids through how they ride using the machine. You must have used one?'

Finn nodded. He taught jockeys the finer points of riding but usually they *could* ride. He had come across Equicisers and supposed they had their place for complete novices. He was more involved in imparting knowledge on the skill involved in race riding, tactics, positioning and so on.

'It's a good cover story though. It sounds like you've given the matter some serious thought.'

Hattie gave him a sideways look. 'Anyway, don't worry about upsetting Kyle. He is a very sensitive boy apparently and could do with an extra layer of skin according to his teacher. I was just teasing, that's all.'

Finn looked relieved. They passed through a small village with a green and a duck pond.

Hattie glanced at Finn. 'I asked my dad about missing people in general and he confirmed that people do disappear all the time. It's scary really. A lot of them stay missing too.'

Finn took this in. 'I suppose it's helpful having two policemen in the family?'

'I suppose. Actually, I don't know that much about the CID, just little bits that Dad and Will let slip every now and then. Mind you my youngest brother is studying Forensics and Criminology at uni, so you know, that might come in handy. So, do you know anything about Sam's family, and do we tell them about him being beaten up?'

Finn took a sharp left turn down a very narrow lane. 'Guess we'll just have to play it by ear. It should be here on the left, number 12.' They saw a row of farm workers' cottages, built in old, mellow brick. Finn drew up outside number 12. The cottage had a dark red door and ornate lace curtains in the two windows.

'Right here goes.' Finn knocked on the door. It was opened by a pleasant looking woman of about forty, dressed in jeans and a blue fluffy jumper. She wore a striped apron and her hands were covered in flour. 'Can I help you?'

'Are you related to Sam Foster? I'm Finn McCarthy, his BHA jockey coach and this is Harriet Lucas from Racing to School.'

The woman looked at Finn's ID.

'Och, you had better come in.' Hattie could see the curtains of the house next door twitching and guessed that the woman preferred to talk to them in private.

The door opened straight into a small but cosy sitting room. A TV was on, with the sound low and a teenager was poring over some books at a table over in the corner.

The woman gestured to a chintz sofa and said, 'Look, I'm Annie, Sam's mum but he's not here. I know he's left. Heck, I must just wash my hands. Excuse me, I'm baking cupcakes trying out some new recipes. Do you want some tea and cakes while we talk?' Her accent was a soft, melodic Scottish brogue.

'Thanks,' said Hattie, who could smell the delicious waft of cooking cake mixture.

While Annie went to fetch some tea, Hattie spoke to the young girl. She could see a maths book open in front of her. 'Oh, poor you, algebra. I hated that. Are you Sam's sister?' Hattie thought she could see a resemblance.

'Yes, I'm Sophie. Are you jockeys too?'

'I used to be. Listen, do you know where Sam is?' asked Finn.

The direct question seemed to unsettle Sophie and Hattie noticed tension, a stiffening of her body when he asked. Hattie went to take a closer look at the maths. She noticed that next to the book was a postcard depicting an ancient castle set in green countryside. Hattie took in the picturesque scene.

'Oh, what a lovely castle. Where is that?'

'Scalloway Castle on the Shetland Islands. My nan runs a post office there.' The girl shrugged, embarrassed. 'She doesn't like using the 'phone or email, she's dead old fashioned. So, we get the postcards instead.'

Hattie nodded looking at the rows of neat working out. Quadratic equations. 'Very good, that looks right.'

'Yeah, I'm in Year 11, GCSE mocks soon.'

'You'll be fine if you can do those. I was awful at maths, until Year 10 when my parents got me a tutor. He was great, and I suddenly got it, you know...'

Annie returned with a tray. She passed round tea in china cups and saucers and then an assortment of cupcakes. 'There's mint and chocolate, raspberry and vanilla and hazelnut and toffee. Those are a new recipe. And some of my traditional drop scones too.' She nodded at the cakes. 'Mum has a coffee shop in Louth,' explained Sophie.

Munching cakes and balancing a cup and saucer on his knee, made Finn look rather uncomfortable. Annie waited for him to speak but after a few seconds Hattie asked,

'So how did you find out Sam had gone missing?'

Annie took a sip of tea. 'Och, that misery guts, Teasdale, rang complaining about him the other day.'

'So, has Sam done this sort of thing before?' asked Hattie in between mouthfuls. The cake melted in the mouth and was delicious.

Annie sighed. 'Sometimes he goes to his Dad's. We split up and his Dad lives in Lincoln. He's English.' She said this as it explained everything.

'Do you think he's there now?' asked Finn.

Annie nodded. 'Aye, he texted to say he was.'

Hattie could see that an expression crossed Sophie's face, a sort of conscious, guarded look.

'Any idea why he'd disappear?' asked Finn. 'I mean he'd just had a winner, he's a good rider, got lots of potential as far as I can see. Although, he was beaten up after his win.'

Annie smiled and nodded. 'Well, we saw the race on the computer, on At the Races. Great, wasn't it? He told us about being attacked and said it was a disgruntled punter. Look, there was a girl, from the stables. They were going out and then there was some sort of row. I think maybe that's what happened. You know how high feelings run at that age? I'm sure it'll all sort out and he'll go back soon.'

Poor Sam. But would he really run off because of a girl? Hattie wasn't at all sure that Henry Teasdale would want Sam back the longer he stayed away, but wasn't going to tell his mother that. Interesting that the family were so relaxed about one of their members disappearing. She imagined her father would have the whole force out by now, TV appeals, people searching, asking questions and piecing together her last known movements.

'Has the girl got a name?'

'Gina someone, I think. What do you reckon? Shall I introduce the hazelnut and toffee cupcake to Annie's Pantry?'

'Absolutely,' said Hattie. 'But the drop scone was gorgeous too, so light, it melted in my mouth. Anyway, thank you, you've been most helpful.'

Mrs Foster looked thrilled but Hattie realised that standing around gossiping about cakes like Mary Berry wasn't going to get them anywhere. They stood up to leave and Finn turned back.

'Can I have your ex-husband's address and the stable girl's contact details too if you have them? Was she local?'

Annie got her 'phone out, turned it on and scribbled down the number and her ex-husband's address on some paper and handed it to Finn.

'Gina left the area, but I don't know why. She came around a time or two and I had her number in case Sam was injured at work.'

'Can I leave my card in case you think of anything else?' Finn passed it over. On impulse Hattie leaned over and took another and passed it to Sophie.

'Yes, thank you. Let's hope we see Sam back at work and riding soon.'

They did not speak until they were back in the car and Finn had driven down the lane.

'So, what did you think?'

Hattie looked steadily at him. 'Well, they weren't in the least bit worried, so he must be at his dad's. His mum would be frantic if she thought he'd really disappeared. All she wanted to talk about was her bloody cakes. I'm not sure about the reason she gave about his girlfriend, either.'

'I agree. How can we find out?'

'We could ask her. Gina wasn't it? That's if we can find her. Listen, why don't you come over to Daisy's, you can look over Kasper for me and we could make an excuse to go over to Teasdale's at the same time. What do you think?'

Finn looked across at her and smiled.

'Sure. You know I'm worried about the lad. Something's not right. It feels wrong. He hasn't responded to my texts and he was doing so well. I'll just try again. If he doesn't respond in a day or so, I'll pop to his dad's place.' He turned to look at her. 'Do you want to ring Gina? It might be better coming from a female rather than me.'

Harriet grinned pleased that he had noticed her skills. She pulled out her 'phone and punched in the 'phone number, her head on one side. The call went to voicemail. 'Damn, I'll text her and hopefully she'll get back to us.'

Finn looked thoughtful. 'Perhaps, they have gone off together for some reason? How can we find out more about her and if she is the key to finding Sam?

Harriet frowned. 'So how about coming to see Kasper?'

'Sounds like a plan. Tomorrow suit you?'

Sunday would be a good day, thought Hattie. Not too much going on, but there would be people around the yard, owners and so on. One of these might know something.

'Great, say eleven o'clock.'

Finn arrived just as Hattie was schooling Kasper in the small arena. The place was quiet as Daisy had gone to a show and it was a rest day for the racehorses in the yard. She popped Kasper over a few fences but noticed a slight uneven movement, especially on landing. She reined in when she saw Finn and he climbed over the paddock railing and came to look the horse over. His eyes were everywhere, noticing the horse's conformation, his movement.

'Nice stamp of a horse,' he said as she halted next to him. 'Not a thoroughbred?'

'No, he's a Dutch warmblood. Did you think he was a bit uneven?' Hattie lived in fear of the tendon injury recurring.

Finn patted Kasper's neck and Hattie could tell he was a horseman through and through just from that small practiced gesture. He narrowed his eyes and looked thoughtful.

'Maybe just nip over those two again and I'll have a closer look.'

Hattie did so, feeling slightly self-conscious this time. Was her jumping position, right? Were her hands light enough? Finn was a proper horseman not a strange jack of all trades like her. She often wondered what use her fencing, shooting, swimming and running prowess were to her now? All that practicing and honing her skills, it seemed like a kind of madness now she was out in the real world. All the pressure to perform well, the targets. Hattie remembered the time her coach Dale tried to persuade her to take the tablets to help her. Christ, she must not go there. It was too shameful! With an effort she dragged her mind back to the present, the here and now, cantering slowly in the school on her favourite horse. Kasper obeyed her aids but seemed to jump a little tentatively. Approaching the second fence, a large upright, he put in an extra stride and made a huge cat like jump at the last minute.

'Hey,' said Finn, 'ever had his back checked? It looks a little sore, you know…'

Hattie dismounted, and Finn unsaddled Kasper and then pressed gently along his spine. At one point, Kasper jumped slightly. Finn pressed the same area again. Same reaction.

'I think you need to get the back man in, you know a horse physiotherapist. Also, I'd exercise him with one of those gel pads under the saddle. You got any?'

'No, I bet someone has though. We could ask in the yard.'

They put Kasper away and walked from the indoor school off into the heart of Vince Hunt's racing yard, about twenty stables arranged in a square. There were several staff brushing up and Hattie could hear noises in the tack room. She followed the sound, Finn trailing behind, eyes flicking left to right, noticing everything. In the tack room, a man was leaning over a sink, running a tap, whilst whistling.

The man looked up, spotted Finn and a huge grin appeared on his face. 'Finn McCarthy as I live and breathe, how the hell are you?'

Finn strode over, grinning, with his hand out ready to shake the other man's.

'Hattie, this is Paddy Owen, a friend, so what are you doing here?'

Paddy had curly reddish hair and twinkling blue eyes. With his short stature and bowed legs, he just had to be an ex-jockey, thought Hattie.

'Sure, I'm the new travelling head lad. Just started a couple of 'weeks ago, I'm working across the two yards, Vince Hunt's and Henry Teasdale's. You?'

Finn explained about the jockey coaching scheme. 'I met Hattie here, who works in racing too, on my travels and came to look at her horse. A showjumper. I think he's got a bit of a back problem. Got any of those gel pads we could borrow, Paddy? You know, the ones that go under the saddle.'

'I think there's one in the other yard, Teasdale's place. I'll walk you both over for a look see…'

Hattie let the two men walk together, interested to see their quiet conversation and body language. She heard bits of it, Finn asking casual questions about the conditional jockeys, and Paddy's predecessor. He heard Paddy say he'd keep an ear to the ground and so on. The two men exchanged telephone numbers. At Teasdale's, a slightly bigger yard than Hunt's, they made their way to a shabby old Portacabin which served as a tack room. While Finn and Paddy walked ahead, Hattie paused to look at the horses, then spotted a fresh-faced girl filling hay nets and decided to try something.

'Hi, I'm just over from Vince's yard. You like working here at Teasdale's? I heard there might be a job?'

'OK. Why, you interested?'

'Might be, someone left then? Or are you getting more horses?'

The girl gazed at her trustingly. 'Well, Gina had to pack it in, what with the baby and all, so yeah there's a space. It's not a bad yard, Teasdale's a moody sod, a bit up and down, I keep out of his way, mostly.'

Hattie wondered if she dared ask more. 'So, Gina, was that a stable romance then? Chance would be a fine thing at ours. Any fit blokes here?' She winced as she said this but hey, how else was she going to find out anything otherwise?

The girl laughed. 'Not really. He's a bit of alright.' She nodded over towards Finn who was approaching carrying a thin, blue gel pad.

Harriet racked her brains for an excuse to ask the girl more about Gina.

'I don't suppose you know where Gina has gone? I am doing some research on female stable staff and their terms and conditions, perhaps she might like to answer some questions?'

The girl stiffened, clearly suspicious. 'No, she's from Ireland so she may have gone back there, but I don't really know her, so I can't help. Sorry.'

Finn came into view. 'Got one,' he told her brandishing the pad, 'right lunch at the local?'

The girl watched as they walked away, Hattie blushed, hoping Finn hadn't overheard the girl's comments. She noticed that women did seem to like Finn. Interesting.

Hattie ordered a white wine spritzer and a cheese toastie at The Yew Tree in Walton. The place was busy and served a low calorie lunch menu, Hattie noted, no doubt for weight conscious jockeys and work riders. They compared notes.

'So, anything?' Finn took a bit of his sausage sandwich.

'Gina, the girlfriend was pregnant...maybe Sam was the father and that's why he's in hiding, but she was Irish and so could have gone back there. But there's no address.'

'Heck, that would be a big thing for a young lad wouldn't it?' He sipped his pint. 'Paddy's going to keep an eye out and keep me informed. I've known him for years and he's a decent bloke. He helped me when I started out.' For a second Finn drifted off. 'He agrees with me that Sam was something special in the saddle.' He bit into his sandwich. 'Paddy has only been there a couple of weeks but a good mate of mine Kevin Allen, a damned good ex-jockey, used to work for Teasdale before he went to a bigger, more successful yard. I could always track him down, I just don't like the smell of it.'

Hattie picked the tomato out of her toasty. 'What do you mean?'

'There's some fuss amongst the owners. They spoke to Paddy about desperately wanting to find Sam as they really want him to ride their horse. It's the Freemans. I know them as I rode my first winner on one of their home bred horses, a mare called Toccata. I might just give them a ring to see if they know anything.'

Hattie's brain was working overtime. 'Anything else?'

Finn suddenly grinned. 'I forgot to say, the cheeky sod Sam sent me a package. I expected some sort of explanation but all I got was this.' He rummaged in his jeans pocket and extracted a small blue metal object. Hattie recognised it as an MP3 player.

Hattie laughed. 'He did say your music was crap. Funny thing to send though. But look if he's up to playing jokes like that surely things are OK. Maybe we're overreacting?'

Finn shook his head. 'Maybe. You can try the bloody music out if you want.' He passed the MP3 player to Hattie. 'Paddy also said he'd heard Connor Moore was unpopular with the owners. Some said he was a weak finisher and they didn't want him on their horses. Paddy hasn't seen him ride yet, but he's going to keep an eye on the lad, try to work out what's going on.'

Suddenly Hattie gave a slight jerk. 'Hey, I forgot I got the photos from the teacher, you know from the Racing to School day at Wetherby when Sam was beaten up. Look, scroll that way…' She passed him her 'phone and watched as Finn scanned them.

'Look there's a face I recognise in the crowd, our GP Dr Pinkerton.' Finn gave her a questioning look. 'So?'

'He's the one who seemed upset when Sam won, the one who said he'd lost money. He never said he'd been there at the races though, odd don't you think?'

'And there's Ross Whitehead, I know him, he runs several syndicates, I think they have a few horses at Teasdale's actually and Jimmy West, of course. West and Whitehead would certainly know one another as they both have horses with Teasdale.'

Hattie felt a little flat. What had she expected? Photos of the men who attacked Sam just as they were putting the finishing touches to their disguises perhaps, their upturned faces identifiable? It was too much to ask, she supposed.

'So, Finn, if Sam or Gina don't get back to you, we'll visit his dad.'

Finn grinned suddenly, a broad smile which gave her more confidence.

'Yes, that's the plan, but don't look now, Henry Teasdale is in here with Vince Hunt and another man.' He shifted in his seat. 'And if it isn't our friend with the skull tattoo, chatting to them.' Hattie craned her neck to see and tried not to look obvious.

'And the other man is the GP, Dr Pinkerton.' There was something rather furtive about the group as they sat in a huddle, well away from the other clients in a sort of alcove. Still, they already knew Teasdale and Hunt were mates and it was no surprise that they all knew each other as they were all locals. No doubt Dr Pinkerton looked after most of their health as there were only two surgeries in the area.

'Hmm. Interesting. How about I leave you to find out about Gina and Dr P and I'll ring the Freemans. And we can schedule in a trip to Lincoln, if I haven't heard from Sam. Where are you next week?'

'Just Doncaster on Friday I think.' Hattie had several assignments and lectures this week. She was also meeting her tutor to discuss her final placement.

'Oh, that's a nice course, another of my favourites. I'll be in touch, probably midweek about the trip to see Sam's dad, assuming Sam doesn't contact me.'

'So, do you think he will?'

'I'm not sure, but I can't believe that someone can just disappear and there's so little real concern from their folks about their welfare. They must know something, or they'd be more bothered. Perhaps he's simply decided to leave because he's had enough and decided that racing is not for him?'

Hattie drove home, replaying their conversation in her head. She knew that Finn was still worried and so was she. She felt like they were trying to complete an eight hundred piece jigsaw, but one where half the pieces had faded and had incomplete pictures on them just to add to the challenge. She thought back to the day when she had helped Sam after he was attacked. He had seemed a nice, normal teenager, who had just had an incredible winner. So why vanish? He should be going from strength to strength, enjoying life. Or maybe he was a flaky sort and they were over thinking it all? Maybe she was just too fond of a good old conspiracy theory and was beginning to like Finn's company? Far from being dour, he actually had a dry sense of humour.

Funny, she reflected, that although he'd chatted about the 'case' as she now thought of it, and seemed keen to work out what was going on with his conditionals, so far, she knew precisely nothing about him, no personal details whatsoever. Was he married? Divorced or unattached she guessed but he gave nothing away, no sign of him having to dash back to see a long term partner. He was good looking, in his early thirties and had, by all accounts, been a good jockey. She felt that he was a complex man and a mass of contradictions. She sensed that it would be hard to get to know him, but that it would definitely be worth the wait.

Chapter 9

Finn found that spending time with Hattie was enjoyable and it made him forget about the other pressing matter on his mind, namely whether he was going to contact Nat. The whole encounter with Boothroyd and Livvy had opened up an emotional hornet's nest and he pounded the pavements, training extra hard the next morning in an effort to find some equilibrium. He felt off kilter, uneasy and apprehensive. After a shower, he sipped his coffee and munched a slice of toast. He could ignore Boothroyd for the most part, except he did wonder what he and West were planning, and he suspected it had something to do with Sam's disappearance. But Livvy and Nat were another matter. He pulled out the piece of paper Livvy had given him and wondered what to do. Part of him desperately wanted to see his old friend, catch up and chat about old times, but he also knew that their friendship was never going to be the same, how could it be when he had been so badly betrayed? Still, he was not a man to bear a grudge forever and besides, he was curious to know what was going on with Nat. Maybe, their friendship wasn't worth throwing away because of a woman, after all?

In the end though he didn't have to contact Nat, as it was Nat who broke the silence. His mobile flashed, signaling that he had had a message.

Liv said she'd seen you. Any chance of meeting up for a drink? I need to speak to you. Hear you work for the BHA. If you're at the races when I'm riding, meet you for a drink? Miss you, mate.

Finn stared at the text for a long time. How typical of Nat to surprise him by contacting him first. He pondered on the matter for a while longer, almost texted back then decided against it, when there was a knock at the door. Finn went to answer it and was greeted by two plain clothed policemen, who flashed their warrant cards and explained that they had come about Sam Foster.

DI James was in his forties, had shrewd grey eyes, a smart suit and very shiny shoes. His companion was younger, taller and had an arrogant air about him.

'This is Sergeant Longton. I gather you are Sam's jockey coach,' began DI James. 'We won't keep you long.'

Finn showed them into his kitchen and offered coffee which they accepted. Finn explained his involvement with the lad and recounted details of the incident in Wetherby when he was beaten up.

'What was your impression of the young man?' asked DI James.

'Well, I only met him on that day at Wetherby, but he seemed a decent enough lad and had just ridden a winner earlier in the day.'

The two police officers nodded gravely, DS Longton making notes in a pocket book in a spiky hand.

'Yes, we're aware that he was doing quite well.'

'So, do you have any idea where he might have gone? We are anxious to get in touch with him.'

Finn explained that he had visited Sam's mother who had told him he was at his father's.

'Do you have that address?' asked DS Longton.

Finn nodded and found the scribbled notes he'd made and passed it over. DS Longton made a record of it.

'Can you think of any reason why Sam may have gone missing?' continued DI James, his grey eyes appraising Finn carefully.

He explained about Sam being assaulted but didn't mention the possible drug issue and Gina's pregnancy. After all, it was speculation and he had no proof whatsoever. He could not go around making spurious allegations that could have serious consequences, so he just kept quiet. He would need to have concrete evidence,

'No, none. I only met him the once as I explained.'

DI James nodded. 'And he never confided in you about any concerns he might have had, why he was beaten up, who was involved?'

'No, on the contrary, he didn't want any fuss or bother at all and certainly no police. I did advise him to report the matter, but he just put it down to angry punters backing another horse.'

'Did you see who had assaulted him?'

'No. I had arranged to meet him to discuss his riding but when I got there he had already been beaten up. Sam said that they wore caps with the peaks pulled down, dark clothing and had big feet.' All the better to kick him with, Finn thought wryly. For some reason, which he was not quite sure of, Finn did not tell them about the package he'd received from Sam with the MP3 player. It seemed, maybe, too trivial. Or more likely he thought, he just didn't know what its significance was, and he wanted to keep it to himself until things were clearer.

The two men exchanged a look and stood up to leave.

'Thank you, you've been very helpful.' DI James nodded.

DS Longton had been studying the photographs of Finn riding various winners. 'So, you're THE Finn McCarthy. I have won quite a bit backing you. I didn't quite recognise you without your riding hat. How are you finding the new job?'

'Interesting,' explained Finn. 'I'm enjoying being back on the racecourse even if I'm not riding, coaching is the next best thing.' He realised that this was actually true. 'Listen, if you find the lad, then would you ask him to contact me and maybe I can help him move yards if he's not fitting in at Teasdale's. He can ride well, you see, he rode Saffron Sun like a pro.'

DS Longton gave him the benefit of a bright smile. 'We will, Mr McCarthy, we will.'

Finn wondered if they were contacting him because of Teasdale. Sam's mother, he decided, would certainly not have contacted the police. Either way, he felt relieved. It felt good that someone official was actually doing something to find the lad at long last, and it also meant that it was not just down to him and Hattie.

He spent some time going over the races ridden by Sam, Connor and Harry. All the conditionals had had thirty or so rides and had clearly improved over time. Their first few rides had run down the field, but all were starting to get some places and even winners. He looked for patterns. He remembered watching real life detective programmes and realised that much of the job was mundane and painstaking, checking facts carefully and looking for coincidences. All of the horses were owned by different syndicates and two were owned by Jimmy West. Had he tried to bully the conditionals to fix races by threatening to withhold rides from them perhaps? He looked at any possible link with Ross Whitehead who ran a syndicate called Equistar, but none of the conditionals rode his horses, so Ross appearing in the photos when Sam was beaten up was probably just a coincidence, he decided, if there was such a thing.

He wondered about Sam and whether Connor Moore knew more than he was letting on about his disappearance. Maybe he ought to pay him another visit? He reached no real conclusions, decided to ring his mother, who was keen to know when he was going to visit and made a point of telling him that his sister had called in just a day ago. He promised to visit and then on impulse rang the owner friends mentioned by Paddy, Mr and Mrs Freeman. They were delighted to hear from their favourite ex-jockey, keen to talk to him about Sam and were very worried about his disappearance. They fixed up a time to catch up with each other over a meal.

He had arranged to meet Mr and Mrs Freeman in York at a French restaurant on Castle Gate. In their fifties, Mr Freeman owned and ran an engineering company, whilst his wife ran their stud farm, alongside a handful of specially selected staff. Finn had had his first winner riding their homebred mare, who was now the mainstay of their stud business. They were a hardworking, likeable couple who had insisted that Finn was given their rides, something he was eternally grateful for.

'It was so good to hear from you,' enthused Mrs Freeman.

'Yes, indeed,' agreed Mr Freeman, or Vanessa and Bill as they liked him to call them.

They chatted about the old days and their horses. The mares that Finn had ridden, particularly their star Toccata, were now broodmares at the Freeman's Stud Farm and as for the geldings, some were sold on as hacks and they still had a couple who were retired and having a marvellous life, turned out to grass.

'Wonderful days and of course, Toccata has had lots of foals. Rhapsody has gone on to hurdle and she's the one we have with Henry Teasdale.' Vanessa shook her head and glanced meaningfully at her husband. 'Which is what why we wanted to talk to you.'

'Yes, congratulations on your new job, by the way, I'm sure you'll be splendid,' enthused Bill. He lowered his voice and suddenly looked serious.

'Yes, Vanessa and I were very worried when we heard about Sam disappearing.'

Finn wasn't sure who else knew about Sam and who ought to know. He was uncertain about how much to reveal.

'Teasdale had to tell us as Sam usually looks after our horses and rides for us too. We asked him and believed that he was simply off sick. I mean the lad was in the best of health and he loves those horses, he simply wouldn't just leave them without very good reason.'

'Rhapsody loves him too. She's been a bit off her food, grieving since he left.'

Finn listened intently. Horses could form very good bonds with humans, he knew, but this did sound rather fanciful. Still, the Freemans were a bit eccentric. Perhaps, there was an element of self interest in there too, in their quest to find Sam.

'Of course, we would like Rhapsody to be fit and well for the Championship Hurdle in December and it would be great if Sam was back to ride her…'

'Ah…'

Vanessa gave Finn a penetrating look. 'Of course, we are still concerned about Sam. You see, he wouldn't have simply walked out, I just can't see it. We have got to know the lad well and it's just not his style.'

Finn nodded. 'I tend to agree. Aside from his riding and talent with the horse, how did you find Sam a person?'

'Well, he was always polite, worked hard whenever we saw him at the yard, and rode like a dream. A sensible, ambitious lad all round, so much so, we don't feel we can entrust our hurdler Rhapsody to anyone else. He rode her out and they have a really good bond. Bloody horse is off her food too, bereft, as I said.'

'That's right,' continued Vanessa. 'I suppose she will get over it eventually, but she's just happier with Sam around. I can't think he's run off, I mean, he had everything going for him.'

'Which is why we spoke to Paddy and then we found out that you were his coach,' continued Bill. 'And then we heard about him being beaten up at Wetherby. It all sounds very fishy. Supposing he's been kidnapped? As I said, he would not go off and leave Rhapsody, he just wouldn't.'

Finn took this in. He explained about the police visit that morning.

'So, you see, they are now involved, and I presume Teasdale reported him missing, so it's in their hands now. If he has been kidnapped, then I'm sure the police will know what to do.'

Privately he thought it was highly unlikely. What would be the motive? The family were not rich, and Sam's mother certainly did not behave as if she had just had a ransom request. The thought made him smile. All she had seemed interested in was her new cake recipes for the coffee shop.

He suddenly thought of something. 'Were you aware of Sam having a relationship with a stable girl called Gina?'

Vanessa shook her head. 'No, I don't know anything about them being in a relationship but then I don't suppose we would. She was a pretty little thing, though, wasn't she?'

She had turned to her husband who grinned sheepishly. Then two pairs of eyes studied him gravely.

'No disrespect to the police, but it stands to reason that it needs someone who knows about racing to find him,' explained Bill. 'It's a BHA matter, surely, if one of their lads goes missing? You're his coach, so it goes without saying you should be involved.'

Vanessa smiled. 'Exactly. Someone who works for the BHA and has all the right contacts, and it needs to be someone who has experienced racing. In fact, someone like you.' Two pairs of eyes studied him. 'When we found out you were his coach, we were delighted. All that riding experience and the true grit you've showed in the past. We just know you can find him. It should be easy for a man like you.'

Finn smiled, a little uncertain. First the Murphys and now the Freemans. Their logic was flawed but he didn't have the heart to say so. They were obviously wanting Sam to come back to ride their precious Rhapsody, as well. But the skills involved in racing and finding missing people were completely different. It was all very well the Freemans having faith in him, but did he have faith in himself?

Finn drove back home, contemplating his meeting with the Freemans. Strange, that they were so much more concerned for Sam than his own mother had been. Obviously, they had their own agenda, but they had seemed genuinely worried. He checked his 'phone for emails or messages from Sam, but there were none. Instead there was a message from Tony Murphy asking him to ring back as soon as possible. He did so.

'Finn, good to hear from you. Now, then, this is strictly confidential, but there's been a development. RaceStraight have received an anonymous tip off about drug dealing and pushing in Walton specifically involving racing yards.' Finn listened carefully. 'So, it puts a different complexion on that missing conditional of yours, doesn't it?'

Finn agreed that it did. RaceStraight was an anonymous phone line that anyone could ring with information about anything that impacted upon the integrity of racing. He went on to explain about the other developments, his conversation with the Freemans, his meeting with Sam's mother and the visit from the police.

'The police are searching for Sam, 'continued Tony, 'but I think you ought to find him first, it needs someone from racing who understands our world. Maybe that other young conditional, the one that had the near miss with the car, perhaps he is worth another visit?'

'By the way do you know Ted Boothroyd? I saw him at Market Rasen. He isn't training again, is he?'

'No, he was banned as you of all people should know. I doubt he'd ever be given a licence again, but I'll check if you like.'

'And Jimmy West?'

'No, never heard of him. Why do you want to know?'

'Because he owned Saffron Sun the horse that Sam won on and I had the distinct impression he was furious with the lad. Suppose he's pressuring conditionals to fix races? He's a bully and I wouldn't put it past him. I saw Boothroyd and West together. Supposing that's their game? Maybe they tried it with Sam, but he wouldn't lose and so had to run away?'

'Look, Finn. These are serious allegations and the publicity, if the press gets wind of it, race fixing or drug pushing, would be very damaging. I think you had better find Sam and find out what's going on, then we can deal with any fall out and get him moved to another yard if needs be. Can you make this your priority?'

'What about the talks about dealing with the press and so on, and the new conditionals you wanted me to take on?'

'No Finn, we'll leave all that for now. This is more important. You focus on finding out what's going on with your lads, right?'

Finn took Tony to mean that the BHA wanted to manage any adverse media fallout that might arise and locate Sam before the police did. That way they could learn the extent of the problem before the press got hold of it. He had a similar view to Tony's that Sam was the key to everything. So, he agreed to try and rang off. He pondered on whether or not to call on Connor first and decided that this could wait. He could visit him again if their search for Sam drew a blank. He was a man who liked to keep his word. He worked out how to find Sam's father's house online and texted Hattie.

No news from Sam, so do you fancy a trip to Lincoln tomorrow?

Chapter 10

Hattie agreed to drive to Finn's home in York. He offered to take them to Lincoln. Finn had a newish Audi whereas Hattie's car, her mum's old Polo, was ancient, needed a service and had a slow puncture, so there was no competition really. Hattie had hesitated about the trip at first, she should definitely be doing some reading and planning for her next assignment, but with only one race meeting at Doncaster this week, she would have two whole free days in which to catch up and how often did adventures like this come up? She found that she was increasingly intrigued by the conditionals. Hattie followed the satnav directions in York to an old, four storey factory which had been converted into flats. It looked like the conversion had been done sympathetically and stylishly. She parked and went to ring the doorbell next to Finn's name, F McCarthy.

He answered the entry 'phone and directed her up and into Flat 4. The flat was a surprise. He showed her into a spacious sitting room with big windows and exposed old brick work along one of the walls. It was decorated in subdued colours, a bit like a show home, brown leather sofas and a cream and brown rug. She noticed that there was little of a personal nature, very few photos, ornaments or pictures. Finn showed her a small business like office, which had a computer and shelving holding several racing trophies in it. No sign of female occupancy either which she found interesting.

'I've not been here that long, my sister helped me buy the essentials…' Finn shrugged and looked apologetic. Ah, she thought so he has a sister. It was the first piece of personal information that he had volunteered.

'Oh, I like it. What sort of factory was it?'

Finn laughed. 'Chocolate of course, one of the Rowntree places. Look, here's some photos.'

Hattie saw workmen and women from the 1930s grinning for the camera in two old black and white pictures on the wall behind the largest sofa. She took a deep breath.

'Mmm, I can almost smell the chocolate.'

Finn looked sceptical. 'Right, are you ready to go or do you want a bite to eat? I know how you're always hungry...'

'Now let's crack on, shall we? We can always grab something on the way…'

En route Finn told her about the visit from the police, his conversation with Mr and Mrs Freeman and finally the 'phone call from Tony Murphy. Hattie was interested to see how quickly what had seemed like quite a small thing, finding a beaten-up jockey, was developing into something else, very much bigger and potentially more serious.

'Do you think it was Sam who rang RaceStraight, or whatever you call the helpline, about the drugs?'

Finn glanced at her. 'Dunno. It all seems a bit too coincidental though, I think if it wasn't Sam it might have been one of the other conditionals. It makes me mad, you know, these young lads need guidance and support. There's plenty of good advice out there, there really is no need for young jockeys to resort to drugs to keep their weight down. Sorry, I'm preaching to the converted aren't I, with your studies…'

Hattie immediately thought of her school friend, Janet. Images of the last time she'd seen her raced through her mind. It'd been just before 'A' levels when Janet had dropped out of school and by then she'd been an emaciated shell of her former self. Eating disorders were surprisingly common and not always obvious to the naked eye. Many normal sized girls were bulimic and there was increasing numbers of boys too, and that was without the added pressure of needing to keep your weight down for a job.

'I suppose some of the lads might just grow too big, it's possible to grow into your early twenties, isn't it? They probably need help working out what weights are possible for their size and then a dietician could devise a sensible diet for them. Even then I suppose some might just cut their losses if it's too draconian or difficult for them. Sounds like a good project for a research in the future…'

'Getting professional advice has got to be much better than starving yourself and getting hooked on booze, fags or drugs. You really interested in working with jockeys then?'

Hattie smiled, 'Oh, I'd love to work for the Professional Jockeys Association or the BHA like you or with other athletes in the future, but I need experience first. I suppose the pressure on jockeys is immense because the weights are so low. It's not such an issue in other sports but good nutrition definitely is.'

Finn laughed. 'Do you know, I'd never really thought of jockeys as athletes exactly, I suppose they are.'

Hattie was wondering what Will knew about the drugs scene in Walton and how much she could find out from him, if anything.

'I'll ask my brother...he's very professional but he might give us a steer in the right direction. So, what do we know about this Mr Foster then?'

'He's an electrician. He told me Sam's not there. Said he could spare ten minutes, if we go to the site he's working on…'

Hattie grimaced. 'Doesn't sound too friendly…'

'He wasn't.'

Keith Foster turned out to be a short, muscular man with a shaved head, tattoos and a bullish attitude. He marched over when alerted by the site manager and looked none too pleased to see the pair. The project he was working on looked like a row of starter homes, but it was difficult to imagine the finished thing with all the trucks, mud, workmen and general bustle. Mr Foster was, she remembered Finn saying, an electrician. He undid his work belt and glared at them.

'So, what's all this about Sam?'

Finn explained about his disappearance and their visit to his ex-wife.

Keith eyed them suspiciously, 'Why are you so interested?'

Hattie guessed that Finn had already gone through his role as a jockey coach before with Mr Foster, but he patiently repeated it. Keith looked marginally less hostile.

'So, is he any good our Sam, got the makings of a good rider?'

'He has, actually. I think he's got great potential. But I'm really worried about why he disappeared. If there's problems at the yard we could look into a transfer elsewhere…'

Harriet couldn't help but chip in.

'It would be a shame for all that potential to be wasted. Sam doesn't need to be scared and think he's wrecked his chances. This sort of thing happens sometimes…' She wasn't sure of her facts here but was keen to reassure his father as she felt that Sam might be languishing at his dad's house, feeling utterly wretched. She remembered feeling overwhelmed herself when she'd performed badly in pentathlon competitions or had an injury. When all the problems blew up with Dale, she'd felt like she'd had no one to turn to. In the end Christopher Pinkerton had come to her rescue and helped explain to UK anti-doping why she'd missed a test and they'd accepted his reasons. Supposing Sam had a pregnant ex-girlfriend and then had problems with drugs at the yard? He could easily feel as wretched as she did then. It was understandable for a youngster to run off. She imagined the call to RaceStraight, if it was him who'd made it, might be some sort of cry for help.

Keith Foster sighed and lit up a cigarette. Narrowing his eyes, he blew smoke in Hattie's direction. He seemed to be considering something. At last he turned to face them.

'He was at mine, but he left a couple of days ago…'

'Was he alright?' asked Hattie.

Keith Foster shrugged as if he didn't care much one way or another. Or as if he did not think the welfare of his son was of any major importance. Clearly, an in depth father and son discussion had not been part of the stay.

'Did he say anything about the yard or why he'd run away?'

Keith took a long drag on his cigarette. 'Said he was taking time out, didn't say why. He was OK, his usual self really.'

Hattie wondered if Keith Foster would notice a hurricane if it hit him in the head, he certainly didn't give her the impression that he was big on emotional welfare.

'Anything else? Did he say where he was going?' Finn sounded as frustrated as she was about this interview.

'No.' A guarded look spread over Keith's face and then he stubbed his cigarette out decisively. Hattie realised that the interview was now over. They watched him walk back to the building site, buckling his work belt back on.

'What do we do now?' she asked.

Back in the car Hattie repeated the question.

Finn grinned. 'How about a spot of breaking and entering?'

Hattie realised she must have looked shocked because Finn gave a bark of laughter.

'Don't look so worried. It's just that we've come all this way and I do have Keith's address, so I don't think there's any harm in having a quick look around, do you?' He wiggled his eyebrows suggestively.

Hattie frowned. 'God, how are we going to do that?'

Finn felt in his pocket and produced some strange looking keys.

'Lock picks. It should be easy enough.'

Hattie shook her head. 'How on earth do you know about this sort of stuff?'

Finn shrugged. 'I just had some dodgy mates as a kid.'

'OK, what is our cover story though?'

Finn smiled. 'I've some tools in my boot and a hi viz jacket, so we could be checking the gas? Someone could have reported a leak.'

Hattie grinned. 'OK, but can we get something to eat first? I'm absolutely starving.'

Finn punched the postcode into his satnav and then they set off to Keith Foster's, Hattie looking out for somewhere to eat on the way. She spotted a McDonalds sign and pointed, 'Look that'll do.'

Finn, with a bemused expression on his face pulled into the drive through and they ordered Big Macs, fries and coffee.

Hattie devoured hers, stopping only to dip her fries in ketchup and chattering in between mouthfuls.

'Can't believe a trainee dietician would eat that!' teased Finn. 'Still it's good to see a girl with an appetite. I don't know where you put it, you must have hollow legs, you're a right gannet. Right ready?'

'High metabolic rate, I reckon. Haven't been to McDonald's for ages, honest. So, what's the plan?'

'Not sure. Park discreetly, slip round the back, have a look around, maybe slip in if we can and look for anything which might help us find Sam. Of course, his dad might be lying, he could still be there.'

Finn pulled up to a compact, newish home on a small estate, not unlike the ones Foster was currently working on, thought Hattie. They parked down the road and then walked quickly to the house, number 17 Bishopsgate's Rise. Fortunately, the place seemed quiet, there was no one about and only a few cars too. No doubt the inhabitants were mostly at work like Keith. Finn hefted a tool box out of the boot, placed it in the driveway and struggled into a hi viz jacket.

'Come on. You go knock on the door and I'll slip round the back…'

Hattie knocked at the white door and tried to peer in the glass window. No reply, she tried again and spotting a doorbell, pushed that too. No answer. She was just about to go around the back when the door opened. It was a smiling Finn.

'Come in,' he said in a low voice.

Inside Hattie took in the carpet, newish but in need of a vacuum and the messy sitting room, its coffee table covered in empty pizza boxes and beer cans.

She hissed. 'So, what are we looking for?'

'Any clues about where Sam might be? If we hear anything, we slip out the back down the side and off to the car pronto, OK?'

He passed her a pair of leather gloves. 'Just to stop prints, you know… I'll do upstairs, you look down here.'

Hattie put the gloves on and went into the kitchen. She felt alarmed and ashamed of what they were doing and tried to think clearly. She remembered what her brother, Dominic, had said about prints. Were leather gloves OK? She reckoned they would be. Right, where would useful information be kept? She spotted a shelf with a 'phone on it and also an address book. She flicked through the book and getting out her 'phone, decided to take photos of the contents of about five pages instead. Next to it was a post-it pad. The top note had no writing on it but there was an indentation, enough to tell her that someone had scribbled a 'phone number on the paper above and then tore it off. Hattie took the top note. Then she scanned the kitchen noticeboard and took a photo of the calendar, the postcards and flyers and so on. There was a postcard from Glasgow showing the city skyline. Hattie pulled it down and examined the back. It read, *'Enjoying my visit to the big city and having a rest from the P.O, love Granny Morag.'*

Hattie noticed, with a pang, that the date of Sam's win at Wetherby was circled in biro. Maybe his dad was more interested in his son than first appeared. She even rifled through the bills piled on top of the microwave. Found nothing of any significance. She peeped in the small utility room that led outside to the garden, spotted outdoor work clothes hung up, a pair of workman's boots, there was nothing that might belong to Sam, nothing even vaguely like equestrian attire. She went to the bottom of the stairs and called,

'Finn, I've done, you?'

He raced downstairs and they slipped out of the back door, down the side of the house and into the car. The whole enterprise could not have taken more than about ten minutes.

'So how did you learn to do breaking and entering?'

Finn smiled. 'You don't want to know. Did you find anything interesting?'

'I think,' said Hattie scrolling through her photos of the address book, 'that the Fosters have relatives in Scotland. His mum had a Scottish accent, didn't she? Sam's sister said that Granny Morag works in the post office somewhere there. I also found an imprint of a number. It might be a 'phone number. I can't quite make it out but if I scribble over it in pencil, I think it'll be clearer, and I might be able to decipher it.'

'Great. And there's more,' Finn looked serious, 'I found this bottle of pills in the spare room which makes me think that Sam left them…' He fished the white plastic bottle out of his pocket.

Later back in York they sat in the car for a few minutes making plans.

'Right, I'll find out what's in these tablets as there's no label on them and you let me know about the 'phone number.'

Hattie nodded. 'OK, I'll be in touch...' She felt a bit disappointed with what they'd collected together, it didn't seem like much and it had taken most of the day. And her essays and assignments, she realised, wouldn't write themselves. Hell.

'Harriet, are you riding this week?' asked Finn, his face in shadow so she couldn't read his expression. 'I thought maybe I might nip over to see Connor Moore and catch up with Paddy and of course Kasper…' He looked thoughtful. 'I think we should talk to Connor again. I'm sure he knows more than he's letting on…'

'OK, I was going to pop down to the yard before Doncaster actually…'

'Perfect, I'll meet you at Hunts' yard, say nine thirty?'

She nodded.

'Harriet, I feel like we've made progress today, thanks…'

She smiled, realising that so had she. 'Hey, don't call me that, I feel like I'm in trouble, like when I had to sit outside the head teacher's office for a whole day for writing on her car in lipstick. See you on Thursday then.'

Finn laughed. 'I can just imagine that, bet you were a right horror. What did you write?'

Hattie pictured Miss Scaife, the tiny, dull woman in her sixties with rough reptilian skin and cold eyes.

'Oh, all I wrote was Racey Scaifey in red lipstick. We all thought it was hysterical, she threatened me with the police for vandalising her car. Luckily Dad talked her out of it, persuaded her that she'd be laughed out of the station and promised to give me a good talking to.'

Finn let out a bark of laughter, dark eyes dancing. 'Quite right, and did he?'

'Yeah, I had to wash her car every week for a few months too.'

Have I got a nickname?'

Hattie thought about Finn's reserve and caution towards people combined with his devil may care attitude to some things. He had either been hurt badly or was just super sensible, then he had to go and mention breaking and entering! He was certainly a man of huge contradictions underneath that gruff exterior, but she couldn't think of anything that wasn't offensive. A moody git? Mercurial, maybe?

'I'm working on it, don't you worry!'

Again, he laughed, his expression lighting up his face like sudden sunshine after rain. 'Honestly, I can see I'll have to watch you. OK. Bye Hattie.'

She got out of the car. As she got into her own Polo, Finn flashed his lights and beeped good night like a close friend might do. It was funny, she thought, how she'd so quickly slipped into this easy friendship with Finn. She shook herself and resolved not to analyse what was happening too much, it would spoil things. All she knew was that she felt safe with Finn, she didn't feel a romantic element to their spending time together, probably because he was several years older than her. But although he seemed reserved, aloof even, except about the case, he was fun, intelligent and she liked him. Don't knock it, she told herself, you could do with another friend and a bit of excitement. After all, during all the years she had pursued her dream to become a champion modern pentathlete she had rather missed out on fun and friends, she could see that now and it was time that changed.

Chapter 11

Finn ate a light meal and rang Dr Jamieson. If his old friend was surprised about his inquiry about how to get some tablets analysed, he didn't show it. He was the soul of discretion and had been a valued friend for a long time. Finn had consulted him when he had injuries and needed quick, confidential advice. Finn promised to drop by with the pills and Dr Jamieson agreed to get the results back to him as soon as possible. He spent the rest of the evening wondering about drug dealing, Teasdale, Connor Moore and their links to Sam. What would make a young man disappear and abandon a promising career? Drugs could be an explanation or bullying. He chased these thoughts round and round his brain, considering the various permutations. Who was the lad running away from? West seemed the most likely person to have put pressure on Sam to lose the race, but if it was drugs, which looked increasingly likely, who was involved? He didn't want to believe that the jockey was mixed up in drugs. Was he being too charitable towards Sam because of his own experiences? Maybe Spud beat him up and he was behind the drug dealing? But he doubted that Spud had the brainpower required to run such an operation and besides those skull tattoos were common enough. God, all this speculation, was getting him nowhere fast.

Then he wondered about Nat and what on earth he might want to talk to Finn about. He googled the horses declared for Doncaster tomorrow and saw that Nat had a few rides, considered texting him but then changed his mind. He wasn't quite ready to hear Nat's justifications and excuses for running off with Livvy, yet part of him was also intrigued. Perhaps, he'd seek him out tomorrow? He wrote up some reports, worked on some figures he'd been asked to give to the Professional Jockeys' Association, submitted his mileage claims and went to bed, thoughts and theories circling until sleep finally overcame him.

Hattie's riding lesson went well. Finn watched from the side of the arena as Daisy shouted out instructions. She was clearly a competent teacher and Hattie a decent rider. Finn's idea to use the gel pad under Kasper's saddle and call the horse physio, had also helped. He left Hattie and Daisy to finish the lesson and decided to try his hand at finding Connor.

Finn looked around the place, spotting that there was still a handful of stable staff sweeping up and replenishing water buckets after coming back from the gallops.

'Won't be too long...'

Hattie followed Finn's gaze and nodded. 'OK. I'll catch you later.'

He found Connor cleaning tack, his arm in a sling. The young man whistled as he rubbed the oil onto the leather. He looked surprised and a little wary as Finn came into view.

'Hi. Just thought I'd look in on you since I'm in the area. How are you?'

Connor nodded. 'On the mend. I can just about manage some stable tasks, but I won't be riding for a bit.'

'Fair enough. You need to make sure you're fully healed.' Finn settled down beside him. 'I wanted a quick word about Sam Foster, you know the conditional who rides for Teasdale.' Connor looked instantly alert. 'I'm sure you've heard that he's disappeared.' He gave Connor a meaningful look. 'I take my responsibilities very seriously and I need to check that he's alright. Might have to take matters into my own hands, if I don't hear from him soon. So, do you have any ideas where he's gone and why?'

Connor swallowed nervously and avoided Finn's eyes. He shrugged rather unconvincingly.

'Nah, can't help you there.'

Finn nodded. 'OK. I have a couple of theories though. I've heard that there's some drugs stuff going on hereabouts. I hope he's not involved in that. You know how it goes, lad wants to be a jockey and starts to struggle to make the weights.' Connor looked at him in surprise. 'Then he decides to do some drugs to help him lose the pounds, only problem is that he becomes addicted, spends too much money and before long, finds he has loads of drug debts and has to do a runner.'

Connor shrugged. Was it Finn's imagination or had the lad turned white? Finn got to his feet.

'And you know what happens then? The friends who supplied the drugs suddenly become your worst enemies and then they apply pressure on you to repay the debt, they will do anything to get their money and I mean anything…'

Connor sighed and continued moving his cloth across the leather in swift, deft movements with his good hand whilst his other arm held the bridle in place. The smell of the neatsfoot oil was both comforting and familiar.

Connor cleared his throat. 'I did hear that Sam split up with his on and off girlfriend, Gina. So, she might know something or ask Paddy. Sam seemed to get on with him. As for any drugs, I wouldn't know. I'm from a tiny village in Ireland, we don't have anything to do with stuff like that.'

Finn studied the lad's pale face. He was pretty sure that drugs were available everywhere, even in Ireland.

'Are you sure about that because I wouldn't want any of my lads to be in that position? I want to help. There's always something I can do, get jockeys moved, get help, legal advice, support…'

For a second Connor looked like he might be about to say something, then a shadow passed the window and a figure appeared in the doorway.

'What are you doing skulking in here when there's work to be done.' The voice was deep and authoritative. Finn recognised the man as Vince Hunt. He frowned at Finn, clearly annoyed to find a stranger in his yard. Finn put his hand out to shake. Hunt pointedly did not reciprocate.

'Finn McCarthy, I'm Connor's coach. Forgive my manners, I should have called to introduce myself before turning up. I came with Hattie actually, so took the opportunity to chat to Connor whilst I was here.'

Vince gazed at Finn. 'Hattie, oh yes.' Vince looked from Connor to Finn, his expression thawing slightly. Finn guessed he could not really stop Harriet bringing a friend to the yard when she was having a lesson, so wouldn't make an issue of him just turning up unannounced, though Hunt clearly felt uncomfortable about it.

'I'm afraid we're short staffed and very busy today, so it's all hands on deck,' he added by way of explanation for his brusque manner.

Finn smiled. 'Of course. I'll go back and see how Kasper is shaping up.' He glanced at Connor. 'I'll be in touch. Nice to have met you,' he called to Hunt as he left. Finn approached the arena deeply troubled. He was sure that he had touched a nerve with Connor and was more and more certain that all was not well. Hunt had made him feel about as welcome as a dose of influenza, and Connor certainly knew much more than he was letting on. He looked around for Paddy but didn't want to push his luck. He sent him a quick text and remembered that Teasdale had a couple of runners at Doncaster that afternoon, so hoped he could catch up with him there. He would also have the chance to look at another of his growing list of conditionals, Aidan Collins. He arranged to meet Hattie there later.

The Yorkshire countryside looked glorious as the trees were turning into full autumn colour mode, vibrant sienna, burnt umber and titian reds. It was God's own country all right he thought, savouring it as he drove. Doncaster was a lovely racecourse set in the heart of the town. It comprised a new Lazarus stand and the old Clock Tower stand, with its steep concrete steps and lovely Victorian façade. Doncaster was the home of the famous classic St Leger race, but it also held decent national hunt cards over its well- kept course, such as the one today. Finn pondered on the fact that he had three people to see, Paddy, Aiden and possibly Nat. He had real mixed feelings about seeing Nat again, as he didn't want to stir up a maelstrom of emotions, not when he was feeling happier and more settled than he had for a long time. Still, although he was not a man given to introspection, he realised it might help him emotionally by giving him what psychologists called 'closure'. It was his opportunity to be the bigger man and that appealed to him, plus he felt a tiny bit of curiosity about what was bugging Nat.

He drank in a couple of lungfuls of fresh air, made his way into the course, bought a racecard and studied it. It was almost an hour and a half before the first race and although the place was steadily filling up, he had time to get a quick coffee and maybe seek out Paddy before the races started. He sipped his latte and enjoyed people watching as he flicked through the card. Teasdale had a couple of runners and one was in the first race, so Paddy was sure to be here already. He also saw that Nat had three rides that day, so he wondered about whether to approach him, contemplated texting him then decided that he didn't want to commit to anything at this stage. He'd see how he felt later. Just as he was about to leave a smartly dressed man, wearing a trilby appeared and eyeing Finn closely made his way over.

'Tim Giles,' he said offering his hand, 'we have met a few times…'

Finn recognised the urbane fifty something year old journalist and smiled. 'Hi, what can I do for you?'

Tim took off his hat, pulled up a chair and glancing round said quietly. 'Well, I just wondered if we could do a quick impromptu interview. You know, well known ex-jockey's new role and all that…'

He waved his hands expansively and then leaned closer. 'I am pleased you've found a new career, is it working out alright for you, Finn?'

Finn smiled. He supposed it wouldn't do any harm to give Tim ten minutes of his time. He knew as well as anyone that the racing public liked to hear how the industry supported its own, how retired jockeys could adapt to new roles in racing once their careers were over. OK, so he wasn't Tony McCoy or Mick Fitzgerald with glittering TV careers, but he did still have a role to play in racing and believed in his new job.

'So, what do you want to know Tim?'

The journalist ordered fresh coffees, whipped out his notebook and with a beatific grin began a short interview. He wanted to know about the Jockey Coaching and Mentoring scheme, who ran it and how Finn had started. Finn relaxed and answered as best he could, mentioning the support he'd received from Tony Murphy from the BHA. Tim's pencil scrawled over his pad using good, old fashioned shorthand. Finn told Tim about the support offered to young jockeys about diet, health, media training, race riding and dealing with owners on race days.

'And you look after Connor Moore, Harry Jarvis, Callum Jones, Aidan Collins and did you say Sam Foster?' Tim leaned in closer. 'I remember interviewing him at Wetherby after he'd ridden a good winner. Is it true that he's gone AWOL?'

Finn's eyes widened, and he wondered how that bit of information had leaked out.

'Well, not exactly. I think he's just taking a quick break, family issues, you know.' Finn was keen to play down Sam's disappearance. He certainly didn't want the press to get hold of it. 'Actually, he contacted me the other day. Even sent me an MP3 player to listen to, said my music was rubbish, the cheek of the lad!'

Tim grinned. 'Well, that's alright then. Once again thanks Finn and I'm sure you're doing a super job, good luck. Now I'm going to write this up as a short piece and send it to a few editors, hopefully it'll appear somewhere soon. Maybe the Racing Post's Sunday section? Good to see you again.'

Tim sprang up, put on his hat and, with a polite nod made his way through the crowd. Finn finished his latte thoughtfully. He felt as if he'd been hit by a charm offensive and wondered idly if somehow, he had said too much. Still, surely not, what after all had he revealed?

And although he was not particularly vain it would be nice to be recognised in his new job and even this small attention was, he admitted, very welcome, after all his difficulties and struggles to get his life back on track after he'd lost Livvy, his best friend and his career.

He made his way to the lorry park and spotted Teasdale's lorry, a mid sized affair with faded livery in varying shades of green. It announced, 'Henry Teasdale Racing'. The ramp was down, and he saw the paraphernalia of buckets, lead ropes and sponges. The yard's Desert Storm was being led round by one of the lads, with bleached blond hair and a refined face and the horse was about to be led over to the racecourse stables. He found Paddy in the cabin of the lorry, munching a packet of crisps. Paddy opened the cab door and shuffled along to the end of the cab seat.

'Now then Finn. Just grabbing me lunch. How are you? Do you have any conditionals riding here today?'

Finn took in Paddy's open face, his features creased in smiles. He remembered his skill in riding, and realised that he would have been a real asset for Sam and someone from whom he could have learned a great deal. It was just a pity he wasn't there today.

'Yeah. I'm watching one lad, Aidan Collins, but I wanted to have a quick word about Sam Foster. I'm starting to get seriously worried about the lad. The police have been in touch with me, but don't seem to think he's vulnerable, so I doubt they'll put the resources in to find him. I just wondered if you could shed any light on where he might be and why he disappeared.'

Paddy scrunched up his crisp packet and squashed it into his pocket. He glanced his watch and athletically swung his body down to the grass beneath.

'Well, perhaps, we could meet later? I need to get our horses into the stables and settled.' Paddy frowned. 'I could meet you in the Owners' and Trainers' bar about four?' He felt his inside pocket. 'I did get a card from him, though. This is the second one, the other is at home. I've still got his stuff too. It's in me cellar. He just asked me to look after his stuff whilst he was away for a few days. I never thought he'd do a runner.'

He thrust a postcard of a rural scene into Finn's hands. 'It is strange him doing a runner because he had it all going for him, he has real talent and a real feel for a horse.'

A lad passed the horsebox leading a horse, wearing a red and cream checked blanket. The horse was lively, and a girl held onto the animal's head from the other side. Finn noticed that the horse was leaping about on its toes and was being led in a chifney, a harsh type of bit, designed to restrain an unruly animal. Clearly the pair were expecting trouble. And then the blond lad leading Desert Storm came over.

'Shall I take 'im to ze yard, Paddy?' His voice was heavily accented. Eastern European, probably Polish, Finn decided.

'Aye, go and settle him. I'll bring the mare in a mo.'

Paddy turned back to Finn. 'Sure, I thought a lot of the lad.'

Finn nodded.

'Do you know anything about Sam having a row with his girlfriend, Gina? Something about her being pregnant?'

Paddy frowned. 'No, I've not heard that at all. Pregnant? Didn't think he had a girlfriend actually.' He paused. 'Look, there are some things I've picked up on.' He looked about him, and his voice tailed off as he saw the tall figure of Henry Teasdale approaching him and worse still, he was accompanied by the owner, Jimmy West. Paddy smiled at the trainer and owner or was it more of a grimace?

'Best get on Finn. I'll meet you later.'

'The Owners' and Trainers' bar at four?'

Paddy grinned. 'Great.'

Teasdale nodded gruffly at Finn and studied Paddy with thinly disguised annoyance. West gave him a filthy look, as though he was completely beneath him.

Teasdale was keen to let Finn and Paddy know who was in charge.

'Come on. These horses need stabling, Paddy. There's no time to stand around chatting.'

Finn began to walk back to the course. 'See you later. Good luck,' he couldn't resist calling adding, as Teasdale glowered back at him.

Finn caught up with Aidan Collins who had ridden a rather cautious and race in the first. He finished sixth of a field of ten, two places behind Teasdale's Desert Storm, who finished a reasonable fourth. He talked Aidan through his race, highlighting that he had made an error in his positioning and had allowed himself to get boxed in at the back. The young lad agreed that it was something he needed to work on, as well as wanting to improve his finishing. They arranged to meet. Finn agreed to come to the lad's yard to watch him school.

He watched out for Hattie and spotted her leading a colourful tribe of children, as usual dressed in jockeys' silks. She was bending her head, talking to one of the girls who looked tiny in her oversized red and black silks. He found himself smiling at the sight of her. She exuded energy and positivity. He texted her and arranged to meet in the same bar as he was to meet Paddy in but later on. He felt momentarily pleased, then chided himself when Nat had a fall in the second race and was taken off to the hospital with possible concussion. Livvy went tearing off after him, her face pale and tight. He felt the usual spasm of jealousy at her reaction, tempered with relief when he realised that he could wander around the course freely without risking bumping into either of them.

He placed a few bets, met some old friends and glanced at his watch. A fine drizzle had begun to fall as he made his way to the Owners' and Trainers' bar. He ordered a cup of tea and a ham salad sandwich and waited for Paddy. He suddenly remembered the postcard that Paddy had given him and fished it out of his pocket. It was a photograph of a rural scene, with a lake and craggy rocks on the background. The postmark was sadly smudged and indecipherable, so there were no clues as to where it was sent from, but it was what was written which caused Finn a jolt of alarm.

Am fine. Just lying low. Can you look after my stuff? They are planning something big. Watch your back. Be in touch. S

Finn pondered this and waited. After an age, it was clear that Paddy wasn't going to show, but he was delighted to see Hattie breezing in, her hair even more curly from the damp, eyes shining.

'What a day! Those kids sure can talk,' she exclaimed slipping off her coat.

Finn reflected that Hattie could probably out talk all of them.

'Oh, you are invited to a party. Chris Pinkerton, Mum and Dad's friend is having a birthday bash for his wife, Honor. It's next week.' Her face flushed as she realised that he might think she was trying to progress their relationship. It endeared her to him, she showed all her emotions on her face. 'I mean, Teasdale and Vince will be there. The Pinkertons are renowned for their lavish parties and, who knows, alcohol might loosen their tongues. So, we could find out something...'

Finn laughed. 'Fine. I'll look forward to it. Do you want a drink?'

He pushed his way to the front of the queue and came back with a couple of glasses of white wine.

'So, have you found anything out?'

Finn nodded. 'I spoke to Connor who seemed about to tell me something but when Vince came along, then he really clammed up. Vince seemed quite off hand.'

Hattie frowned. 'Really? Vince is usually a sweetheart. He probably didn't like you interrupting his staff at work. Daisy said people were off with the 'flu so he's probably just stressed.'

'Hmm. And I was due to meet Paddy, you remember the travelling head lad from both yards, but he hasn't turned up.' He shrugged. 'Must have got caught up in something, perhaps there was an injury to one of the horses. He did give me this though. It's from Sam.'

He handed the postcard to Hattie who scrutinised it. It was then that the doors of the bar were flung open and a man came rushing in, his eyes searched everywhere. He was middle aged, dressed head to toe in tweed and was perspiring from the exertion of running. He wore a lanyard which announced that he was the clerk of the course,

'Anyone seen Teasdale? Has he been here? Only it's urgent, there's been an accident.'

Everyone craned their necks to look at the man.

Finn approached him. 'I saw him in the lorry park earlier, but he's not been in here, I'm afraid. Can I help at all?'

The man sighed. 'I've just come from the stables. One of his staff has been involved in an accident, so I need to find him urgently.'

Finn put on his coat as a terrible sense of foreboding crowded in.

'Who is it? I'll come and help you find him…'

The man gulped. 'It's his travelling head lad. I'm afraid he's been severely injured. He fell.'

'Where?'

'Down the steps of the Clock Tower stand.' Finn was aware that he had been holding his breath as alarm coursed through him. He remembered the steep concrete steps of that particular stand, and realised that this could be serious, very serious indeed.

Chapter 12

Hattie saw the colour drain from Finn's face so that it took on the colour of cold, congealed porridge.

'You mean Paddy Owen? Is he OK?'

The clerk of the course's face looked guarded. 'Look, I really need to find Teasdale…'

'Haven't seen him. If he's not here he might be with his horses, he had a runner in the last. Or maybe he's gone to hospitality with the owners?'

Hattie had seen both Desert Storm and The Purple Panther, Teasdale's horses run reasonable races.

The clerk turned abruptly, and Finn followed. Hattie drained her wine in one long draught and went with him. Finn half jogged past the paddock towards the main stand which had a distinctive square tower and gave a great view of the course. Hattie saw an ambulance and a crowd gathering around it. As she reached Finn's shoulder, she saw the paramedics carry a stretcher which bore Paddy's prone figure and load it into the vehicle. Hattie suddenly spotted a familiar face. Dr Pinkerton. Thank the Lord for a reassuring presence. She sprinted over.

'Christopher, I'm so glad to see you, what happened?' She noticed him looking at Finn. 'This is a friend of mine, Finn McCarthy. He's a mate of Paddy's too.'

Dr Pinkerton looked rather serious and clearly was considering how much to say.

'Your friend,' he said gravely, 'has sustained a head injury as a result of a fall.'

'Is he conscious?'

'No. Look, we need to get him to hospital as soon as possible. There's nothing you can do Hattie, darling.' Dr Pinkerton put his arm around her shoulders. 'Probably you ought to go home. I've told Teasdale to get home too, he'll need to sort the horses out. I'll travel with Paddy.'

Hattie felt relieved that Paddy had an experienced doctor to travel with him but also pleased that Dr Pinkerton was there to comfort her. Just his steady presence consoled her. Still, another accident at the races? Who would have thought that a day out to the races could be so dangerous?

'I'm going with him too,' Finn told them. 'He's a good friend and I owe him that.'

Hattie made a lightning decision. 'I'll follow you in the car and catch you there, OK? I'm sure it'll be alright.'

She did not know why she felt obliged to offer such mechanical reassurances because clearly, she had no damned idea if Paddy was badly injured. But somehow the devastation on Finn's face made her want to comfort him. It was as if a line had been crossed, his concerns were now hers. Especially if they related to the investigation.

'We're going to the Doncaster Royal Infirmary because it's just down the road,' said the paramedic. 'It'll be a blue light, miss, so you just follow at your own speed, we don't want another accident.'

'See you later, Hattie.'

Finn and Dr Pinkerton disappeared inside and then the blue lights and siren blazed, and the vehicle zoomed off, whilst hi viz jacketed officials kept racegoers out of the way.

Hattie texted her family.

Hi, have been held up, will be late Hx

Then, mindful of the investigation and feeling responsible with Finn out of action, Hattie decided to hang around discreetly and try to find out what had happened. Didn't they say that most of the clues to a serious incident were present in the first hour and it was vital to get as much evidence in that first period as possible? She was sure Dominic had told her something of the sort. She wished he was there suddenly and resolved to 'phone her youngest brother soon. Not that she knew exactly this was serious, it was likely to be a horrible accident, but one thing she had learned from having two detectives in the family, was that there was no such thing as a coincidence.

Hattie approached a group of racegoers who had watched the ambulance leave.

'Did you see what happened?' she asked.

One woman wearing a cream mac and a maroon beret looked at her with interest.

'Do you know him, love?'

'Yes, he works at my friend's yard. Do you?'

Maroon beret shook her head.

'I was just about to go and get my winnings,' said her friend, who had long dark hair in a plait. 'We watched the race from up there and all of a sudden there was a clatter and the man fell down those stairs, hit his head on that post there.'

Hattie looked over to the Clock Tower stand where a racecourse official was inspecting the scene, and a man in a staff jacket stood at the entrance stopping people from going up to the oldest part of the stand. The steps there were very deep, almost thirty centimetres, she guessed and a fall down them would be very painful. The post Paddy had hit, she noticed, was concrete and looked very solid too. She suddenly felt clammy.

'Did you see what happened before, I mean was he on his own, did he trip or what?'

Maroon beret took up the story again. 'We were going up to that rail there to watch the race, but we didn't because he was with this other man and they were blocking the stairs at the top. They were talking…'

'Friendly, were they?'

The woman with the plait rolled her eyes. 'No, that's just it love, they were arguing, a heated conversation at any rate.'

Hattie had to ask the next bit. 'I don't suppose you heard what they were arguing about?'

'No, love.'

'What was the man like?'

Maroon beret shrugged. 'I only saw him briefly, smartish, youngish, blondish.' Hattie felt exasperated. The 'ishs' were just far too vague. It could have described half the young men at the racecourse.

'Was he pushed? And where did the blond man go afterwards?'

Both of them shrugged and said they didn't know. It was a busy day at Doncaster, Hattie realised, and someone could easily slip away into the crowd unnoticed.

'Come on Elaine, I reckon we need a drink to steady our nerves before we go home.' Both walked off to the nearest bar. Hattie scanned the crowds looking for someone else to ask. But the racing was now over, the light was beginning to fade, and most racegoers were beginning to drift off to their homes after a good day of racing. Hattie went over towards the stand looking around her, at the ground and generally listening to people's conversation. She spotted a blond lad who she recognised from somewhere talking to Henry Teasdale. Henry looked grim faced and solemn as he clapped the blond man on the arm, and the pair turned to walk towards the stables. As they strode away Hattie took a quick photo of them with her 'phone, just in case she needed to identify the lad again. Feeling anxious and worried about Paddy, she decided her work here was done and it was time to go off to the hospital to see how he was faring. Maybe the injury wouldn't be as bad as it first appeared, mild concussion or something.

It took a while to drive the few miles or so to the hospital. All the way, Hattie went over what might have happened to Paddy. Obviously, she didn't know him really, he was a fairly recent appointment, but he did work at Vince Hunt's yard and she knew enough to know he was well liked and respected. Clearly, Finn thought a great deal of him too. Hattie remembered Daisy telling her that he lived in a small cottage in Walton, somewhere near Henry Teasdale's large, grand house. She didn't think he was married, there was certainly no sign of a Mrs Owen at the yard with him. Finn had said something about a separation and she thought he mentioned children too. Of all the rotten luck, she thought, for him to have safely negotiated what was by anyone's standards, a hugely dangerous career, only for him to have an accident and hurt his head falling down some steps at the races. Still, people did fall and hit their heads all the time and they were all right in the end, she told herself. But it was the vision of Paddy's face as he was carried to the ambulance which ran, again and again, through her brain. Somehow his terrible translucent colour, the whiteness of his cheeks and his total stillness worried her. He had, she realised, looked like a waxwork, rather than a real man. She pulled into the hospital car park at around five thirty, parked, read the instructions, put money in the meter and followed the signs to the Accident and Emergency department which she presumed was the right place.

Hattie asked the matronly woman at the desk where Paddy Owen had been taken. She was busy and irritable and said,

'Are you a relative?'

Hattie sighed and explained what had happened. The woman said she'd ask if Hattie would sit down and wait. Hattie sat amongst the injured, a man with a profusely bleeding finger, a child with a cut on his head, a woman who looked like she'd fallen and broken her hand. The child with the cut was about ten, a brave boy who was dressed in a tracksuit. He had two younger sisters who were dancing around the chairs and fighting. Their mother, a frail looking blonde, appeared exhausted and Hattie wondered if she should try to entertain the girls but thought it might appear too pushy. After ten minutes of pretending to read the various leaflets on display, Hattie approached the desk again. The receptionist hit her own head with her hand,

'Sorry love, I forgot to ask. What was his name again?'

The nurse disappeared through one of those doorways covered in clear plastic hanging strips. Hattie waited, felt like a nuisance and then sat down. The boy with the cut suddenly began to whimper and Hattie seeing the two girls fighting, said to the mother,

'Look, shall I read to them while you try to calm him down?'

The woman nodded, and so Hattie grabbed a dogeared copy of 'Funny Bones' from the toy box and began to read, one girl settled on each side. She was about halfway through the book when Finn walked through the fringed doorway. He looked around as if in a trance and Hattie jumped up to intercept him.

'Finn, here!'

Finn stood, dazed and Hattie raced over, the first prickling of alarm travelling down her neck.

'What's happened Finn. Is Paddy OK?'

He turned, expressionless and slow as if drugged.

'He seems to have fallen and hit his head several times as he fell down the stone steps.' Finn looked exhausted and choked. 'He didn't make it, Hattie. He's dead…'

Hattie raced towards him and instinctively reached out to hug him.

'Oh my God. I can't believe it.'

'It was a terrible fall. He must have hit his head over and over on the stone steps. Catastrophic brain injury they said...'

God, she could picture him tumbling helplessly. She found herself leading Finn over to a chair and sitting down next to him. Then her legs nearly gave way. She didn't even know Paddy properly, she had just had a brief nodding acquaintance with him but, even so she still felt utter disbelief.

God, they couldn't just sit here like shocked, stone statues, she realised she needed to take charge.

'They've contacted his ex-wife, she's coming…' said Finn tonelessly

'Right, do you want to stay or what?'

'She won't get here until tomorrow, she lives in Bristol…'

Hattie made a decision. 'Look, why don't I drive you home? But before that let me buy you a drink Finn, you look like you need it.'

'I'd rather go straight home…'

'Hey, what about your car?'

Finn stirred. 'I'll get it from the racecourse tomorrow, take the train…'

Harriet shook her head. 'No, I'll drive you, I insist.' She could not leave Finn alone at a time like this.

Back at Finn's flat in the old chocolate factory Hattie poured him a stiff whiskey. He still had the haunted look, but it was easing and his colour was returning. On the way he'd spoken a little, and they'd listened to the radio. But now, at home he seemed to have revived a little and had told her where to find the whiskey. Hattie made herself a coffee in the stylish chrome and glass kitchen.

When she took the drink through to the sitting room, Finn had dug out an old photo album.

'Look, there's Paddy the day he won the Midlands Grand National at Uttoxeter. Look at him, he was so made up. It was his biggest race, you know…'

Hattie studied the smiling, mud splattered face of Paddy Owen. His grin showed a few missing teeth, but his exuberance seemed to leap out of the photo.

'You were pretty close, then?'

'Yeah at one time, he was one of the lads I just got on well with, always cheerful, ready with congratulations if you won and commiserations when you lost. Everyone loved Paddy. He never had a bad word to say about anyone.'

Hattie sipped her coffee and nodded to indicate that Finn should continue. Surely, it would do him good to talk?

'He was older than me by about ten years and he looked out for me, you see he rode for Reg Hollings when I was a conditional there. I had a really bad experience at Ted Boothroyd's yard. He was a brutal man, brutal to horses and staff, especially conditionals. He beat me up badly when I tried to challenge him about the lack of pay, overtime and poor conditions. He was drunk and just left me. A stable lass found me and got me to hospital. I had fractured my leg in two places and punctured my lung. I would have died if she hadn't have found me. She's still a friend, Rosy moved to Hollins place and I moved with her. Now he was a true gentleman and great with his jockeys. Paddy worked as his stable jockey and life improved from then. Paddy was always pleased to pass on what he knew, said the old hands had a duty to help the youngsters, you know. He really looked out for me and I owe him a lot.'

Hattie let Finn continue to talk, his voice thick with emotion. He was clearly upset, and the revelation explained why he had wanted to be a jockey coach. Hattie guessed he hadn't spoken about this for years. And certainly, to hardly any people. She felt happy that he trusted her enough to confide in her about his past.

'So, what happened to this Boothroyd man?'

Finn turned and smiled. 'Oh, I went to the police and then all the tales came out about his ill treatment of not just horses but staff too. He was banned from keeping a training licence and went to prison for a bit.'

'Why did you stick it so long?'

Finn turned to her. 'Because it was my dream to be a jockey and I wanted to be one so badly, nothing else mattered. And I was scared of whistle blowing, and too bloody obstinate to go home and have my father gloat. That's why we have to find Sam. Something's not right, and these lads and lasses are so vulnerable, they're just so desperate to follow their dream.' Finn sat for a moment, deep in thought. He was a complex man, Harriet realised, and liked him all the more for that.

'So, what do they think happened to Paddy?'

Finn shrugged. 'I'm not sure. Did he fall or was he pushed?'

Hattie was about to ask more when Finn suddenly turned to face her.

'My God, I forgot, listen they found some drugs in his pocket at the hospital.'

'Drugs? What were they?' Hattie's mind was buzzing suddenly. Was this something to do with the amphetamines? Maybe Paddy had been a supplier?

Finn shook his head. 'I can't remember the name, but your friend Dr Pinkerton found them and knew what they were. I suppose we'll find out in time.'

Hattie drained her cup. 'Listen, I forgot 'til now but I asked around at the course after the accident. Apparently two women saw Paddy arguing with a man on the stands, the next minute there was a loud thud as he fell…'

Finn knocked back the amber liquid, his eyes narrowing. 'So, it wasn't an accident. What did he look like, this bloke?'

Hattie shrugged. 'The ladies I spoke to, gave me a very general description. It wasn't that helpful.'

Finn frowned. 'Look, call me crazy but this feels wrong. There was something bothering Paddy, and I'm pretty sure that he was going to tell me what it was when we met up. Something feels off about the whole thing and I'm going to find out what. God, I owe Paddy that much…'

Hattie remembered the photo she'd taken of the blond youth who'd been talking to Teasdale. She showed it to Finn.

'Oh yes, I know the lad, he was with one of their runners today. He came past when Paddy was arranging to meet me. When Paddy gave me the postcard. Could it be him who Paddy was arguing with?'

'Could be, but then the two ladies I spoke to were just too vague. Youngish, blondish, smartish, could be anyone really.'

Finn nodded continuing to stare at the photo. 'Look, that looks like our old friend Spud.' He pointed at a tall, broad plain man in the background who Hattie had failed to notice. 'Wonder what he was doing there? I'm sure it was him that beat up Sam. Mind you, the skull tattoo is not conclusive. I suppose they're common enough. We'll just have to find Sam.'

Now, more than ever before, everything seemed to come back to Sam and the time he was beaten up at the races. None of the information seemed to piece together. It was rather like trying to plait fog, with swollen arthritic fingers in total darkness. Both of them were just too exhausted to be rational. Hattie glanced at her watch.

'Look, I had better shoot, I've got loads of Uni work to do tomorrow…'

'Right. I'll try and find out who Paddy could have been talking to. I'm going to speak to his ex tomorrow. Then we've got to work out a plan because we need to find out what the hell is going on. I can't see him just falling like that…'

'Maybe he was ill and slipped or passed out for some reason. Or maybe he was pushed? Perhaps we're just being paranoid and seeing trouble where there is none?'

Finn rummaged in his pocket and passed over the postcard from Sam. Hattie read it with a feeling of disbelief. They are planning something big. Hattie gulped. This was surely proof that something dodgy was going on. Clearly Sam thought so, and he didn't even know about what had happened to Paddy yet.

'And Paddy said he had another postcard at home. So, we need to search there too, probably before his wife arrives. She's bound to want to stay there. She's got loads to sort out and now a funeral to organise.' He shook his head sadly. 'Look, Hattie I'm too tired to think. I'll 'phone you tomorrow and sort out what's best. There's the Pinkerton's party too. Do you think it will still be on after Paddy's death?'

Hattie was glad he'd mentioned that, not her.

'Yep, bound to be. Dr P and his wife have everything planned. Besides, they don't really know Paddy, although Teasdale and Vince Hunt might not feel up to it. Now try to get some rest…'

Finn leaned over and gave her a quick peck on the cheek. 'Thanks for driving me, for listening to me going on, you're a mate, Hattie.'

Hattie drove home, her head spinning, thoughts tumbling around her brain in a random, jerky, disassociated manner. Uppermost in her mind was shock about Paddy's death and then fear. Maybe he had taken drugs and fallen, but he hadn't seemed the type. Supposing it wasn't an accident and he was pushed? She switched off the radio irritably, it was annoying her, and she needed quiet to think. Suddenly she gripped the steering wheel and sat up straight. Just supposing the smartish, blondish man had seen the postcard being handed over, guessed who it was from and wanted to stop Paddy telling Finn whatever else he knew? Christ, she realised they had to be careful, otherwise both she and Finn could be in danger especially if they were seen asking awkward questions. For the first time the utter seriousness of what they might be involved with hit her.

She could talk to her father and brother but then she rejected the notion. If they thought she was in danger they would probably come over all protective, and before she knew it there might be a heavy handed action. But there would, she realised, have to be some sort of investigation into Paddy's death so they needed to let that run its course. But as for the rest of it, she decided, she and Finn were on their own for now. They needed to tread very carefully because she also reckoned that not only were they in danger but, almost certainly, Sam Foster was too. She and Finn needed to find him before 'they' did, or whoever was master minding all this anyway. If Paddy had been pushed, then whoever did the deed didn't much care about the harm they inflicted on other people and that included them. They needed to think very carefully and trust absolutely no-one.

Chapter 13

Finn felt appallingly shocked by the incident. Then shock had given way to anger and renewed his determination to find out what the hell was going on. His mind turned over the events of the day, Paddy's death muddled with Sam's disappearance. Once Harriet had left, he spent an age going through his old photos and drinking. He replayed the conversation with Paddy over and over. Whichever way he thought about it, Finn was convinced that Paddy had been troubled by something that was going on at Teasdale's yard and he was more and more sure that whatever it was, it had something to do with Sam's disappearance. He wished now he hadn't spoken to Paddy about his concerns in a busy area where horse boxes were parked. There had been lots of people milling around. And there could have been others lurking around in the other boxes, out of view. With the clarity of hindsight, he realised that they could easily have been overheard. But if Paddy had been pushed over on the stand and it was a big if, then it might relate to what Paddy wanted to tell him. He kept staring at Sam's postcard with the strange message.

Am fine. Just lying low. Can you look after my stuff? They are planning something big. Watch your back. Be in touch. S

Sam had been so afraid of something he felt he had no other option but to disappear and hide away. Finn racked his brain to think back to who was in the car park, who could have overheard him arranging to meet Paddy in the bar later. He remembered a blond stable lad and a few other people were also milling around. Maybe one of the stable lads was in cahoots with Jimmy West and even Boothroyd? He wished he had paid better attention but, of course, he had no idea what was about to happen next. There must be something either written on the other postcard or in Sam's belongings that might provide some clues. He knew it wasn't rational, but he felt he was to blame for Paddy's accident and therefore, it was up to him to find out who was responsible. Sam's disappearance, Connor's reluctance to ride, it all pointed to something very unsavoury. He put on his jogging gear, pounded the pavements extra hard that morning, showered, and ate toast as a plan began to form. He thought that Paddy's ex-wife would reach Walton in the early afternoon but go straight to the hospital or police station. She was likely to stay at Paddy's, so they had to act quickly. He texted Hattie.

Think we need to go to Paddy's house and get his stuff before his ex-wife arrives. Are you up for going this afternoon at about 1?

He smiled when Hattie immediately pinged back a reply, yes. At least now they had a plan.

It was easy enough to locate Paddy's address. Hattie had parked in the town and Finn picked her up from outside the library and drove the short distance to Paddy's street. It was a dim, dull autumn afternoon. Paddy lived in a mid-terraced cottage on Knight's Lane in Walton. They drove past the picturesque old brick and timbered row of cottages until they came to number 9. The front garden had a picket fence around it and a vast array of shrubs.

'So, do you have a key or what?'

Finn shook his head. 'No, but I do have my lock picks.' He pulled the set of thin lengths of metal out of his pocket. 'The front is far too exposed. How about you keep watch and I'll nip round the back.'

He reversed the car into a parking space just opposite with a good view of Paddy's front door.

'Right. If anyone calls at the house, you need to leap out and distract them. Think you can do that?'

Hattie's eyes gleamed. 'I'm sure I can think of something.' In the gathering gloom he saw her smile. 'Got it. Leave it with me.'

Finn climbed out of the vehicle and left Hattie as look out. With that, he jogged round the back into the little alleyway which led to the back of the properties. He pulled out his torch and made his way along the alley. The cottages were bordered by half brick and timbered fences. Each property had a gate which led to the back garden. Finn quickly found the correct gate and lifted the latch to enter the garden. Outside, number 9 was well tended with a square of grass, broad borders, a shed and a small greenhouse. He followed the path to the back door and reached in his pocket for his lock picks. He hoped to God that there wasn't a bolt on the inside of the door, and fortunately after he had twisted his picks for a short while, he heard the familiar click, pushed down the handle and the door opened easily.

The door led into the kitchen. He looked around, it revealed neat wooden units, a small table and two chairs and a draining board with washed breakfast dishes in place. He felt a huge lump in his throat when he thought about Paddy's last breakfast here. He had eaten, full of anticipation of a good day's racing, not knowing that he was going to suffer a horrible accident which he would never recover from. Still, there was no time to dwell on that now.

He quickly looked in the cupboards and drawers. There was a cork board on the rear wall which had several photos of horses pinned to it and amongst it a postcard depicting a rural scene, similar to the one that Paddy had shown him. He pocketed it and then scanned the kitchen for another door. Paddy had said that Sam's belongings were in the cellar, and he found the cellar door in the hallway adjacent to the staircase. He opened the door and advanced gingerly down the old stone steps. The temperature dropped immediately and as he shone the torch light around, it was clear that the property was far older than he had originally thought, although it had been well modernised. He shone the torch around the domed brick ceiling and back to the floor. There was an old sofa, a bookcase, a hoover, and closest to the steps a very large rucksack and a small holdall next to it. This had to be Sam's. Surely Paddy would place his gear close to the door for easy accessibility? Finn quickly unzipped the backpack and found underwear, breeches and jumpers. In the bag he found riding boots, undershirts, a body protector, a whip and a riding helmet. He grabbed both bags, quickly exited and fumbled with the lock picks until he was sure the door was locked. He hefted the backpack on his shoulders, grabbed the holdall and raced back to the car, shoving them in the boot.

There was no sign of Hattie. Finn was about to start the car when she slid into the passenger seat, her face pale.

'Are you OK?'

Hattie turned towards him. 'I'm fine. One of the neighbours was looking out the window so I got up and popped into the shop just in case. I didn't want to arouse suspicion.' She pointed at the small shop cum post office in the adjacent road. She pulled out a couple of chocolate bars, shrugged and threw one at him. 'And I was starving. Look, they're proper curtain twitchers round here. We'd best go.'

Finn noticed the lace curtains of number 7 flutter almost imperceptibly. He fired up the engine. 'You did well.' He nodded at the Mars bar in his lap.

'Cheers,' replied Hattie through a mouthful of Snickers. Finn grinned and indicated left and waited for a dustbin lorry to pass.

'At least if they were looking out the front then they won't have seen me going through the back way.'

'Did you find Sam's things?' Hattie's eyes were wide.

Finn nodded. 'Oh yes, the postcard and his bags are in the boot. I suggest we go back to mine and have a good look through.'

He heard the satisfaction in Hattie's voice. 'Brilliant.'

Finn suddenly felt apprehensive. What were they going to find? Maybe there was a stash of drugs, or money from drug dealing?

He supposed it would all become clear. Finn took Hattie back to fetch her car and she then followed him on the short drive to York.

At Finn's apartment, Hattie rummaged through the fridge and decided to cook them a steak, potatoes and salad whilst Finn went through the contents of Sam's bag. He was still wearing lightweight gloves, as he was aware of fingerprints and didn't want to incriminate himself.

'Right, got any garlic?'

Finn pointed her in the right direction. He realised when he smelt the delicious aroma of the steak frying in the pan, that he was very hungry too.

Finn spread everything out onto the floor in the sitting room, whilst Hattie looked on. The postcard of a loch simply said;

I'm safe. Had to get away. Be in touch soon. S

'Anything so far?' she asked whilst he sorted through pants, socks, riding clothes, trainers and a couple of smart shirts and trousers. There was an opened packet of condoms and a men's toiletry bag containing a toothbrush, shampoo, razors and a contact lenses case. He began to feel oddly deflated and emptied the sponge bag onto the floor besides these items. He found riding boots, clothes and a warm coat and helmet in the holdall. He shook the bag again and a small, black notebook tumbled out. He began flicking through the pages, rather confused. All the effort of breaking in and this was all they had found?

'Well, there doesn't appear to be anything much in this lot.'

'OK, I'll have a look through in a minute when we've eaten.'

Hattie passed him a plate of steak and salad. He couldn't help but notice that Hattie had served it up with a colourful side salad and it looked and tasted delicious. It was so nice to do something simple like eat a home cooked meal with a friend. Finn opened a bottle of red wine and poured Hattie a glass.

'What are you looking for anyway?' Hattie took a mouthful of steak, scooped up the notebook and flicked through it.

'I've no idea really.'

Hattie frowned. 'Well, this makes no sense.' She held up a page which read:

20/10, DN, Dragon, HJ, NW

11/1 MR, Pick me up, BJ, DD.

Finn focused on the other letters following these, pointing them out with his finger. 'Look these letters could refer to places, these to people involved.'

1/3 UT, Snow, BJ, CM,

15/3 WY, Genie CM, NW.

8/10 CH, Bud, CM, DD, NW.

Hattie frowned. 'Hey, I know, could it be a record of drug deals? Isn't Snow, cocaine, Pick me Up, amphetamine? Not sure about the rest though.'

Finn peered at the page, puzzled.

'What was that?' He read the list back. Could it be a list of deals? There appeared to be some sort of sequence to the letters and numbers. There were numbers, possibly a date followed by two or three letters. He focused on these letters. TW, MR, UT, WY, CH. He felt as though he had been doused in cold water. 'These initials could be referring to racecourses and these to customers, maybe jockeys or other dealers?'

Hattie frowned. 'God, it is to do with drugs then?'

Finn shook his head, yet something didn't make sense. He studied the letters and numbers again, willing them to give yield a clear clue. What on earth did the initials mean and did the names refer to horses? He sighed and pulled out his 'phone turning to the camera function, and took several photos of the code. He then emailed them to both Tony Murphy and Harriet. Then he sent a copy to his own email to be on the safe side.

'Why on earth did you do that?'

Finn shrugged. 'I just thought it might be an idea to keep a copy, you never know. Besides, I can look at it when I'm out and about and puzzle over it.'

Harriet frowned. 'I still can't see Sam being involved in drugs though, can you?'

Harriet seemed deflated and he had to agree he was disappointed in their haul. Yet, he couldn't see Sam being a drug dealer either.

'No. I think it's more likely that Sam discovered something so big he had been forced to go into hiding for his own safety. Paddy also knew and was pushed from the stand to stop him telling me.'

They both looked at each other as the implications of what they had discovered sunk in. Neither of them questioned Finn's assertion that Paddy had been pushed because they suspected it was true. They looked at each other and wondered what on earth they had stumbled upon. One thing was now very clear, whatever it was, the stakes were much higher than either of them had first thought. After a further hour in fruitless discussion, Harriet yawned.

'Look. I'd better make tracks, Finn.'

Finn slept fitfully that evening, images of Paddy falling and being pushed by some unknown person and of Sam lying low, scared of some malevolent force, bounced around his brain. He eventually nodded off only to wake again, his senses suddenly alert. He looked around his room in the dim light, his eyes becoming accustomed to the dark and felt curiously uneasy. There was the merest hint of light which crept around his bedroom door, yet he was sure that he had turned the lamps off when he went to bed. He listened, his ears straining and heard the soft hiss of what sounded like his drawers being pulled out, followed by the sound of papers rustling and a shuffling noise. Realisation hit him like a cold shower. Someone was in the flat.

He tiptoed out of bed, grabbing his mobile and turning on the narrow torch light, shined the beam around. The light flickered over his golf clubs, a remnant of his racing days, which had been gathering dust in his bedroom. Some of the lads had played golf and tried to get him into it. He had never taken to it, but now he suddenly saw a good use for the equipment. He gently pulled the nearest club towards him, tiptoed step by step towards the door and slowly pushed the door handle down. When he had enough space, he leapt towards the light switch, his club raised ready to strike.

Light flooded into the room and a figure, dressed in black turned towards him, froze momentarily and then turned and ran. Fury coursed through Finn at the intrusion and he screamed and gave chase, brandishing the club like a man possessed. Everything happened so quickly, and he found himself lashing out instinctively. He managed to whack his quarry on his ankle with the makeshift weapon and heard him yelp in pain. He was gaining on the intruder when the black clad figure ran into the communal stairwell and suddenly seemed to get a second wind. The man leapt down the stairs four at a time before disappearing into the night. Finn gave chase but was breathing heavily, suddenly conscious that he was dressed in only boxer shorts and a t shirt and was not wearing any shoes. His feet sunk into the damp grass as he rushed outside, the cold air engulfing him. He ran down the street, his eyes scanning the empty road, but the figure had vanished into the night. Finn wandered around the block, his feet catching on the cold pavement, sharp stones digging into the bare soles of his feet. Defeated, he walked back to the apartment. He was suddenly conscious of how he must look wandering around at three o' clock in the morning, half dressed, with a golf club over his shoulder.

He studied his front door and saw that there was no damage which meant that whoever had broken in must have been a professional lock picker or have had a skeleton key. He resolved to change the locks and add some substantial hardware in the form of bolts to the inside. He pushed an armchair against the front door for now and surveyed his living room. Papers, books, ornaments and photos were strewn all over the place, their contents spewed all over the floor. He filled the kettle made a cup of tea and began to tidy up. The intruder had been wearing all black with a baseball cap pulled over his face and a polo neck pulled up to cover the lower part of his face. He was also sure that he was wearing gloves, so there would be no fingerprints for the police to check.

He tidied up, his mind buzzing. it was clear that whoever had broken in was looking for something particular. His wallet, car keys, iPad and laptop were all untouched, as were his bronze horse trophies and paintings in the study which were originals he had won or been given by grateful owners. He wondered what on earth the intruder was searching for and found himself at a loss. Was it a random break in, a sneak thief? He dismissed the idea as surely someone on the ground floor would have been much easier to burgle. Nothing of any value had been taken, so it was clear that he had been targeted for some reason and his skin became clammy as he realised that it could only be something to do with Sam's disappearance. Damn! Of course! The article that Tim Giles had written. In order to play down the fact that Sam was missing, he'd mentioned that Sam had sent him an MP3 player and probably Tim had added this to give the article a bit of colour. At least he'd had the foresight to give the MP3 player to Hattie. Perhaps someone knew he had Sam's bags? He pulled out Sam's holdall, rummaged around in the front pocket and found to his dismay that the small notebook had vanished. He felt utterly bereft until he remembered that he had had the foresight to photograph the pages. He flicked through the photos on his 'phone and enlarged them. He laughed out loud when he saw that the quality was excellent, and he could read them more clearly. At least now he knew that the code was vitally important. But maybe it was the MP3 player that was the target as that was all he had mentioned in his interview? What music was recorded on there? Suddenly several pieces of information settled in his brain and began to make sense. Couldn't MP3 players be used as general storage for other files or documents? That was it! Maybe it didn't contain music after all?

Chapter 14

As she drove home, Hattie felt pleased that she'd managed to tear herself away before she got too absorbed, she had a great deal of work to catch up on and she didn't want to fail so close to finishing her degree. Hattie also knew that she was in danger of becoming totally immersed in the shadowy world that their investigation seemed to be opening up to them. She forced her mind to concentrate on the fragments of the coded list they had found in Sam's notebook. She needed to do some research because, being naive in the ways of drug dealers, she had no idea how they were sold. Presumably, they were weighed so the figures surely related to either the weights of the drugs or the value of what was owed? Or they could mean something else entirely. She toyed with the idea of asking Will for his advice but knew he would immediately guess why she was asking and then the lectures would begin. Her every move would be monitored, and she would alert his suspicions and invite interference or at the very least robust questioning.

At home, her mother was washing up in the kitchen. Dad was poring over the crossword, calling out clues every so often to his wife.

'Hi, had a good day?'

'Yep love, you? How did you get on with Kasper, is his back all right now?'

Hattie filled the kettle up. 'Mmm, the gel pad seems to be helping. Finn suggested it…'

'Ah, the ex-jockey, Christopher says he was a talented rider in his day, he won a great deal on horses ridden by Finn McCarthy,' said her mother. Hattie recognised that her mother was trying to find out more about Finn without actually asking outright. 'Talk of the devil…'

They could hear the sound of their friend, Dr Christopher Pinkerton, entering the house through the hall. He always let himself in like this and Mum never seemed to mind but her Dad, she noticed, rolled his eyes and tutted. Hattie had noticed that her father wasn't quite as friendly with the good doctor as he had used to be. Probably because me and Mum are always pleased to see him, she thought, and Christopher could be a bit overpowering with his easy charm and bonhomie. Her Dad, she reflected, was a quieter, more thoughtful man and had seemed more so since he'd retired. Maybe she should talk to Mum about the way Dr Pinkerton let himself in. If he could knock and wait, that would probably suit her father better.

'Evening chaps,' came the booming voice, 'just calling by to ask your advice about the party next week…' The GP pulled up a chair and sat round the table. Christopher seemed his usual urbane, well-groomed self, except he looked tired, dark rings underscored his eyes and even his voice sounded weary.

'Cup of tea, Christopher?' asked Hattie.

'Yes, yes although if anything stronger is on offer, I'll go for that instead…'

Dad nodded and rose to fetch the bottle of Glenmorangie from the kitchen corner cupboard. He poured a generous measure for himself and the doctor and waved the bottle at the two women. Both shook their heads.

'How can we help?' asked Philippa.

'Booze…' said Christopher, 'how much shall I order? It'd be bad form to run out, wouldn't it? It's my one job and Honor won't advise me she's too bothered about doing up the venue.'

Philippa grimaced, and Hattie guessed that she was wondering about Honor's decision to hold the party in Vince Hunt's indoor school. Honor had persuaded the trainer into renting her the facility and was convinced that this would give them lots of space for dancing. Like everything Honor did, Hattie suspected, the large scale of the party was about being bigger and better than anyone else's. Honor was, by all accounts, desolate by reaching the ripe old age of thirty. She was twelve years younger than her husband but had decided to throw herself into marking the milestone, in an attempt to lessen its magnitude and effect on her mood.

'Still don't know why you can't use your place, I mean, you've got that new conservatory and the best house for parties I know…' grumbled Philippa.

'Well, since we are using Vince's school, he might take the opportunity to showcase one of his new horses, there's a syndicate forming to fund Snow Storm's racing career. You might want to buy a share in him Bob, Pippa?' the doctor looked at his old friends.

'Quickest way to waste a lot of money,' said Hattie's father, taking a decisive swig of whiskey, 'racehorses. Might as well burn it and be done with it.'

'Anyway, seems like going to the races is a dangerous pastime, after what happened to that poor man at Doncaster,' the doctor replied.

As he sipped his whiskey, Hattie's ears pricked up. Christopher was bound to know the details surrounding Paddy Owen's accident, he'd actually gone to the hospital with him and Finn, all together in the ambulance. With his medical knowledge, she knew he'd have pieced the incident together, and the medics would surely have talked to him.

The doctor eyed them all with an air of gravitas. 'Well, between you and me, the head lad Paddy Owen had epilepsy medication in his pocket. Seems like the poor chap had developed the condition following a fall. But he kept it quiet, I suppose nobody would have employed him otherwise.' He swirled the amber liquid around the cut glass. 'But it puts a whole different spin on the fall. The consultant from Doncaster, Teddy Friend, thinks Paddy Owen's fall was the result of a seizure. It's terribly sad, really. Think he must have hushed it up to get the job 'cos if he was epileptic, of course, he shouldn't have been driving. He could have killed a lot of people if it had happened when he was behind the wheel.'

Phillipa poured more tea for herself and Hattie. 'Oh, so that's why he fell and hit his head, poor chap.'

'Yes. We think so,' Christopher continued swirling his drink. 'The fit made him fall and because of the location he fell down some steep, stone steps. The resulting damage to his brain was just too severe to recover from.'

Hattie took this in. Paddy didn't seem the type to try and conceal a serious health condition which could place people and horses at risk. She wondered about the information the two female racegoers had given her straight after the fall. They seemed to suggest that there had been an argument and a possible push, but Hattie now revised this view. Christopher Pinkerton was a trusted source of information, he'd have all the facts at his fingertips. It really must have been accidental. She couldn't wait to tell Finn that things weren't as bad as they thought, after all.

'Finn was really worried.' Hattie told them, 'Paddy was a sort of a mentor to him when he was just starting out.'

Philippa looked at her carefully. 'You and he seem to be spending quite a lot of time together. Are we ever going to meet him?'

Damn. Hattie knew she shouldn't have said anything. She could feel her cheeks flushing. 'We're just friends, he's helping me with Kasper.' Her brain whirled. 'But Christopher, is it alright if he comes to your party as my plus one?'

Dr Pinkerton smiled. 'Of course, Harriet darling, the more the merrier. Anyway, I would like to have a proper chat about racing with him. We didn't really get to talk about that in the ambulance, as you might imagine.'

Hattie excused herself and went up to her room. She must plan out her latest essay and then submit it to her tutor. Only then could she start and write the damn thing. Then there was the presentation next week. Time to get her head down and focus on Uni work for a bit.

The next couple of days for Hattie passed in a blur of lectures, meetings and finally writing essays. She did not even visit the yard and had asked Daisy to look after Kasper. The livery was flexible, Hattie did most of the week but there was always a couple of days that Daisy covered for her. They were also due at a team meeting for the Racing to School staff, which was at Doncaster races on Wednesday morning followed by working together at the racecourse that afternoon.

Daisy picked her up just before eight. Daisy turned down Ed Sheeran singing about The Castle on the Hill.

'So, how's Kasper?'

'Greedy as ever. You get lots of work done?'

'Yeah. I'm up to date, for now. How are things at the yard?'

Daisy swerved to overtake a dustbin lorry in the village. 'Bloody burke. Oh God, home is tense. Dad's really upset about Paddy and, of course, there's the usual stuff about who should take over his job. It leaves us even more short staffed. Connor's injuries are slow to heal, and he can't do too much, certainly not work ride. Mum's quite worried about Dad, he seems right moody at the moment, biting mine and Alice's heads off. Honest, I wish I had your parents sometimes...'

Hattie laughed. 'Yeah, they're OK. But yours are just too stressed I reckon…' The long hours, the trouble with not only jockeys but stable staff must take its toll, she supposed.

'We're broke, that's what Hats. Dad is owed loads of training fees too. That's why Dad's rented the indoor school to Honor Pinkerton for an exorbitant fee, trying to keep the yard afloat. He's setting up some syndicates too, so we can have some new, slightly better horses.'

Hattie sympathised. It seemed like careers in horse racing were hard to keep on track. Not for the first time, she felt grateful for her parents' steady incomes and now her father's solid pension. They always had cash to help out if she was struggling and were, while not rich, certainly comfortable.

'Don't worry, something will come up. Your dad is such a good horseman…'

'Mum is thinking of taking on more liveries too. Anyway, don't mind me, I'm just being a moody cow today.'

Hattie took the cue to change the subject. 'I'm looking forward to the party. What's it going to be like and who will be there?'

Daisy concentrated while she indicated to join the motorway from the slip road. Hattie knew her friend was a good, safe driver and waited for her to move into position.

'Daisy?

'Yeah, well Honor's been around every day this week. The school is out of action while she and her friends do it up.' Daisy rolled her eyes. 'Nice woman, dead glam, but more money than sense.

There's going to be a live band, The Tomcats, great catering from Tatty Livermore and Dad's even got in on the act with a parade of Snow Storm, the new horse he's trying to drum up a syndicate for.'

'Sounds fab.'

'Yeah, but things are weird. Dad and Henry Teasdale had a row, I heard them shouting. Something about the new guy, I think. Henry says he should take over Paddy's role as travelling head lad. He's that blond guy, from Latvia or somewhere Eastern European, Pavel, he's called. Dad says he's no good with the youngsters, is too impatient and tends to belt them to make them box…'

Hattie felt a stirring of interest. 'The blond guy who was at Doncaster the other day?'

'Yeah, he's quite hot though. Got these amazing pale blue eyes like a husky dog. You should get to know him, he's going to the party.' Daisy looked suddenly tearful. 'It's awful to talk like that though, with Paddy dying. He wasn't with us long, but he seemed a really nice chap…'

Harriet patted her hand, thinking that no one seemed to have a bad word to say about Paddy.

Hattie wondered about this Pavel character. He'd been in a very animated conversation with Henry at Doncaster. Interesting, she thought. The rest of the day passed quickly. At the meeting they were given details of other developments in the Racing to School initiative. Classes of children could now be offered stud and training yard visits and school workshops where staff would 'bring racing to the classroom.' It all sounded exciting, but Hattie was careful not to sign up to deliver too much, fearing that her academic work would suffer with the time the investigation was taking too.

That afternoon, Hattie and Daisy had an excitable year 6 class to manage, showing the kids around the racecourse, the weighing room and walking the course. Outside the weighing room, before racing began, Hattie was interested to see Nat Wilson and a glamorous woman with long dark hair.

'Livvy Jordan,' hissed Daisy, 'used to go out with Finn McCarthy. But then ran off with his best friend, jockey, Nat Wilson.'

Hattie felt a stab of what she recognised might be jealousy followed by the thought that Finn must think she was very plain compared to the gorgeous creature she'd just seen. Just as well we are only friends, she thought. Now Finn's reserve, his slightly wounded persona all made sense, the poor guy was heartbroken. She thought back to the photos she had seen on the internet when she had googled Finn. She recognised Nat from them, and suddenly the motive for the fight before the Grand National suddenly made sense. Hattie knew that Finn was busy today but wondered if he had heard anything from Sam. She wondered whether to contact him before the party and tell him what Dr Pinkerton had said about Paddy Owen. Just as she and Daisy were seeing the pupils back to the bus, ready to go home, she had a 'phone call from him.

'Hattie,' he said in an urgent tone. 'Listen, I've just intercepted the last postcard that Sam sent to Paddy. I had a hunch and popped down there just to see the postman delivering the card. I gave them some guff about taking it to his wife. It says, '*the big thing is coming up in the next 10 days. Please destroy this card and the others because they may be onto me, Sam.'*

Harriet took this in. 'God, that doesn't leave us long to find Sam, does it?'

'No, that's just it. If they have something big planned and they think that Sam knows, they will want to find him to keep him quiet. Maybe it's a shipment of drugs or something, I've no idea. There's no time to lose. We need to find him before they do.'

Harriet found she had been holding her breath. She wondered what lengths the gang might actually go to in order to silence Sam. It didn't bear thinking about. She was in the habit of regularly checking her 'phone to see if there were any messages from Gina. There were none, so in desperation, she sent another text, explaining that Sam's safety might well be at risk and could Gina contact her immediately. As she pressed send, she just hoped that this time Gina would respond.

Chapter 15

Finn chose a dark grey suit and white shirt for the party, and even added some aftershave. He couldn't have felt less like going to a party than he did now, grieving as he was for his old friend Paddy. But he knew he had to show some steely grit if he was going to ever resolve the suspicions he had about the strange happenings of the last few weeks. Hattie had told him what Dr Pinkerton had said about the epilepsy drugs found in Paddy's pocket, but he found it frankly unbelievable. All the years he had known the jockey, he had always been a straight down the line sort of a chap, thoroughly honest and decent. It just didn't ring true that he would potentially put others at risk by hiding the fact that he had epilepsy. That just wasn't like Paddy. He often drove the horsebox and he most certainly wouldn't jeopardize the safety of his horses either. Could the epilepsy medication have been planted on him? If so by whom? Finn rejected this notion, it sounded too fantastic by half. But something felt wrong and he just knew it was tied up with Sam's disappearance.

He looked in the mirror and a handsome fellow looked back at him, belying the worrying thoughts reverberating around his head. He picked up Sam's postcards and then his own notebook in which he'd scribbled ideas, trying to make sense of the code. He copied it from the photos on his 'phone. It still looked like complete gobbledygook. Was Sam involved in a massive drugs operation and was that what got

Paddy killed? Or had his death just been a tragic accident? He couldn't rest until he was satisfied with the answers. Maybe he might be able to find something out at the party? He decided to drink very little and keep his ear to the ground. Who was behind it all? If Spud was involved, and that was in doubt as the tattoos were pretty common, he was just the hired help but there must be a Mr or Mrs Big masterminding the operation. Hattie had also told him about the two witnesses she had spoken to at Doncaster, who were adamant that they had seen Paddy arguing with someone at the top of the Clock Tower stand. Surely that had to be very significant? He hated the fact that the enemy was hiding in plain sight and he had no idea who he was looking for and therefore, everyone was under suspicion. He sighed, tried to think more positive thoughts and reached for his coat. And then there was the last postcard from Sam hinting at the next big job. What and where? He had no idea. He was looking forward to seeing Hattie, but other than that he felt like he was a soldier about to go into battle across enemy lines with unseen snipers at all sides, and landmines strewn across the terrain.

By the time Finn had picked up Hattie and they'd arrived at Hunts' yard, the party was in full swing. The indoor school was beautifully decked out, with a dance floor to one side where a jazz band were currently playing. The place was kept warm by vast heaters and was festooned with colourful bunting and fairy lights. There were several tables with huge floral displays and formally attired waiters and waitresses circulated with trays of nibbles and flutes of champagne. The sawdust floor had been covered with tarpaulin and even the horse odour had been masked by huge bowls of potpourri. Finn and Hattie gazed at the place in amazement. She was wearing a fitted green dress and black high heels. The dress set off her auburn hair and slim but shapely figure and she had applied a little makeup which suited her, Finn couldn't help but notice. She also wore a subtle but expensive perfume which was quite light and fresh.

'So, what are we looking for,' she asked, her eyes bright.

'I'm not really sure. Let's just keep our ears to the ground and try to enjoy ourselves, shall we?'

Hattie grinned and then noticed her friend Daisy.

'How about I introduce you to some people and we'll go from there. OK?'

'Sounds good to me.'

Finn was introduced to an extremely glamorous woman who looked like a model. She was a classically beautiful blonde with killer cheekbones and bright blue eyes. She looked almost Danish in appearance. She was dressed in a sparkly, skin tight blue dress, skyscraper heels and a great deal of expensive jewellery. Diamonds, Finn guessed, definitely the real thing if their sparkle was anything to go by. Livvy had often told him what to look out for, no doubt hinting she would welcome some, he now realised. The woman greeted Hattie with a hug. Hattie introduced her as the party girl, Honor. Finn was genuinely surprised and said so.

'You don't look a day over twenty,' he said truthfully, knowing full well that it was her thirtieth birthday. Her beauty was only marred by a scar from her cheekbone to her jaw on the lefthand side of her face. It was concealed by makeup but still visible. He wondered how it had happened. An accident as a child perhaps?

Honor beamed showing off perfectly white teeth.

'Oh, you are a perfect darling, isn't he Hattie?'

Finn was introduced formally to Dr Pinkerton who shook his hand delightedly explaining that he had backed many of Finn's winners.

'Great to see you in happier circumstances,' added Finn, remembering the stressful journey in the ambulance with Paddy.

'Absolutely. I'm just sorry that your friend did not survive his fall. It's just such a tragedy.' He frowned momentarily. 'Well, it's great that you could come. 'Finn was a marvellous jockey on his day,' he announced sagely to no one in particular. 'Hear you have been seeing quite a lot of Hattie.' He winked. 'Lovely girl, great family all round...'

Hattie flushed. 'Yes, but we are just good friends, Christopher.' She flashed an apologetic look at Finn.

Dr Pinkerton smiled. 'Oh, of course, darling.'

Finn couldn't help observing that the doctor and his wife did not look well suited. He looked every inch his age and then some. Despite his bonhomie and charm, he was balding and paunchy, whilst Honor could easily pass as a supermodel. He noticed that the good doctor's eyes never left his beautiful wife and she attracted a lot of attention, much of it from men, who could not take their eyes off her either.

Finn and Hattie each picked up a champagne flute and surveyed the other party goers. Hattie knew most people and introduced him to her parents who he liked on sight and several other couples. Finn noticed Henry Teasdale, Vince Hunt and Jimmy West talking urgently to one another. Teasdale glanced at Finn, then gave him a nod of recognition. Hattie decided to make formal introductions.

'Hi. Lovely party, it's so clever how you have managed to transform the place. Finn, I know you have met Vince and Henry, but do you know Jimmy West? Finn mentors conditional jockeys.'

Jimmy gave Finn an appraising look.

'Yes. You used to ride for me. You mentor that useless conditional, don't you?' He muttered turning to Henry. 'Any news on your runaway conditional, Henry? I suppose you have been on his trail, McCarthy?'

'Do call me Finn. Yes, I have. I felt an obligation to the lad, you see. But the trail has gone cold, so I'll leave it up to the police now. I suppose there could be lots of reasons he ran away.'

'Hmm. Who knows what's in the heads of young men these days,' replied Henry. 'But do let me know if you hear anything from him. I still have some wages for the lad.'

Finn assured him that he would, noting that he seemed keen to get hold of Sam, as it was the second time he had mentioned this.

'Terrible about Paddy's death. He and I went way back.'

The effect was instantaneous. Jimmy's jaw tightened, and he glared at Teasdale and Hunt even more. The other two men looked most uncomfortable, but whether it was because they feared Jimmy's reaction, it was hard to tell. After an awkward silence, Jimmy wandered off to talk to someone else. Vince glanced at Henry.

'Yes. It was truly awful. Very unlucky to fall down the Clock Tower stand. Those steps are lethal,' continued Vince mournfully.

Henry looked serious too.

'So, was it an accident?' Finn inquired, studying them closely.

'Apparently so. Seems he had some sort of fit which caused him to fall,' explained Vince carefully. Finn noticed that Hunt was avoiding his eye. 'Look. I feel like we got off on the wrong foot the other day. I took a keen interest in your riding career, you were a great talent. We should get together and perhaps you's like to ride out for me? There are some horses I'd like your opinion on.'

Finn nodded. He recognised an olive branch when he saw one. 'Great, I'd love to.'

However, he realised there wouldn't be a reciprocal offer from Teasdale. Henry's gaze had drifted off into the middle distance, his face a curious mixture of anger and grief. Finn turned slightly to see who he was staring at and was surprised to find that it was Dr Pinkerton. Interesting he thought, very interesting indeed. He wondered what on earth was going on. The body language was all wrong, off key. Did Henry have some reason to dislike Dr Pinkerton? Maybe Henry admired Honor, perhaps that was it? He couldn't help feeling that there were strange undercurrents and by discussing Paddy, had certainly upset everything. He was almost certain that they knew far more than they were letting on. Were they involved in Paddy's so-called accident?

Hattie reappeared with Daisy who Finn had also met previously and her younger sister, Alice. Finn recognised her as the young girl who had answered the door when he was first making inquiries about Connor.

'So, how is the jockey mentoring going?' Daisy asked. 'Any news on Sam?'

'Nothing, not a dickie bird. I am worried about Sam, and then what with Connor having his accident, it seems a hazardous occupation being a conditional and that's without the riding. Quite a few get into drugs too, or so I'm told.'

Daisy nodded. 'Well, I think you're safe with Connor and Sam there. They are both very health conscious, almost religious about their health. They even used to go jogging together and frowned on people smoking. But it is strange that Sam should go off like that, because of the two, I'd say he was the much better jockey.'

Her younger sister glared at her. 'That's not fair, Daisy. You can't say that!'

'Just because you like Connor, Alice. Well, maybe it's not strictly true, but he can't ride a finish. Dad has put him on at least three red hot favourites and he's lost out every time. Honestly, I wonder why Dad keeps putting him up. I know he has a weight allowance but really, he needs to get a grip. Now, that is something he needs to work on. He'll be riding Mississippi in a few weeks when he's fully recovered.'

Finn smiled back taking in everything that she had just said. 'Yes. I will certainly bear it in mind when he's back in action. Is he here tonight? I could have a word…'

'Yeah, he's somewhere. I saw him earlier. I think he's going to lead Snow Storm around. He loves that horse. Anyway, he might like a chat, he's been very upset since he was injured and then Paddy died. Fancy him having epilepsy all along?'

Daisy shot her sister a sharp look.

'Let's talk about something more upbeat. What do you make of our hostess, Honor?' she asked swiftly changing the subject.

'Absolutely charming and very beautiful, of course,' he replied.

Alice frowned. 'Yes, she's lovely. Mum says that she's far too good looking for poor old Christopher and he's struggling to hold onto her.' Alice glanced at her hostess chatting away to a tall, good looking blond man who was hanging on her every word. 'Oh look, she's there with Giles Henderson. He is always chatting her up. Wherever Honor is, Giles is not far behind…'

Daisy shot her sister another sharp look. Finn smiled at Hattie who also looked amused. He decided he liked the frankness of the two Hunt girls, particularly Alice, who was probably unaccustomed to the champagne. It had certainly loosened her tongue. In vino veritas, Finn thought dryly, committing her comments to memory. He couldn't resist finding out more.

'Who is this Giles character?'

Alice smiled. 'Oh, some mega rich city type who made a fortune on the internet. We're hoping he'll have some horses with us actually.' She smiled. 'He's much better looking and far richer than Christopher.' Again, she was rewarded by a scowl from her sister.

Finn eyed Honor and Dr Pinkerton. 'Well, she is stunning. How did she get that scar on her cheek, it's such a pity?'

'Well,' said Daisy, 'I think it was from a fall from a swing or something when she was little. It's actually much better than it was. Christopher has spent a fortune on plastic surgery for her. He hates the fact that she has a flaw. I don't think Honor minds though and Giles certainly doesn't.'

'What time is the parade for Snow Storm?' asked Harriet, aware of an air of expectancy about the place.

Daisy looked at her watch. 'Probably about now.'

With that, there was a lull in the music and Dr Pinkerton grabbed the microphone. After the inevitable 'testing, testing 1,2,3' he began to speak.

'I'd just like to say a few words before the parade. I'm so pleased that you are all here to celebrate the birthday of my darling wife, Honor. She has truly been the light of my life since the day she consented to become my wife and I hope you will join me in wishing her a very happy birthday. I have a special present for you, my dear.' He fumbled around in his pocket and pulled out a gold envelope and presented it to her.

Honor opened it, her face lit up with happiness. 'Oh, my goodness.' She took the microphone from her husband. 'It's a holiday to Barbados and a part share in the syndicate for Snow Storm. How absolutely wonderful. And I'd just like to thank you all for coming and for my fabulous presents.'

The couple embraced to loud applause and Vince took the microphone.

'A toast to our dear friend, Honor Pinkerton.' Everyone raised their glasses and waiters and waitresses circulated with slabs of birthday cake and yet more champagne. A cold buffet of salads, ham, chicken and beef had been served, together with a dessert table complete with gateaux, cheesecake, trifle and a vast chocolate fountain.

'Please eat. But before you do, please take some time to join us in the lunge ring for Snow Storm's parade. If you are interested in following Honor in owning a share of this most promising and well bred horse, then please speak to me or my wife. Do hurry as I do know that shares are selling like the proverbial hot cakes.'

Finn pretended to drink but tipped his wine away in a pot plant that decorated the school. He had to keep alert. He spotted Teasdale, Hunt and Jimmy leave, but not in the direction of the lunge ring. Then he saw the blond stable lad Pavel following them.

'I'll join you in a minute,' he said to Hattie as the guests went to watch the parade. He followed Pavel walking purposefully towards the rear of the building. There was something about the man's build that reminded him of the intruder in his flat, something about his gait, but then he dismissed his thoughts. He couldn't be at all sure. He followed Pavel, who disappeared into an adjoining storage area. He lost sight of him but heard voices coming from a nearby room. Finn walked past and tried to listen to what was being said. He could hear muffled phrases and tried to tune into the conversation. It was indistinct and impossible to distinguish who was talking. He heard the words;

'Bloody fool. Didn't sign up for this ... Draw the line.'

The other voice was deeper but less clear. 'It was a bloody accident, that's all…'

Another voice was higher and sounded like it belonged to a younger man said, 'He's right. One last time. Everything is in place... find Sam.'

There seemed to be some murmurs of assent and Finn hid around the corner to see who came out of the room. Still, he had no time to consider the meaning of what he had overheard or see who came out. Shouts and gasps were coming from the guests at the parade. He heard someone calling for help and ran over to assist.

There was a large crowd hovering and a buzz of apprehension as the beautiful dapple grey horse, Snow Storm, he presumed, reared and pulled at his rope, causing the young man leading him, Connor, to cry out in pain as the horse reared again, wrenching the rope and Connor's healing collarbone at the same time. The bloody idiot, thought Finn. Why had he insisted on leading the horse round when the horse was clearly a flighty sort? Surely, he knew it could set back his recovery if it played up and wrenched his arm?

There was a murmur of alarm and no one seemed about to step in and assist, so Finn barged his way through the throng, dipped his head under the taped fence and approached the horse.

'Whoa boy. Come on now. It's alright there.' He took the rope from Connor and stroked the horse, murmuring as he led the animal around the lunge ring. Snow Storm's black tipped ears flicked back and forwards, and he started to settle down, stopped pulling and his breathing began to calm down. Eventually, the horse started to nuzzle in Finn's pocket for treats.

'He's alright, ladies and gentlemen. He was just spooked by something, that's all.'

He nodded at Connor and was shocked by the expression on his face, as bystanders helped the injured lad to his feet. Finn imagined he might be embarrassed, grateful even, but he did not expect the look of pure venom that crossed the lad's face as he stared at Finn. Then it came to him. He had wanted to be injured by Snow Storm's antics. As Hunt joined the group to explain about the syndicate arrangements, Finn continued to lead the horse round, his thoughts spiralling wildly. Hattie had been right about them coming so see what the lie of the land was, but now he had picked up so much information, that he had absolutely no idea what any of it meant.

He went to find Hattie who was dancing and told her what he had just witnessed and about what he had overheard. He beckoned her over and whispered in her ear.

'Something strange is going on with Jimmy West. Teasdale and Hunt seem scared of him and then I followed Pavel and overheard some of them talking about finding Sam and doing one last job.'

'Who was talking together, what did they say?' Hattie swayed to the music.

'That's just it. I'm not entirely sure. It sounded like West was in there, but no one is above suspicion…Teasdale and Hunt. Maybe even Pinkerton. Maybe he planted the epilepsy medication on Paddy?'

Hattie suddenly became serious. 'Look, you can't just go around accusing people. Christopher is an amazing guy, and this is his party after all.' She stretched her arms about her in a dramatic gesture. 'These people are my friends….' Her eyes were glazed, and it was clear that she had had a lot to drink and was at the stage where she was about to become very emotional. 'You must be wrong, Finn. I'd trust him with my life, I have actually and he's a complete professional. You're just a suspicious arse.'

Finn sighed but made no comment. He, rather than anyone else, knew that it was pointless to argue with someone who had drunk as many cocktails as Hattie had. He decided that he had no option but to agree. He couldn't afford for Hattie to go blurting out his suspicions to everyone. He would talk to her tomorrow after she had slept and sobered up, then she'd see sense.

'Of course, it's just pure speculation,' he added. Harriet smiled beatifically, reassured as Finn decided to extricate himself and make his excuses. His head was full of questions to which he had no answers and he needed time to make sense of what he had witnessed, and he needed Hattie sober before he could share his ideas with her properly.

Chapter 16

Hattie woke up feeling groggy. Hell, was that the time? Hell, she put away quite a lot at the cocktail party yesterday. God, they were drinking Bellini's, Margaritas, mixing all sorts of cocktails. Christ the thought made her groan. Her head ached, and her mouth felt like a suction pump had sucked all the moisture out it and put sawdust in its place. She rolled over and tried to go back to sleep but felt slightly sick and she desperately needed the loo.

In the bathroom she caught sight of herself, bugger what a terrible state of collapse, black rings all under her eyes, clogs of mascara on her lashes like a cliché of the morning after the night before. Details from the party slipped back into her mind. Hattie vaguely recalled a sober Finn driving her home, and before that he had told her about what he'd overheard. He'd gone on and on about the importance of finding Sam and there been some new compelling reason why, another postcard and then a conversation he'd overheard about 'the something big' being in ten days. She'd been of the same mind as him until then, had agreed that they needed to find him as soon as possible. They had even arranged to meet on Wednesday at Catterick. She remembered being enthusiastic but silly, giggling when he came in for a coffee. Hattie may had tried to get him to dance too, called him a square and had even play punched him.

Oh my God, then the room had started to spin, and he'd had to support her to the downstairs loo where she'd thrown up noisily. Christ, she cringed now in shame and hot darts of humiliation flared on her skin. Finn had even held her hair while she vomited. And hell, hadn't there also been some sort of disagreement? Something that Finn had said had annoyed her. Hot darts of shame moved up her scalp. Bugger, she remembered it was when he said that no one was above suspicion, even suggesting they consider Christopher Pinkerton. Finn said he could have planted Paddy's tablets in his pocket and said, 'Funny how he's the only one who thinks Paddy may have been epileptic.'

Hattie remembered her crazy, drunken comments in defence of Christopher. Now she recalled going on and on saying thing like,

'I trush him with my life... absolutshley... luuve the guy…'

If she remembered rightly, she'd been very rude and ended up telling Finn he was 'a suspicious arse' are something similar. Finn's words came back to her. He had only suggested that she keep an open mind about everyone she knew, including Vince and Christopher. God, Finn must think she was such an idiot. Still, Christopher was a family friend and she could not believe he was capable of planting medication, but she had been rude rather than robust in his defence. It was stupid really because with so many police officers in the family, she knew that Finn was right. Everyone was under suspicion until proven innocent. Damn. She staggered back to bed and vowed never to drink any alcohol ever again. She drank thirsty gulps of water which someone had left on her bedside table. Then she spotted a pack of ibuprofen next to the glass with a yellow post-it note on it. She looked closer.

Take these tomorrow. See you Weds Finn x

This paradoxically made her feel worse. She'd been a stupid drunken cow and he had behaved thoughtfully. Christ, what must he think of her? Cheeks reddening, she grabbed the post-it-note and held it in her hand as she dozed off. Her last thought was, at least he had said see you Wednesday and put a kiss at the end. He can't hate me that much, she thought. The knowledge that all was not lost comforted her.

Downstairs a couple of hours later, her mother was reading the paper at the kitchen table.

'OK Hattie? Good party, wasn't it? Listen, I'm teaching this afternoon, then I'll call in at the shop, need anything?' She raised an eyebrow. 'Painkillers?'

Hattie grinned sheepishly. 'You're alright, Finn left some for me…'

Her mother eyed her speculatively. 'Hmm, I did like him. Are you sure you're just friends? I thought he was quite the gentleman…handsome too, anyway your father's helping clear the indoor school and putting it back to normal.'

Hattie looked down. 'Mum, I know I drank a bit too much, did I make a right fool of myself last night?'

Her mother laughed. 'Nothing I saw no, you were just merry like most other people. Hey, but you should have seen what happened after you left, that poor young jockey, Connor someone, he seemed to hurt himself leading Snow Storm around. The stupid horse reared up and fractured Connor's collarbone again. First, he was injured in a hit and run and now this. How unlucky can you get? Mind you your father swears he did it deliberately, you know what he's like, always thinks the worst. And then there was a right carry on with Honor and that man called Giles...'

Hattie poured herself a coffee from the pot on the stove and topped up her mother's. This was, she thought, part of the fun of a party, dissecting events afterwards.

'Well go on, what happened next?'

'Giles started dancing with Vanessa Freeman and Honor marched up and pushed her out of the way. It was so embarrassing. Anyone would have thought she was jealous of someone being close to Giles and not married to Christopher at all…'

'Oh, she's not having an affair with him, is she?'

'She says not but I don't know, she would say that, wouldn't she? Sometimes I think it's only a matter of time, she certainly likes to flirt. Anyway, I better dash…'

Hattie spent a quiet afternoon trying to read up for yet another essay, she was too wrecked to think clearly. Although she knew there were things about the case which didn't make any sort of sense, she also knew that things would look clearer tomorrow. She had a text from Finn which read,

'Hope you feel OK, meet you at 3, members' bar Finn x'.

The next day Hattie went to ride Kasper. She could see the indoor school was now operational and spent a session putting the horse through his paces. Kasper was fit and moving well, he was jumping cleanly too with no sign of his back problems. The gel pad had worked like a charm. Hattie sighed, the thing was with people like Finn, they were steeped in horses and knew so much about when an animal was in pain or off colour, it was almost unnerving. Not like her, who had a smattering of skills over lots of disciplines. As she unsaddled Kasper, she heard a familiar voice,

'Hi sis, so this is your new nag?'

'Blimey, Will, what are you doing here?"

She felt immediately suspicious. Will never did anything without a good reason, and she imagined that today's visit would be about something important, even if her brother didn't exactly tell her what it was.

'You know, had to see a man about a dog.'

Hattie knew a load of flannel when she heard it.

'So, you must be here about work?' She turned to face him, curry comb in hand, 'Are you going to give me any clues?'

Her brother opened the stable door and hovered rather nervously in the corner.

‘As long as you control that beast.’ He lowered his voice. ’You know the drug thing I mentioned, you heard anything sis, around the yards and that?’

Hattie made a quick calculation, deciding what she could and couldn’t tell him, yet anyway.

‘No, nothing definite. It’s mostly gossip about disappearing or injured jockeys.’

‘Mmm. You listen out Hat, because there’s something big coming and we’re trying to catch the organ grinders not the monkeys.’

‘Sure, but what am I listening out for exactly?’

‘We think there’s some new guys on the drugs scene. We think they’re operating in this area. It could be dangerous but if you hear anything, will you let me know? Keep your wits about you, alright?’

Hattie thought Will sounded more like an actor from a cop show but agreed to help and pass on anything definite that she did hear. Did he think the racing yards were involved? Damn. She was just about to ask him but found Will had already gone.

On Wednesday she drove to Catterick mulling over what she’d found out. She also resolved to apologise to Finn for her drunkenness and the rather pointless argument about Christopher Pinkerton. She still didn’t believe the doctor had anything to do with planting epilepsy medication on Paddy, but she could see how it might look to someone who didn’t know him as well as she did. She played around with various scenarios in her head, Christopher dealing in drugs to make money, maybe trying to keep Honor happy. Mmm, that would just be possible with someone with dodgy morals but not Christopher. He had always been a source of sound judgment and a speaker of good sense to her as she grew and matured. It was him she confided in when she was scared about the problems with Dale and Christopher had really helped her. Turning into the racecourse car park, she suddenly remembered what Finn had said about finding another postcard from Sam. It'd said something like '*the big thing is coming up in 10 days. Please destroy this card, they may be onto me.*'

Oh my God! That fitted perfectly with what Will had said. And Finn had told her about overhearing men talking and about how they had to find Sam. Christ, no wonder Finn was convinced the poor lad was in danger. Then she thought about what Mum had said about Connor Moore. Had he volunteered to lead Snow Storm round knowing full well he was skittish and prone to rearing? It did seem terribly unlucky to be rammed by a car, break a collarbone and then when you were recovering, struggle to hold on to a rearing horse and fracture it again. It was almost as if the two conditionals at Hunt's and Teasdale's were jinxed and someone didn't want them to ride in any races for some reason. But why? And how the hell was that related to drugs?

Hattie worked with Bob, completing the Racing to School activities with a lively Year 5 group from one of the local schools. At Catterick they had also got the Equiciser set up and one of the ex-jockeys, Kevin Allen, had agreed to show the children how it worked and talked about the importance of balance and the centre of gravity. They all piled into a room next to the weighing room, just as the jockeys were arriving with their kit bags. Kevin was well into his demonstration and had the children's attention, when a loud shout from outside took Hattie's attention. She walked over to the entrance of the weighing room and saw two young men, clearly jockeys, pushing and shoving one another. Then one lad, a strawberry blond, baby faced youth yelled,

'Sod off, you wanker, you know piss all about it,' and lunged at the other jockey, punching him with an almighty thud and flooring him. Several men came to intervene and one man, who Hattie recognised as one of the valets, helped the blond jockey up. The jockey already dressed in blue and pink colours pushed away any helpers.

'I'm OK, just let me get to the ring and on with my rides.'

Hattie returned to see Kevin finishing off his demonstration. The man should teach, she told herself, he was a natural. She looked at her watch. Two o'clock. Time to watch a couple of races with the kids and then she'd arrange for Bob to finish off, so she could meet Finn. Hattie went off to talk about 'Parade Ring Possibilities' with the kids. When they arrived, she explained about colours, owners and trainers as the children watched the horses in the ring. When the jockeys walked out, Hattie spotted the lad in the pink and blue colours who she'd seen fighting earlier, approach his owners and she was that he was riding number 13. She checked in her racecard to see that this was a bay horse called Regency Belle. She watched as he was legged up into the saddle and then cantered down to the start. Then Hattie and Bob ushered the children to the stands to watch the race. 'They're off,' said Hattie to the chattering children, whose eyes were all trained on the horses as they began to race.

'Blimey, there's some sort of problem,' said Bob pointing up at the big screen opposite the stands, 'someone's fallen off before they're even reached the first flight of hurdles!'

'Number 13 has unseated his rider,' said the racecourse announcer.

'Looks like the saddle slipped,' Bob told her,' and the jockey must be injured because they're fetching a stretcher.'

Number 13 thought Hattie. Unlucky for some.

It was just past three when she reached the bar. She spotted Finn over by the window studying his 'phone. A wide smile broke across his face as he saw her approach,

'Still alive, I see? I hope you're feeling a bit brighter.'

'Oh God, I'm so sorry…' Her ardent apology was waved away immediately.

'Save it, Hattie.' He looked intently at her as she settled herself at the table. 'There's been some new developments.' He looked round as if checking for listeners and lowered his voice. 'I've just come from dealing with one of the jockeys, Harry Jarvis. He's been involved in a fight outside the weighing room and then he fell off right after the start.'

Hattie recalled the incident. 'On number 13?'

'Yep,' said Finn when she explained what she'd seen. 'That jockey, Harry, looks like a choir boy but it's misleading. Anyway, he's only gone and broken his leg. Seems like the girth was loose and the saddle slipped. Talk about a rookie error, I can't believe he didn't tighten up the girth properly. By the way, this same doctor analysed those pills we found in Sam's room.'

'Really what were they?'

'Bloody antidepressants!'

Hattie took in Finn's exasperated tone.

'What is it with these conditionals, why are they so much trouble?'

'Christ alone knows, but we've got Sam missing and depressed, Connor so terrified that he's throwing himself around the place like a madman, almost as if he wants to be injured.'

'Can we get some food and then you can have my fullest attention.'

Finn grinned attractively. 'Sure, I'm peckish too.'

Hattie laughed with relief. Finn clearly wasn't bearing a grudge else he wouldn't be teasing her as usual. 'OK, let's find somewhere before I fall over…'

The bar had a restaurant section and Finn soon caught the eye of one of the waitresses. As he ordered Hattie noticed the young woman casting him admiring glances. He did look good in a slightly dishevelled way, with just enough dark stubble and tousled hair.

Whilst they waited for their food, Hattie told him about Will's visit to the yard. She leaned closer.

'And he said something big is going down in the next few weeks and his team is investigating drugs, as you know. There's a new gang, he thinks, operating in and around Walton.'

Finn waited while tea and sandwiches were laid out in front of them. He hesitated until the waitress was out of earshot.

'Hmm. Could be connected... Obviously we need to find out what the hell is going on, who's involved, which jockeys are involved. Yep and we need to talk to Connor and Sam… and maybe Harry.' Finn noticed Hattie's questioning expression. 'He's a conditional too.'

Harriet hadn't realised.

'Oh my God, not another one! That's one missing lad, two injured and counting…'

Chapter 17

Finn found that his brain was spinning, and worry gnawed at him about his conditionals. And worse, he felt that it had stirred up a powder keg of old hurts and injuries. He thought he had dealt with all that happened to him when he was a conditional at Boothroyd's but found the anger, humiliation and shame now resurfaced with a vengeance. The only way he could make it right, somehow, and redeem himself was to help other lads in the same position, otherwise, what was the point of his job? He forced himself to concentrate on his current charges. There were so many leads that ended up going nowhere. His mentor career seemed to be floundering badly. Harry had broken his leg after the fall, and he needed to find out what was going on with Connor pretty damned quick. He knew that Sam held the key to everything, and they must find him, but he was conscious that they had already tried the obvious steps. He had no idea what to do next. He peered at the postmarks on the cards Sam had sent hoping to find some more clues, but they were smeared and completely indistinct. And there were also pieces of information that didn't fit. He remembered what Alice and Daisy had said about Sam and Connor, that they were very into health and fitness and were appalled by smoking, never mind taking drugs. Yet, Hattie's brother was convinced that there was drug dealing going on within Walton and that it centred around the racing yards, so that had to be a factor didn't it?

He stared at the photos he'd taken of the notebook in Sam's luggage with its strange notation. This also pointed to drug deals, but was there something else? Finn resolved to ask Harry some questions before going to Market Rasen for the afternoon where he was meeting his boss, Tony Murphy.

Melvin Pike's place was nestled on the outskirts of Walton yet near enough for him to use the town's gallops. Melvin was a trainer with a small yard but with a reputation as a no nonsense type of chap who had trained one or two excellent horses. He was still furious about Harry's accident.

'I just don't understand it. He was doing great, so well that the owners for Regency Belle were dead keen to have him ride her in the next race. The weight allowance would have been very helpful. Then, he forgets to tighten the girth on his last ride at Catterick and blasted well falls off. He knows that I check it when saddling up, but he should check it too. That horse is known for puffing its stomach out.' Melvin frowned.

'Can I speak to Harry?'

'No, well what I meant to say is he's not here. His fracture is quite bad, so I've sent him home for a few weeks.' Melvin shrugged. 'He can't muck out or ride and I can't have him moping about the place. It was such a basic mistake not to tighten the girth. Regency Belle's owners were so disappointed.'

'Where does his family live?' Damn. Finn had Harry's local address but not his family's. He could always visit.

'Oh, somewhere in Cornwall, Penzance, I think.'

Finn nodded remembering the lad's accent. Well, he wasn't going to be going down that way for a while, so he would have to try and ring him instead. He could understand Melvin's annoyance especially when Regency Belle was one of his best horses and stood a great chance of winning that day. Trainers had to please their owners and made every effort to do so, otherwise they could move their horses at the first sign of trouble. Owners were the lifeblood of the sport and every trainer knew it.

'Hmm. I'm wondering if there was anything going on personally for him, something bothering him, money worries, debts, girlfriend problems, anything like that…?'

Melvin looked bewildered. 'Hang on, are you saying he did it deliberately?'

'No, no I just wondered if he was distracted and maybe wasn't thinking straight, that's all.' Melvin nodded. 'I just put it down to him being young and a bit daft, but honestly everyone knows to check a horse's girth before mounting. Many horses blow their stomachs out and God knows I've told him time and time again to check.' Melvin looked thoughtful. 'Look, maybe the ride on Regency Belle was too much too soon? He seemed very confident but maybe he was struggling. Lots of conditionals don't make it and many of them just don't have what it takes.' Melvin frowned. He appeared to be having an internal battle about Harry. He was torn between feeling compassion and sheer irritation for the lad. Irritation won out in the end. 'But I run a tight ship here and we all have to work hard and if he isn't prepared to then he's better off walking. I am not running a charity, Mr McCarthy and I can well do without time wasters.'

Finn glanced around the small but very neat and tidy yard. There was an air of calm efficiency and organisation about the place, all hallmarks of a well run operation.

'Yes. I understand, and I can see that the place is beautifully maintained, and the horses all look wonderful, so you obviously know what you're doing. I'll contact Harry at home and find out what's going on, but whilst I'm here do you mind if I talk to some of the other staff? Did he have any particular friends?'

Finn's compliments about how he kept his yard, seemed to have mollified Melvin slightly.

'Well, he did speak to Jamie and Mo. They are stable lads and he did spend a lot of time with them, so they might know something.'

'OK. I won't keep them long.'

Melvin nodded and pointed into his yard. 'Jamie is the red haired lad and Mo is from Pakistan, doesn't speak English too well but he and Harry seemed to communicate alright.' Melvin gave the ghost of a smile. 'Don't ask me how…'

Finn found Jamie brushing a huge bay gelding with a tiny white star on his head. The animal nosed in Finn's pockets for mints.

'Hi, I'm Finn McCarthy. I'm Harry's mentor. I'm just checking if everything was alright with him. Do you know if he was in any sort of trouble, anything bothering him?'

Jamie paused. 'Search me. If he was upset by something, then he certainly didn't tell me.' Jamie frowned. 'Course he was keen to prove himself and make it. He seemed to ride OK, he was pretty confident so no worries on that score. I'm not sure about anything else. I suppose he'll come back when his leg is healed?'

'Yeah, I'm sure he will.' Finn had no idea either way but decided not to worry Jamie with his doubts.

Jamie picked up his body brush and resumed his vigorous brushing, then paused. 'Mo might know more.'

'Does he speak any English?'

Jamie grinned. 'Nah, but he's sort of good at communicating, you'll see when you meet him.' He suddenly looked serious. 'But if you do find Harry, tell him to give me that twenty quid he still owes me.'

Finn agreed to do just that thinking that everything seemed to come down to money and love in the end. He found Mo shovelling horse muck into the muck pile.

'Hi there. I'm a friend of Harry's. I'm wondering if he was OK? Was there anything bothering him?' Finn tried not to shout.

Mo was a small Asian man wearing riding boots and a navy padded jacket. He grinned. 'Harry, yes. He my friend.'

'Yes, yes. Did he talk about any problems he was having? Was he OK?'

Mo smiled and waved his arms about. 'He upset. Harry angry.'

'Yes. Do you know why?'

Mo grinned again. 'Harry, he upset. He my friend.'

'Yes, yes, but why was he upset? What happened?' Finn shrugged, raising both his shoulders, emphasising the movement in an impressive Gallic fashion, worthy of a mime artist.

Mo grinned and nodded. 'Ah.' He frowned speaking in a torrent of what Finn assumed was Urdu or something. 'Men...tell him….' Mo made a tugging gesture with both his hands as though pulling something towards him. 'Harry good.'

Perhaps these men had physically threatened Harry?

'What is it that they asked him to do?'

Again, there was a rush of fast words in a foreign tongue and the tugging gesture.

'Harry, he good man. He say no.'

'Right, Mo. Thank you.' Finn turned away, well and truly baffled.

'Hey,' called Mo. 'You tell Harry to come see me. Yes?'

Finn smiled. 'Yes, my friend, I will certainly tell him.' Though, he didn't feel that he had made any headway at all, in fact he was now more confused than ever.

Finn texted Harry asking him to get in touch and made his way to Market Rasen and once there, enjoyed the brief glimmers of radiant sunshine in the late November afternoon, although the wind was biting. He bought a racecard, studied form and quickly texted Harriet.

Visited Harry's yard but no joy there. Any ideas?

Finn then rang Lisa, Paddy's wife, to offer his condolences. She sounded absolutely wretched.

Finn listened and said, 'I have some photos of Paddy from when he was riding, so I thought you might like them. I can't believe he's gone...'

Lisa sighed, and it was a sound full of regret. 'Even though we were separated, we were still close. I always thought that maybe we'd get back together...'

'I know. He always spoke highly of you and adored the kids, of course.'

Lisa sounded tearful but pleased.

'I've also had the police round saying he had medication in his pocket, and he may have had epilepsy and lied about it to get a job. I can't think he would do such a thing, can you, Finn?'

Lisa sounded close to the edge and utterly bewildered by it all. Finn agreed that Paddy wasn't capable of knowingly placing anyone in harm's way. He had been the most generous of men.

'I suppose they will check with his doctor to see if he was diagnosed or what medication he was on, so that should clarify things, but I agree, it's not something Paddy would have been capable of.'

Lisa sounded relieved at his reassurances. 'Listen, the police might want to come and see you as you were one of the last people who saw him.'

'Right. Fine, I'll wait to hear from them.' Finn wondered what the police had picked up and whether or not he ought to tell them about his plan to meet Paddy and his suspicions that what Paddy might have had to say, could have got him killed.

'Did Paddy ever mention that he was having fits or headaches? Was he in any trouble?'

Lisa almost laughed at the idea. 'No, nothing like that. He seemed his usual self, a few gripes about child maintenance but nothing more.' She paused. 'Listen, Finn, I'm glad to hear from you. I would love those photos. I really appreciate your offer of help. It's just great to talk to someone who knew Paddy from the old days and who knows how talented he was. It's important the boys know what a great dad they had and all about his riding.'

Finn agreed to visit and thought about his two sons growing up without their father. They really did need to know what a wonderful jockey and man he was. They also deserved to know the truth about his death, whatever, that might be.

Finn placed a few bets and chatted to one or two people he knew. Seamus and Rosy had a runner and he was pleased to see their horse, Cardinal Sin, romp home to win at 20-1. Better still, she was ridden by another conditional, Lily Graham, who had just been allocated to Finn. He had studied her race carefully and thought she had ridden very well.

'I'm thrilled for her,' Rosy said later when he caught up with her. 'Especially if you're going to be her coach. Maybe the girls will cause you less problems. Did you hear anything from your missing lad?'

Finn shook his head. 'No, but we are following up some leads.'

'Oh, that reminds me, I saw Nat Wilson on the way in. He was asking after you.' She sighed. 'He'd really like to talk to you and it's high time you made it up. You know that.'

Finn shook his head.

'Come on now, Finn. Even you can't bear a grudge forever…'

Finn was sure that he could.

He felt churlish so decided to have a celebratory drink with Rosie.

'Perhaps you're our lucky mascot! I'm just so delighted.' Rosie repeated.

Finn had forgotten what a positive person she was and how she was always so genuinely surprised at her and Seamus's success and delighted for everyone else too.

'Mind what I said about Nat.'

Finn was non-committal. Later, after watching another race, he made his way to the members' bar where he had arranged to meet his boss, Tony Murphy. Tony raised a hand to greet him.

'What'll you have to eat? Drink?' They sipped beers as Tony pulled out his notebook and pen. Not many jobs allowed for supervision to be conducted in a bar at the races, and Finn was grateful he wasn't stuck in some boring office somewhere where he guessed most supervision took place. Tony was an ex-jockey, a small wiry man with a keen sense of humour and bucket loads of common sense. They went through some of the formalities before getting to the crux of the matter.

'So, what the hell is going on with your conditionals? Do you reckon they're just a bad lot or is there something else?'

Finn filled him in on Sam's disappearance, Harry's accident, Connor's reluctance to ride, and the information about drugs being dealt within the racing yards at Walton.

'But I'm just not convinced about the drugs stuff. We must be missing something.' Finn explained about Paddy's fall and how he suspected it was not an accident and the postcards from Sam to Paddy suggesting that something big was being planned.

Tony listened quietly. 'God, it sounds like a proper mess. When I checked, the BHA Integrity team have nothing further to add about the drugs, so I can't help you there.' Tony sighed, deep in thought. 'Who do you think is behind it all?'

'Well, that's just it, I'm not sure. Teasdale and Hunt are the trainers where Sam and Connor are based. Perhaps, they are involved and then the chap I've visited today about Harry, Melvin Pike, seemed a decent enough type, so God only knows? Then, there's the owner, Jimmy West. He seems to hate all conditionals and is a bully. He is pally with Boothroyd and that is certainly a worry. You remember Boothroyd?'

Tony nodded sympathetically. Tony had been a good friend to Finn and had supported him when the authorities had taken action against Boothroyd. A steady stream of conditionals and stable staff had come forward and the tales were all the same, some even worse than Finn's experience. Boothroyd had promised them the earth and meted out beatings and dodged payments just because he could. It was a classic tale of power and control over those who were vulnerable. Finn shook his head as he tried to rid himself of his bleak memories.

'Then there was the incident with Paddy. He fell down the steps of the Clock Tower stand, but they found epilepsy medication on him and now everyone thinks the fall was an accident and that Paddy had hidden his condition to keep his job. But some eyewitnesses stated that Paddy was seen arguing with someone prior to his fall. Someone meeting the description of a stable lead called Pavel. Supposing he pushed Paddy?'

Tony frowned. 'I know it's awful, but you can't just go around making wild allegations. I presume the police are looking into Paddy's fall? What other evidence do you have to indicate it wasn't an accident?'

Finn explained that Paddy had arranged to meet, and he was sure he was going to pass on vital information. 'I think I need to find Sam as soon as possible.'

Tony nodded. 'OK. Let me take down the names of the trainers and the stable staff, Jimmy and Boothroyd. I have some unofficial lines of communication with the police and I need to call in a few favours. Let me see if I can find anything out.' He drained his glass. 'Look, if you do go on some wild goose chase to find Sam, then try to keep me informed. We could do with the information if it looks like racing has a big problem, so we can head off the media and do a spot of damage limitation. But be bloody careful. We all know what drugs gangs are capable of.' Tony clapped him on the back. 'Oh, that reminds me, I saw Nat as I was coming in and when I said I was meeting you, he was very keen to see you too, in fact he gave me a note.' Tony fished a crumpled folded piece of paper out of his pocket and gave Finn a stern look. 'You should consider it, talk to him at least. Life is too short to bear grudges. Now, you look after yourself.' He raised his hand as he walked away into the crowd, leaving Finn staring at the note and the scrawl written upon it. First Rosy and now Tony. Nat must be really desperate to speak to him.

'Meet me after the last race, Owners' and Trainers' bar. Nat'

Finn watched the races, chatted to several people that he knew and pondered on the investigation and whether or not he should meet Nat. He pocketed some winnings from a few well placed bets, at least two on horses Nat was riding and found his way to the Owners' and Trainers' bar. He was about to order a coke when he decided he just couldn't face Nat, not today. He wasn't ruling out some reunion in the future. Tony was right, life was too short but today wasn't going to be the day. With a sigh, he turned on his heel and headed home.

The drive was long, and it was when he pulled off the motorway and on to the dark 'A' roads, that he noticed that he was being followed. The same pair of blue rimmed, oval shaped lights had been behind him for the last few miles. The lights were so unusual that it had to be the same vehicle tailing him, there wouldn't be two.

Finn felt a cold finger of alarm trace down his back. As he came into York, he quickly turned left then right and double backed on himself. He strained to look in his rear-view mirror and waited to see if the blue lights followed him. Just when he thought he had got away with it, the familiar lights reappeared behind him again. Damn. Who the hell was it? Teasdale, West even Boothroyd himself? Adrenalin coursed through him as he thought about the fear and evil which had driven Sam underground, scared off the other conditionals and which might be behind Paddy's death. He would not be another victim. Senses alert, he drove off at a fast pace, around the one-way system, over the river and veered sharply left, then right past the railway station. The traffic lights were on his side for once and he pulled into his private car park without the company of the blue lights. He felt relief and then concern. If he was being followed, then did they know he was on to them and what would be their next step?

Chapter 18

Hattie sighed and decided to take a break from her essay about the rise of type two diabetes in the UK. In fact, it was true to say that these days her thoughts were constantly interrupted by racing, about troublesome and disappearing conditional jockeys and accidents at racecourses. She shut down her laptop and went downstairs to make a coffee. As she settled down to drink it there was a knock at the door. It was Daisy.

'Oh, great you can distract me from my essay, how are things with you?'

Her friend settled down and grimaced. 'Bloody awful. I just need to get out of the place for half an hour. Dad's in a right mood. There's no one to ride the horses with Sam disappearing and Connor breaking his collarbone again.'

Hattie wondered how much to tell her friend Daisy. It was worth asking a few questions. But she didn't want to put her friend in danger or in a difficult position.

'Have you any idea what might be going on, have you heard any whispers from the other staff?'

'Christ, first things first, have you got any biscuits, I'm starving?'

In between crunching bourbons and custard creams, Daisy talked about the yard.

‘I’ll tell you one thing for nothing, ever since Dad became matey with Teasdale the whole atmosphere has changed. Dad seems on edge, unhappy and as for that stable lad of Teasdale’s, Pavel, he’s really rough on the horses and isn’t above thrashing them for no good reason. I don’t trust him at all. I know I said he was hot, but the more I’ve seen of him, the less I like him.’

Hattie smiled. Anyone who hurt horses would be hated by Daisy who was the polar opposite of Pavel. She’d starve herself rather than see her horses go without anything. Still, Hattie couldn’t see her standing by and letting someone harm her horses either.

‘How do you mean he’s not above thrashing them? And what are you going to do about it?’

‘Well, I haven’t actually seen him hit a horse but I’m sure he has done. They all recoil from him, as though they’re afraid so he must have done something to them. I caught him coming out of a stable with a whip a couple of times, but he said it was just to protect himself. But I don’t know. He’s a right bully if you ask me and he’s always watching, whatever you do, bloody Pavel’s there watching you. Now I know him better, I wouldn’t trust him as far as I could throw him.’

Hattie frowned.

‘And what about him and Teasdale? Surely Henry wouldn’t put up with him hurting his precious thoroughbreds?’

Daisy sighed. ‘Well, that’s just it. They are close even though it seems unlikely. It’s almost as though Pavel’s there as a tough guy, he’s certainly no horseman. As you know, you can’t force a horse to do anything, you have to sort of gain their trust first. Brute force or fear doesn't work.'

At the back door, Daisy paused. 'And Teasdale and Dad were arguing about something too. They were in the office talking and then Teasdale got into a strop and left.'

Hattie's ears pricked up at this. 'Oh, I wonder what they were arguing about?'

Daisy shrugged. 'I dunno. Probably something to do with Connor not being able to ride. And Dad's really upset about Paddy too. Anyway, Teasdale went off muttering about dad having to wise up and smell the coffee or something.'

Hattie looked at Daisy's forlorn expression. 'Maybe they're just struggling and having a lean spell?' Daisy was always going on about how the yard was a different place when they had winners. All the hard work seemed worth it then.

'Yeah, maybe you're right.' Daisy rolled her eyes, tutted and gave her a final wave.

Hattie knew she wouldn't get much done on her essay today. She wondered about the tension between Vince and Henry and Pavel's role at the yards. Why employ someone if he hadn't got a clue about horses? She was struggling to concentrate and decided to have a walk around the town to try and clear her head. She drove into Walton and decided to call in at her favourite coffee shop 'The Singing Kettle.' She was just waiting for her cheese and onion toastie and taking a sip of her mocha, when she heard a familiar booming voice nearby.

'Hello Hattie. Mind if I join you? You look miles away? Are you alright, sweetheart?'

Hattie looked up to see Christopher Pinkerton beaming at her. Great. She felt a rush of affection for him. 'Course help yourself. How are you?'

Christopher smiled. 'All the better for seeing you actually. I hope you enjoyed the party?'

'Yes. It was great fun. Thank you so much for inviting me and Finn too. We had a great time. Shame about Connor hurting his collarbone again.'

Christopher looked mournful. 'Yes. Well, it just one of those things I suppose. I'm glad you enjoyed it. Honor was delighted with the whole thing.' He suddenly looked serious. 'I was meaning to ask you if you'd mind giving me Finn's number? I wanted to talk to him about another of his conditionals, actually.'

Hattie was immediately curious. 'Oh, who?' She noticed Christopher's wariness. 'Oh sorry. I know you can't say anything to me. Forget I said anything.'

Christopher nodded. 'It's quite alright. I don't think you would know them anyway. These conditionals certainly seem to be giving Finn quite a hard time, I must say. Is there any news on the missing lad, Sam, wasn't it?'

Hattie sighed. She looked at the big man sitting opposite her, as she ate her sandwich and thought how nice it would be to talk to someone other than Finn about her worries. She delved in her pocket for her 'phone and scrolled down to Finn's number. Then she wrote it out on a paper napkin.

'Here you are. No. Sam seems to have vanished without trace. I think Finn has some leads. He does take it very seriously, the duty of care he has to them. Anyway, I'm sure Sam'll turn up at some point.'

Christopher looked at the napkin thoughtfully. 'I'm sure you're right. I presume Finn lives locally. I'll give him a ring and pop round. It's always best to deal with delicate matters face to face, I always think.'

Hattie nodded and explained that he lived in one of the old Rowntree Factory buildings in York.

Christopher pocketed the napkin. 'Wonderful. His conditional has probably met some girl or has gone to stay with a friend or a relative. Just leave well alone, Hattie. I mean if the lad doesn't want to be found then what good will come from trying to find him? I'm sure Finn will have thought of that, surely…'

Hattie nodded, confused. 'Well maybe. I suppose he's an adult. Sam's mum is Scottish so I'm sure he has lots of relatives there. Maybe he doesn't want to be a jockey and can't think of another way out…'

Christopher drained his coffee and took a bite of his sandwich. He seemed pleased.

'That's it, just leave him to it. Anyway, how are you, Harriet? I always worried about you when you decided to stop competing. I know it must have been hard for you to readjust, but I just hope you've found your niche with this University course. I'm sure you'll be excellent at it. We don't always get the chance to talk like we used to in the old days, do we?'

Hattie looked into Christopher's brown eyes and remembered how unfailingly kind he had always been to her. When she had been competing, he had advised her on nutrition and how to come back from injuries when she had felt at rock bottom, he had been ever ready to lend a listening ear. He had even covered for her when she had a positive test. Her coach had convinced her that she could get into the UK Olympic squad, hadn't even really told her what was in the supplements, just that it wasn't harmful, and she'd been furious when she found out. When she'd confronted him, he'd convinced her that no one would find out and everyone was using the stuff and she had to use it to keep up. God, she didn't even like to think about it now. She was immature and had really trusted Dale, idolised him even and he had become so much more than a coach. Then the whole thing had gone horribly wrong. That was why she was so anti drugs and why in the end she could not resist getting involved with Sam's case.

She squeezed Christopher's hand. 'Of course, I'm fine. I'm enjoying my course. Actually, I need to get back and finish off my essay actually or I'll never pass it.' She grinned and got up to settle her bill.

'Don't worry. I'll get it, Harriet. I just wanted to say, I'm very glad that you're happy. Rest assured, your little problem is safe with me. I'm really proud of the way you have coped, you know. If you ever need to talk to me about anything, anything at all, you know where to find me.'

Hattie smiled. 'Thanks, Christopher. For everything. It means a lot.'

She drove back home and started to feel rather uneasy. Christopher was right that they didn't get the time to talk about what had happened, mostly because her parents were there. They didn't know the full details and she didn't want them to find out. Feelings of guilt and self loathing crowded in. She had allowed the testers to take her sample knowing full well it would come back positive. In a total panic, she had told Christopher what she had taken, and he had vouched for her, stating to the authorities that he had given her a steroid prescription for a fictitious illness, so that had accounted for the positive steroid test. His statement had been taken seriously, he was a well respected GP of course, and he had literally saved her reputation and put his own on the line for her. He had never revealed her secret to anyone. Her family would have been utterly ashamed of her and she couldn't bear that. She had been desperate and had been sick with worry. Dale was clear he would deny all knowledge, and it was then that she realised how stupid she had been to trust him. Thank God, she'd had Christopher Pinkerton to turn to. She would always be grateful to him. Despite the fact that she decided to give up the sport just months later, he had protected her from being exposed as a cheat and for that she would always be grateful. But it was hard to shake off the feelings of self loathing. She wondered why Christopher had brought up the subject after all this time? He had said that her little problem was safe with him. She had presumed that anyway, but the fact that he needed to say it made her worried, as though he might actually tell someone. Then she realised it was just a figure of speech and that she was reading too much into it. She was being stupidly paranoid.

Back home she tried to banish her gloomy thoughts and made herself focus on her essay. An hour later, she had made some progress and began searching for some old notes. As she looked, she found the piece of paper she had taken from Sam's father's house, the one with the indentations, where a number had been written down on the sheet above and then torn off. Satisfied that she had done enough Uni work for now, she took out her pencil and delicately shaded over the top of the marks to reveal the number. After while it became a little clearer. 01595 was the code followed by another number which she couldn't make out. The first digits must be an area code but where for? She searched through the yellow pages which was no use so googled the number instead. The answer surprised her. Lerwick. Where the hell was that? On the Shetland Isles apparently. Bingo. As she was taking this in, the door banged. It was Mum, so she went downstairs to chat.

Her mother hefted a huge pile of marking onto the kitchen table.

'Hi darling. How's the essay coming on? Shall I put the kettle on?'

'Fine. Hey Mum, where are the Shetland Islands?'

Her mother looked at her curiously as she filled the kettle. 'Off the coast of Scotland, I think. Why do you need to know?'

Harriet feigned indifference.

'Oh, no reason. I just wondered that's all. One of my friends from Uni lives in Scotland and has invited me there.' She quickly texted Finn. Maybe they had just had the breakthrough they needed. Then her 'phone started to ring. It was an unknown number. Hattie punched the buttons to receive the call. A hesitant, unfamiliar woman spoke.

'Is that Harriet? I'm returning your call. It's Gina.'

Chapter 19

Lisa smiled at the sight of Paddy, grinning back at her from the photograph after winning the Champion Hurdle. Finn took in Lisa's white face, framed with her dark hair. She looked absolutely exhausted. He realised that she was very attractive, but that stress and grief had dimmed her beauty.

She smiled. 'Paddy talked about you a lot actually. About how you'd been at Holling's with him and how well you'd done. He followed your career, read about every race.'

Finn nodded. 'Yeah, well I always had a lot of respect for him. I owe him a great deal. He was a great guy. Listen Lisa, if there's ever anything I can do to help, I could teach the boys to ride when they get older. Anything...'

Lisa nodded and gulped back tears and he hugged her for a minute. She felt fragile and birdlike in his arms. Finn tried to think of something to say that might help, but it all sounded so cliched. Lisa pulled away.

'It takes something like a death to make you realise how much someone means to you,' Lisa added, her eyes sparkling with tears, as if to reinforce his thoughts. 'I'll just miss the old sod and so will the kids. We've two boys aged four and six, you see.'

Finn nodded. 'Where are they now?'

‘At my parents.’ Suddenly her face clouded. ‘God, how am I going to tell them that their father has died? I have no idea.’

‘Just be honest with them, explain they and you are going to feel sad for a long time and tell them what a great man he was and how much he loved them. But tell them it will get better because it will.’ Finn thought that was the sort of thing his sister Jenny would say, and her advice was generally very sound.

Lisa nodded. ‘Something isn’t right though. The police seemed cagey and when I went to stay at his place, there had been a break in, stuff was everywhere. It was an awful mess. I called the police and went to stay at the local Travelodge. I daren’t stay there.’

Finn made a mental note to pay Lisa’s hotel bill, it was the least he could do. He felt slightly dizzy. He wondered what the culprits were looking for and realised he had a pretty good idea. Probably Sam’s postcards and the MP3 player Finn had given to Hattie. He thought about the blue tinged lights of the vehicle that had been following him last night and wondered.

‘Oh God, how terrible for you.’ At the same time, he didn’t want to terrify her. ‘I suppose it could have been opportunism?’

Lisa studied him and raised an eyebrow. She clearly didn’t believe it and neither did he.

Finn drove home, his mind in turmoil. He was pretty sure that whoever had done over Paddy’s place knew that he was close to Sam and was probably looking for Sam’s belongings, maybe the notebook, with its odd code, but that had already been stolen. Maybe there were two sets of people after it? He patted his pocket to make sure that his 'phone was still there. The notebook must contain incriminating information. It was a good job he had photographed the relevant pages after the break in to his flat. It was clear from the postcards that something big was being planned and highly likely that they would try to find Sam to stop him going to the authorities. From the Racesafe information and Will's comments, it had to be drug related and they must be worried about what Sam knew. His mind whirled with the possibilities of who they were. Was Jimmy West involved? He had to be the most likely suspect, but he wouldn't be acting alone. Teasdale and Boothroyd, maybe even Hunt? It was about four in the afternoon as he drove, and the darkness had descended. In his rear-view mirror, he noticed a car behind him, their familiar blue tinged, oval lights blinding him as he drove. He turned into his street and the car followed. He was being followed again. He drove past his flat and deliberately took a circuitous route, turning sharp left and left again, then suddenly right. Each time after a short delay, the blue tinged lights reappeared in his rear-view mirror. The hairs on the back of his neck stuck up as he realised what was happening. Who the hell was it? Just when he was thinking of pulling up and confronting whoever it was, he heard a police siren and he pulled over to let the vehicle past. Then he swiftly turned left again and waited to see if the blue lights would follow him. This time he thought he had shaken them off and he drove to his flat. Sure enough, they did not appear. He pulled into the private car park for his flats and locked up. There was a chill in the air, and he looked about him as he made his way to his flat, deep in thought. Then he almost jumped out of his skin as his 'phone beeped signalling that he had received a message. It was from Hattie.

'I think I know where S is. Think of the home of those lovely Thelwell ponies! We need to go asap. Meet early tomorrow? Text me!'

He laughed and punched the air in glee. He was glad that Hattie had been circumspect in her text, but he knew exactly where she meant. The Shetland Isles. He loved the Thelwell cartoons and the characterful, native Shetland ponies they frequently depicted. He texted her back arranging to meet first thing and plan their trip. He pottered around in the flat, worry gnawing at him when his intercom buzzed and the same policemen who had visited about Sam made their way up to his flat. He remembered DI James and the rather more arrogant DS Longton.

'We must stop meeting like this.' Finn's remark was met with a scowl from DS Longton. 'Any news on Sam Foster?'

'We are following some leads, but it seems he doesn't want to be found and as he's not classified as vulnerable, we will probably keep his disappearance on file for now,' replied DI James. Finn wondered whether or not to mention their Shetland lead but decided against it. He wasn't sure about the information and he didn't want to do all the work for the local plod, after all.

'We've come about the death of Patrick Owen. We gather you were at Doncaster and may have seen him prior to the accident.'

‘Yes, that’s right. I saw him in the horse box car park and chatted to him. I had arranged to meet up with him later in the Owners’ and Trainers’ bar but, of course, he didn’t turn up and I later found out why.’

‘Did you know him well?’ DS Longton managed to make this sound accusing.

‘Yes, we worked together years ago. We met up recently and it was great to see him after almost ten years. He was a great chap.’

‘When you saw him earlier in the day, how did he seem?’

‘Fine. I had the impression he wanted to tell me something, though. I had spoken to him about Sam disappearing and I think he may have wanted to talk to me about that.’

DS Longton scowled. ‘You really have a bee in your bonnet about Sam Foster, don’t you?’

Finn shrugged and decided to bite back an angry retort and ignore the jibe. At least he was bothered which was more than could be said for the police.

DI James gave his colleague a hard stare. ‘Were you aware of any problems that Patrick may have had, financial, health or otherwise?’

‘No. He seemed in good health, he was working and was in good spirits.’ Finn sighed. ‘I have heard that Paddy had some medication for epilepsy on him, but I wasn’t aware that he had the illness.’

DI James nodded. ‘But he may have concealed his condition in order to get the job. Hunt and Teasdale would certainly not have employed him if they had known about his condition as the role included driving.'

Finn shook his head. 'I can't see Paddy lying about something like that. He was too decent a chap. He'd never put any person at risk by driving with the condition and I'm one hundred percent sure he would not have risked the lives of any of the horses either.'

Finn was aware that he sounded defensive of Paddy, but he just knew that Paddy wouldn't have done that. 'Anyway, did he have epilepsy?'

DI James pursed his lips. 'The results of the post mortem are inconclusive, I'm afraid. But there is the possibility that he was an addict.'

Finn couldn't believe what he was hearing. 'No, you've got that wrong. Paddy a drug addict? I don't believe it! Why would he take epilepsy medication anyway?'

'Well, you'd be surprised what drug addicts will take and maybe his particular drug of choice was epilim. It is surprisingly popular with opiate addicts. It's accessible and legal.'

Finn stared at both men in bewilderment. 'I still don't believe it, I'm sure you've got that wrong…'

DS Longton read back through his notes. 'You did say that you'd not seen him for about ten years, so how would you know?'

Finn had to admit that he didn't know for sure, but he could not believe that his friend was a drug addict. He realised, though, that the police would accept that Paddy was either an addict or had epilepsy and tried to conceal this from his employers. If he wanted justice for Paddy, then it was up to him and Hattie to prove otherwise.

Finn showed the officers out and decided to walk around the block to clear his head. Grief, shock and confusion nibbled away at him. It was dark and cold, and he buttoned up his coat and wrapped the scarf around his neck. He walked at a fast pace and began to feel a little better as he made his way back to the flats. As he approached the entrance, a shadow flitted across his path and a figure loomed. Finn instinctively pulled back his fists, prepared to finally unmask his foe. It was hard to see who it was, as they were wearing a beanie hat pulled down to cover their face. He leapt forward into the slight black clad figure and struck him on the nose.

There was a howl as the figure fell backwards and Finn advanced to pull off the beanie hat and reveal his tormentor.

'Bloody hell, Finn! You still have one hell of a punch on you.' He wiped his bleeding nose.

'Nat? What the hell are you doing here?'

Nat ran his fingers through his tousled curls and pulled himself to his feet.

'Well, when you won't talk to me despite my best efforts, then I decided to find you and so here I am!'

Finn scowled. Bloody hell. Of all the people he expected, Nat certainly wasn't one of them.

Nat grinned and held out his arms in a conciliatory gesture.

'Look, I'm sorry about Livvy and all that shit and I probably should have said something earlier, so I'll get it out of the way, but I just miss you mate…' He sighed. 'And I'm in a bit of trouble and who better to talk to than me old mucker, Finn.'

Finn sighed and shook his head undecided what to do. Relief made him more conciliatory than he wanted to be. Trust Nat to turn up out of the blue and make him feel sorry for him. He looked at him as he weighed up his options.

'OK. I think you'd better come up then, hadn't you?'

Finn felt awkward and wrongfooted by Nat turning up unannounced. All those times he had planned what he would actually say to him when he saw him, and now he struggled to remember any of it.

Nat looked round the flat and whistled appreciatively.

'Nice place you've got here. Glad to see you did alright in the end.'

'No thanks to you.' Finn found himself clenching and unclenching his fists. 'By rights, I should beat you to a pulp for what you did to me. You smug, two faced, backstabbing bastard!'

Nat held out his hands again. 'OK, OK. Get it out of your system. Hit me again if you want to, if it makes you feel any better.' He proffered his cheek to Finn and pointed at it. 'Go on then, do it!'

Finn shook his head. Suddenly he didn't want to fight any more. He pulled out a whiskey bottle and two glasses, pouring them a good inch of the amber liquid.

'Right. You'd better tell me what's on your mind. I don't have long. I'm going away first thing tomorrow.'

Nat took a sip of Scotch and suddenly looked serious.

'I'm in trouble, mate and I don't know what to do…' Nat ran his fingers through his curls. 'Someone is trying to blackmail me to pull the favourite in a race in a week's time and they are not taking 'no' for an answer.'

'Who?'

'That's just it, I have no idea. They just ring me and threaten to expose me.'

Several drinks later, whiskies for Nat and cokes for Finn, he could hardly believe what he was hearing.

'So, you are being blackmailed to pull a race over something that you did years ago when you were a conditional?'

'Yes, that is about the size of it.' Nat took a sip of his drink. 'God, who would have thought that something from way back would come back to bite me. I could lose everything.'

'So, when you were a conditional back in the day, you took cocaine and had a bit of a problem and now someone has got hold of this, says they have the evidence and are threatening to expose you?'

Nat looked at him morosely. 'Yeah and now it's suddenly big news. I was riding at the time and, of course, it's against the rules. I suppose I had a bit of a habit until I got myself clean. It gave me a bit of courage, if you must know.'

'How much of a habit?'

Nat shrugged. 'Recreational use only, I swear.' He suddenly looked serious. 'Look they keep ringing, threatening to tell the papers, Livvy, everyone.' He swallowed hard. 'They even threatened Livvy, well, it was some sort of veiled threat about what a lovely girlfriend I had, and they hoped she would keep her looks and stuff like that. I think they meant it. They might cut her, throw acid in her face, anything…' Nat frowned. 'I know how you felt about her, mate, and I'm sorry for everything, but she means the world to me. We're even thinking of having a nipper…'

Finn took a deep breath. He did care about Livvy and these threats to her were too much. His mind was in overdrive. How had Nat had a cocaine habit and he had never even suspected it? They used to spend so much time together.

'So how old were you when you had the coke habit?'

'Seventeen, nearly eighteen, as I recall, and a bit daft, as lads of that age often are.'

'Were there any charges?'

Nat shook his head. 'No, nothing.'

Finn sipped his drink. 'So why don't you just let the blackmailers do their worst? It seems years ago, and they can't have any proof, surely?'

Nat sighed gloomily. 'Well, that's just it. They say they have hard evidence and I can't put Livvy in that situation.' Nat glowered. 'I can't bloody well risk it. I'm happy as anything with Livvy and riding high in my career. Can you imagine it when the press gets hold of this and I'm seen as a junkie? Besides, Livvy'll get rid of me too. We were even thinking of getting hitched…'

Finn winced at that bit.'

'Sorry,' added Nat. 'She's a great girl.'

Finn did know, he knew better than anyone, but he found it hurt less than he thought it would.

'And you've no idea who they are?'

Nat shook his head. 'No, he rings me, has done for the last few months telling me I owe them, that they have a job for me. I think it's in the next couple of weeks, the calls have increased lately along with the threats…'

'What sort of voice?'

Nat sighed. 'Look, it's disguised, alright, sounds all sort of muffled, nothing I can recognise anyway.'

'Have you thought about going to the police?'

'No. I'd be prosecuted for sure. They couldn't just do nothing with that information, could they?'

Finn took this in. 'Who else knows?'

'A couple of lads at the time, neither works in racing now.'

'Anyone else?'

Nat frowned as he thought. 'Maybe, can't think of anyone else, my supplier at the time, I suppose.'

'Who was that?'

'Oh, some low life. I'm not even sure he's alive now…'

Finn glanced at his watch. He needed to get some sleep. He was picking Hattie up bright and early.

'So how do they plan to do it? It's alright pulling the favourite, but any other horse could come through to win.'

Nat nodded. 'They could bet on the horse to lose or try and blackmail some of the other jocks in the race, that way they'll have the whole thing sewn up.'

Finn suddenly sat up very straight. 'What did you say?'

Nat shrugged. 'Just that if they had got to some of the other jocks then they would be certain who was going to win.' Nat took in Finn's expression. 'Wait a minute, you know something, don't you?'

Finn shook his head.

'Come on, out with it. You always were the brainy sort and with you working for the BHA, you must be in the know…'

Finn shrugged. 'Where did you work as a conditional?'

'Walton in North Yorkshire. I was with a trainer called Cuthbertson, he was a decent enough sort. Ben Jamieson went there after me, you know him. He's doing quite well now.' He gave Finn a shrewd look. 'Come on, you do know something, don't you?'

Finn wasn't at all sure that his disappearing conditionals had anything to do with the scam that Nat was implicated in, but suddenly he felt the need to confide in someone. Nat listened to the story his expression changing from disbelief to one of excitement.

'So, you're going to Shetland to find Sam Foster, you and this Harriet girl?'

'Yes, we've been sort of working on it together.'

'And you're leaving tomorrow? Well, I'm coming too!'

'Oh no, don't even think about it...'

Nat had set his mouth in a determined line.

'I'm coming with you. I'm the one with everything to lose here and it can't be a coincidence what's happened to your conditionals. I bet they are being blackmailed too. Your missing young jockey holds the key.'

Finn had to admit he was curious though he wasn't at all sure that the two cases were related. Sam's disappearance was related to drugs, surely? But then maybe he had done some drugs too and was being blackmailed because of that? Maybe they had been given freebies to get them hooked and owed money too? He knew how aggressive some of these drug gangs could be.

Nat pulled off his shoes and tried the sofa for size.

'Just get me a blanket mate, and I'll kip down here.' He gave Finn a considering look. 'Besides I like the sound of this Harriet, good looking, is she?" He had recovered some of his good spirits and gave Finn a dirty wink.

Finn shook his head. Nat was never going to change, he always was a flirt. He went off to find a blanket, deep in thought. Nat was a wily character and had a reputation for toughness. He also had a vested interest in getting to the bottom of the scam, so having him along might prove useful. He threw the blanket at Nat and by the time he had left the room he heard him emit a loud snore.

In the privacy of his own room, he pulled his 'phone out and scrolled to the photographs he had taken of Sam's notebook and examined the code again. His head was buzzing with Nat's revelations. The notebook had to be what the thief had been looking for, the evidence that Sam had about them. It must be very important if those responsible were prepared to break into Paddy's house to find it. If Nat was right, then it could be a list of races in which the jockeys had been blackmailed to pull horses and fix races. Who was involved? West and Boothroyd most likely. While Boothroyd had been a violent bully he had never openly tried to get Finn to pull races. He had hinted at things like this though and said vague things like, 'we're not here to win,' or 'it's a training run today, so don't get carried away, lad.' Maybe the bullying would have turned into race fixing if he'd stayed there. He thought about Rosy, the stable girl who had found him and taken him with her to Hollings, with immense gratitude. In Reg Hollings, he found a fair but firm boss who had been generous in assisting him in getting a professional licence and supported him all the way. That was what he wanted for his conditionals. Most trainers were decent and keen to help their young charges, after all it was a win win situation for them. The young lads gained experience, and the trainers made the most of the conditionals' weight allowance. Maybe Boothroyd, having been struck off from training, was keen to make his way in the world and he and West had come up with this betting scam? Both of them, from what he knew of them, were more than capable of blackmail.

He felt heady with anger and relief that Boothroyd would soon get his just desserts. He sensed that it was all coming to a head and he needed time to think, to second guess his enemy so that he could be prepared for them. He began to pack his things, warm clothes, hat, gloves, a selection of tools, then shut down his computer and willed himself to sleep, but it was hard with all the thoughts swirling around his head. He was very conscious of Nat's presence in the next room. He felt relief that it was only Nat who had been following him, but more than that it felt good to have him close. He no longer felt so devastated about Livvy and his anger at Nat had dissipated as a result. He realised that, at long last, it was time to move on.

Chapter 20

Hattie met Finn in a local supermarket early, where she had already stocked up on basics, food, matches, warm blankets and a torch. She was surprised when she saw that he was accompanied by another man. He had brown wavy hair and sparkling, blue eyes and was very attractive in a slightly dissipated way, more so when he grinned broadly when Finn introduced them. He looked very familiar, surely it wasn't him, was it? Then she realised it was the man that she had seen Finn photographed with. He made introductions.

'Nat Wilson, Harriet Lucas. Nat is coming along with us.' He lowered his voice. 'Nat thinks he can help us. We'll tell you later.'

Hattie looked from one to the other. She knew Nat Wilson by sight, he was a very well-known and successful jockey after all, but hadn't Daisy talked about Nat and Finn falling out over Finn's fiancée? Still, she supposed that Finn knew what he was doing by bringing him along. She wanted to ask a lot of questions but knew to wait until there were fewer people around.

'So, how about we grab some things and have a quick coffee whilst we discuss how to get there?'

Nat grinned. 'Brilliant.'

They settled down in a quiet corner of the café. Finn and Hattie ordered bacon sandwiches. Nat declined to eat with a shrug.

'Nah, I won't. I've got to keep me weight down. I hope to be back riding in a couple of days.'

'What's going on?' Hattie asked after they had agreed to travel to Aberdeen by car and then catch the ferry to Shetland. She had opted to drive first. She looked from one to the other, waiting for some sort of satisfactory explanation.

'Does Nat know about Sam and the other lads? I'm not going anywhere until I know what is going on.' Hattie also wanted to discuss her conversation with Gina.

Hattie couldn't really explain it except to say that she felt very uneasy. Only she and Finn knew all the details of Sam's attack and subsequent disappearance and Connor and Harry's suspicious injuries. Then there their concerns about Paddy's accident. They were going to the Shetlands to find Sam, help him, not bring trouble to his door. Could they trust Nat? She wasn't at all sure.

Nat looked at her appraisingly. 'It's fine, Hattie, I don't blame you for being suspicious. Listen, I came to find Finn because I was in trouble and even though we fell out, he was my most trusted friend. I know, in spite of everything, I can trust him to do the right thing. You see, I am being blackmailed to pull a race in about a week. I think whoever is behind it is planning something big that also involves your conditionals. Let me explain.'

Hattie listened as Nat told her his story. Finn nodded every so often as if to emphasise a point.

'You see, my career and relationship will both be in tatters if I don't find out who the hell is behind the scam, so believe me I am as keen to find Sam as you are.'

Hattie nodded. There was no doubting Nat's sincerity and anger about the situation. She even felt sorry for him. But then she remembered that he had run off with Finn's fiancée, though, so maybe he didn't deserve her compassion. She considered the complex story.

'Right. So, you think that several jockeys including you, are being blackmailed to fix races? A particular race, especially?'

Nat nodded. 'Yes, and they are trying to get conditionals involved but not having much luck by the sound of it. If the gang choose a race where they can get several jockeys to pull their horses, then they bet heavily on the rank outsider and that comes through to win and they make a fortune. If they pick the right race and a horse with long enough odds, they could make thousands, a real killing!'

'Wouldn't the bookies be suspicious of large bets being put on an outsider?' Hattie was sure there were safeguards in place to prevent criminals profiting from race fixing, weren't there?

Finn nodded. 'But there are ways around it. They could get lots of people to put small bets on within a short time frame, so it goes unnoticed. It's been done before. It takes a lot of organising, but it's doable.' He rummaged around in his rucksack, pulled out his 'phone, found the photo he had taken of Sam's notebook and passed it to Nat.

'Hey. See what you make of that…' He looked at Hattie. 'I'm sorry, Hattie. I should have explained about Nat coming along, but I do think whoever is blackmailing Nat could well be behind all the incidents with the lads.'

'OK. By the way, Gina rang back.'

'And?'

Hattie looked from one to the other. 'Sam isn't with her, they weren't in a relationship, though she did like him as a friend. '

'Does she have any idea why he ran away?'

'Not really, just that he was noticeably moodier approaching a race. He hated riding West's horses and felt he couldn't do anything right.'

'Anything else?'

'She hadn't heard about Paddy and was very upset. Although she barely knew him, she said he was such a kind man. She thinks Sam will be at his nan's as he always seemed very close to her.' She suddenly remembered something else. She fished the MP3 player out of her pocket. 'I tried looking at this to see if there were any word files on it, but there were just music files.'

Finn nodded and pulled out his car keys. 'OK. Right, we'd better get going and see if we can find our missing conditional.'

Hattie studied the route on her 'phone. They were to drive to Aberdeen and get the seven o'clock overnight ferry to Lerwick.

'We could fly there in sixty-five minutes from Aberdeen…' she pointed out.

'But then we'd need to hire a car which on balance might be more obvious than taking this car.' Finn turned to talk to Nat who was still looking at the photos of Sam's notations on Finn's 'phone and checking out some information on his own mobile.

'Does it make any sense to you?' asked Finn.

Nat moved his head from side to side in a non-committal movement.

'Maybe. I'm still working it out and texting my agent. I've told him I have some personal issues to work out, so I won't be riding for a few days.'

Hattie studied Nat in her rear-view mirror. He was frowning in concentration. She supposed insider information might be just what they needed to crack the code.

'What do we do when we get to Shetland?' asked Finn.

Hattie had already got this worked out.

'Well, you remember when we went to see Sam's mother and his sister mentioned that their nan runs the post office in Scalloway? Well, I reckon he's bound to stay there, don't you think?'

'Brilliant. I'm sure you're right.' Finn scowled. 'Listen, did I tell you that Paddy's wife told me that his place was broken into?'

'What were they looking for? The notebook?'

Finn nodded grimly. 'Yes. I think they broke into mine and Paddy's place. And I thought I was being followed by a 4x4 with blue tinged lights, but thankfully it was only Nat after all. I can't tell you how relieved I was.'

Nat sat up straight. 'What? That wasn't me. I don't drive a 4x4. I have a Merc, a saloon car.'

Finn looked at Nat with horror. 'Are you sure?'

Of course, I'm bloody well sure. I didn't need to follow you. Tony gave me your address.'

'Shit. Well, that means that they are onto us, whoever they are.'

'I can't wait to meet them. Bring it on,' said Nat, his eyes glittering, whilst he clenched and unclenched his fists.

'Absolutely,' replied Finn, with equal relish. The two of them exchanged a glance full of male bravado. Hattie swallowed hard. The seriousness of the situation and the danger they were placing themselves in suddenly became all too apparent. Her father and brothers had given her advice on self defence and advised her to keep a handbag sized deodorant spray in her bag which could double as a weapon in case she was mugged. A squirt of deodorant in the face might delay a villain. Hopefully enough for her to get away. She looked in her rear-view mirror for the millionth time checking for a car with distinctive blue lights.

They swapped over so Nat was driving, Finn slept in the back and Harriet was in the passenger seat.

'So, how did you meet Finn?' Nat asked.

'Well, we met when I found Sam Foster, his conditional, beaten up at Wetherby. I'm finishing off a degree and work part time work for the charity, Racing to School. I happened to be there that day and helped Finn with Sam. Some of the kids I was with were nearby when it happened and were able to describe the attackers. I passed the info onto Finn and we sort of worked together after that.'

Nat turned and grinned. 'Hmm. What are you studying?'

'I'm training to be a dietician.'

Nat turned to her and grinned. 'University, hey? Brains as well as beauty…'

Hattie blushed. He was very attractive, and she could imagine the full charm offensive would be very hard to resist. She found herself floundering.

'We thought it might be to do with drugs actually, but what you're saying makes sense because of what happened to the other lads.'

'Right, I see. I heard about the other lads, Connor and Harry.'

'Yeah. Connor hurt his collarbone and Harry had an accident when his girth slipped, so neither are riding at the moment.'

Nat pursed his lips. 'But they could have been trying to get out of riding, because of the pressure applied to them by the same person who is trying to blackmail me.'

'Yes, it certainly sounds possible. What did you make of the information in the notebook?'

'Interesting. The first column initials could refer to the racecourse, the second could be the horse and the third column the initials of the jocks they were trying to blackmail. I can remember that there was racing on each of those days, I've got some idea of the horses and I can guess at the jockeys.'

Hattie was impressed. It seemed so obvious now. She turned and picked up the notes Nat had taken which was lying next to Finn. He was snoring softly.

'So DN is Doncaster, MR?'

'Market Rasen, UT Uttoxeter, WY Wetherby and CH Cheltenham.'

'Right. I see.' Hattie's gaze slid to the end column where NW was referred to twice. 'So, the last column is the jockeys involved, you said?' Nat followed her gaze.

'Well, they tried to get me to pull those races. One I lost anyway, despite my best efforts.' Nat smiled. 'The horse had to be pulled up as he was lame. Honestly. And the other I suggested to the trainer that the conditional ride the horse instead to get the weight allowance, but I can't do that forever, can I?'

Hattie took this in. 'How do they contact you?'

Nat sighed. 'They or rather he uses a voice disguiser thing. He sounds like Darth Vader and just rings me out of the blue. They have got more and more threatening over time, made veiled threats about Livvy too.' Nat scowled. He was clearly more rattled then he was letting on.

'Have you any idea who it might be? Is there anyone you may have annoyed?'

Nat grinned broadly. 'Well, you do make enemies in any sport, but I haven't made more than anyone else, apart from perhaps the odd husband or boyfriend, you know how it is? Once you have a bit of success, the girls start hanging around.' He shrugged. 'Then

Finn started going out with Livvy and I fell for her, big time. We just couldn't help ourselves.'

Hattie found herself flushing again. She could well imagine the havoc that this good looking, charmer could create.

'How did Finn find out about you two?'

'One of the other jockeys let something slip, unintentionally, and Finn put two and two together. It was just before the Grand National, and we were both on fancied horses. Finn was furious, and we had a fight in the weighing room, the other lads had to pull us apart. He blacked my eye.' Nat grimaced at the memory. 'He couldn't concentrate on the bloody race and kept trying to force me onto the rails instead of riding his race, so I took a chance on a gap or two and only bloody won. There was a huge drama from the stewards not to mention the owner and trainer after the race. I had me photo taken and went to a press conference and all that, with a massive shiner from the punch up. The media would have had a field day, so I had to make up some story about how it had happened during the race.' He shook his head. 'Finn was on a fancied runner and lost because he couldn't concentrate, I suppose.'

Hattie remembered the photos and the speculation about it all when she had looked Finn up on the internet. How could Nat have done it to his friend?

'Didn't you feel bad about running off with Livvy?'

Nat nodded. 'Yeah, I did. We were as thick as thieves before then, but then I met Livvy and wham, that was that. I was utterly hooked, still am, actually…' He flashed her an embarrassed smile. He nodded at Finn crouched in the back. 'He is a mardy git sometimes, but a better man I've yet to meet. What about you and him?'

It was Hattie's turn to blush. 'Oh, no. We were sort of thrown together over the Sam thing, and we're just good mates now, that's all.'

Nat gave her an appraising look then his gaze shifted to the rear-view mirror.

'Hey up. We've got company. We've got blue headlights behind us.'

Nat turned to Hattie with an impish grin, as his foot pressed down hard on the accelerator. The car hurtled forward at an alarming pace.

'Come on. Did I tell you that like most jockeys, I also love car racing and speed? You're about to experience the finish of a lifetime! Let's see what Finn's car is made of. Hang onto your hat!'

Hattie took a deep breath and prepared herself for the burst of speed. Christ, what had she let herself in for? Yet, they had to get away from the vehicle behind them. She clutched her seat as the car lurched forward.

Chapter 21

'You bloody idiot, Nat! What the hell!'

Finn scowled at Nat as the car leapt forward and sped past others on the motorway. Nat was driving at over a hundred miles per hour as he twisted and turned from lane to lane. Eventually, he settled down at a more sedate pace.

Hattie turned around from the passenger seat. Her face was white, as her eyes peered through the rear windscreen and beyond.

'Wow! I think you've lost them! Well done!'

There was a loud whoop from Nat and the pair of them high fived each other.

'We were being followed again,' explained Hattie.

'I'll just pull off at the services and see if they tail us,' added Nat.

Finn felt anxious about the possibility of coming face to face with the brains behind the operation. He suddenly had an awful thought.

'Did either of you tell anyone where you were going?'

Hattie shrugged. 'I just told Mum I was going to Scotland to stay with friends.'

Nat shook his head. 'I didn't even know we were coming, if you remember. Livvy thinks I'm looking at some horses in Ireland.'

Over coffee in the services, they speculated on who might be behind the scam.

'My money is on Jimmy West and Bert Boothroyd. It's gotta be those two trying to make a killing by blackmailing jockeys, with Spud and maybe Pavel used as heavies. If you think about it, West's haulage business would be a great front for drug smuggling.'

Nat took a sip of his skinny cappuccino. 'Well, I'm not so sure. West maybe but Boothroyd was a bastard. Mind you, I heard that he's terminally ill and had found God, so it doesn't fit. The last I knew he was running around trying to make amends for his sins, not about to commit a load more.'

Finn pondered this. That accounted for Boothroyd's weight loss and frail appearance the last time he saw him. Strangely, he felt absolutely no sympathy for the man.

'Surely, we need to think who would be in a position to know all this information about the jockeys. Nat, who would know about your history, especially if it was years ago?' Hattie pursed her lips. 'We just need to be logical. There must be someone who knew about you and the others?'

Nat shook his head. 'Finn already asked me this. There were a couple of other jockeys who also had a habit, neither ride now, and of course, my supplier.'

'So, what has the blackmailer got on Sam, Harry, Connor and what was the name of those other jockeys?' asked Finn and pulled up the photos of Sam's notebook. Nat leaned over to look at the final column.

'I reckon BJ is Ben Jamieson and DD is Danny Doyle.'

'Do any of those lads have anything in common?'

Nat frowned in concentration. 'They are all jockeys. Maybe we've all had complaints made via RaceStraight and someone there is using the information to their own ends?'

Finn didn't buy it. 'Possibly, but if it's not proven then it would be too risky. Besides Tony Murphy would no doubt have mentioned that they had had all these complaints.'

'Just try and think back to anything you and the other jockeys have in common, maybe you use the same valet or something like that,' continued Hattie.

Nat shook his head. 'God, this is tricky.'

Finn sighed and cast his eye around the service station. It was full of truckers, ordinary men, women and children.

'So, do you see anyone you recognise round here?' he asked.

'No. We definitely shook them, mate.' Nat grinned. 'You worry too much.'

Finn agreed but couldn't help but fret that their enemy was there, hiding in plain sight amongst the coffee shops and restaurants. He just wished that they would show themselves.

Finn drove the rest of the way. He thought it was best, he didn't quite trust Nat's crazy driving. The man was a thrill seeker and a daredevil, even more so than he was. Nat had nerves of steel but still, Finn would rather get to Aberdeen in one piece. They needed to be ready for when they finally met their nemesis.

As they approached Aberdeen, Finn was suddenly sick of all the radio programmes and decided to play the MP3 player that Sam had posted to him. The sound of Coldplay, Adele and Ed Sheeran floated over him. For someone who had made a point of complaining about his musical tastes, Sam's were pretty middle of the road, Finn thought. He didn't know what he was expecting, maybe some rap or grime artists. The music finished and there was silence. He was just about to switch back to the radio when a voice rumbled through the loudspeakers. It was eerily distorted and rather creepy.

'You need to pull number 5 in the 4th race tomorrow, lad, if you know what's good for you. Just do as you're told, then rest assured, your little problem will be safe with me. If you disobey me, your secret will be spread around the racing papers the very next day and make no mistake your career will be over. Do you understand?'

Then the sound died away. There was a pause as they took this in.

'Well, it's definitely the same guy. It's a carbon copy of the calls I get, except in mine he has started to go on about how my beautiful girlfriend might not stay so beautiful. Where did you get the MP3 player from?'

'Sam sent it to me. My guess was that he intended us to find the voice recording,' added Finn.

Hattie tried to be positive. 'At least we know for certain it's a race fixing scam, I suppose. All we need to do is find out the person who would be privy to all the information on jockeys.'

Finn had to agree that it was progress. It sounded deceptively easy to find out who knew all that information, but in reality, he had no idea where to start.

Finn turned off the satnav as it rang out with the message 'you have arrived at your destination.' Nat was resting in the back, and Hattie stirred in the front.

'Hey, look we're here. I'll go and get our tickets.'

Hattie yawned. 'I think I'll go in search of a coffee and a cake.'

'OK.'

Did that girl do anything but eat, he wondered? She was slim, so she must have the sort of metabolic rate all jockeys dreamed of, lucky or what? He left Nat snoozing and wandered off to the ferry terminal ticket office. It was six o' clock. The skies were dark and gloomy, illuminated only by streetlights and stars. The temperatures had plummeted. Finn pulled up his collar and looked about him. There were a few vehicles waiting in line for the small ferry, a compact but new looking vessel. There were some lorries, but the majority were smaller cars belonging to people who regularly made the trip across the sea to experience the bright lights of Aberdeen, he guessed, not tourists, so late in the season. He heard the thick Scottish accents and tried to tune in what was going on around him. There was a strong smell of diesel and fishmeal. The ticket office was manned by a surly looking man with dark curls and huge shoulders.

'Can I help you?'

'An open return to Lerwick please, for a vehicle and three passengers.'

After explaining that that he was visiting relatives with his mate and her boyfriend, he would explain to Hattie and Nat later, he paid in cash, not by card, as he did not want to leave an electronic trail. The man behind the counter eyed the new banknotes keenly as Finn counted them out.

'Are your relatives Shetland born and bred?' continued the man. 'Only you don't sound like you're a local.'

'No, they moved there from the Home Counties,' he improvised, not wanting further questions.

'Wanting peace and quiet, I shouldn't wonder,' the man continued. 'They'll get that right enough!'

'Yes, well they love bird watching, so it's ideal for them.'

The man beamed and started rabbiting on about the bird population in the Shetlands. Finn smiled weakly at the mention of the puffins, skua, the red throated loon and the glossy ibis that his friend had seen, a rare find indeed, apparently.

'Brilliant,' muttered Finn, hastily picking up his tickets, 'well, thanks.'

He strode down the pathway and pulled up his collar against the cold just as a black 4x4 came crashing around the corner almost mounting the curb where he was walking. He leapt out of the way. He was so close to the vehicle, he felt the air rush past him and was showered in water from a nearby puddle. Idiot. Finn stood glaring at the vehicle as it disappeared around the corner. The windows were blacked out and it was dark, so it was impossible to get a good look at the driver. But he did recognise one thing about the car, the blue oval headlights. Damn. Despite Nat's crazy driving, it looked like their nemesis had found them after all. He wondered if he was making too much of the blue headlights, after all a lot of cars might have similar lights but this was also a dark 4x4 with blacked out windows. Surely that was too much of a coincidence?

The ferry was small but comfortable. Hattie had come back with burgers and chips for them all as they were queuing. Then once aboard they had a quick cup of tea, watched a sci fi film showing in the lounge and made their way to the reclining seats. They all sat in a quiet corner, away from the other passengers. Nat looked up and down scrutinising their fellow travellers.

'Anyone suspicious?' Finn asked.

'Not that I can see.' Nat pulled Finn to one side. 'I think we should take it in turns to keep a watch out. After all, I'd hate it if anything happened to Hattie. You and I are big enough and ugly enough to be able to look after ourselves.' He nodded at Hattie. 'I like her, are you and she …?'

Finn shook his head. 'No, we're just friends.'

'OK, I get you,' muttered Nat giving Finn a large nudge as though he didn't believe him. Finn resisted the urge to thump him.

The crossing was a little turbulent but fortunately they all found their sea legs and quickly got used to the rolling motion.

'Glass of wine?' Finn asked.

'Why not?' Hattie replied with a smile. 'And some chocolate?'

As Finn made his way to the bar, he looked around him but saw no one who looked suspicious, no drug dealers or anyone resembling Boothroyd or West. There were a few lorry drivers, couples and families. The Scottish burr was very much in evidence, rather than the flat vowels of Yorkshire. Reassured, he began to relax.

'So, what's the plan?' asked Hattie, downing her wine. They were sitting in a secluded side of the ferry, the lights were dimming and outside they glimpsed the grey, icy North Sea crashing against the side of the vessel.

'I suppose we get to Scalloway, find the post office and hopefully Sam. We might need to find him somewhere to stay if his safety is compromised and alert the authorities. I have Tony Murphy on standby and I suppose Will should be able to advise too?'

'Course he will. What did you mean about Sam's safety being compromised?'

Finn smiled. He didn't want to alarm Hattie, but she had the right to know.

'Look, it might be something or nothing, but when I came out of the ticket office at the ferry port in Aberdeen, a black 4x4 almost ran me over. It partially mounted the pavement and I had to leap out of the way. It had those blue headlights.'

Hattie gasped. 'Christ Finn! Why didn't you say anything? Did you get a look at the driver?'

'No, I didn't see them. It was too dark. Mind you those blue headlights are more common than I thought.' But not in 4x4's, he added silently.

Nat frowned. 'I suppose we have to assume the worst. They need to find Sam to stop him telling the authorities. Listen, I've been thinking about the race that they may be trying to fix. I am booked to ride the favourite in a three miler at Cheltenham next week and I reckon that would be the perfect race to go for.'

Hattie looked blank and Finn shrugged and nodded for him to continue.

'The race itself is fairly nondescript, there is a firm favourite and I've checked and all the jockeys we think are involved are booked to ride.' He ran his finger down his 'phone. 'I think they plan to get all the lads to hold up their horses so Cococabana comes in. Alfie Dwyer is booked to ride him. He's an older guy, an amateur, known for being very strait laced. We call Alfie the vicar, he's so proper. And Cococabana's odds are long, about 35-1.'

'So, the stewards wouldn't suspect him?'

Nat grinned. 'Exactly. The gang could net a fortune.'

'So, we're looking for a blackmailer who is also a trainer or who works closely with a trainer…' added Finn. 'Teasdale?'

'That's my guess, yes. And Sam has worked out who is involved which is why they need to find him to silence him. I reckon they still intend to go ahead if they can find Sam. We have to be careful not to lead them straight to him.'

'Did you have any more thoughts about who might know about you and the drugs? Anything at all, it might help us.'

For a split second something flickered across Nat's face. 'Nah, I'm afraid not.'

Finn studied him for a second. He was sure that he wasn't telling the whole truth, there was something but now was not the time to press him. He glanced at his watch.

'Right, it's getting late. You two try to sleep and I'll wake you Nat, so you can keep an eye out in a few hours.'

Hattie and Nat began to settle down into their recliners.

Finn surveyed the other passengers, who were all doing the same. None of them looked threatening, just ordinary people going about their daily lives. Thoughts and questions, to which he had no answers, swirled round his mind but the quiet hum of the engines and the rocking motion soon sent him off to sleep too as the ferry drifted in the North Sea, towards Shetland and the unknown.

Chapter 22

Hattie awoke around six thirty, yawned and stretched. It took her a few seconds to remember that they were on a ferry bound for Shetland. She was starving and as her stomach rumbled, she was rewarded by a nudge from Finn who she thought was still asleep. Nat was nowhere to be seen.

'Breakfast I think, don't you?' He glanced at his watch, 'we'll be arriving in about an hour.'

Nat appeared then, looking fresh and bright eyed.

'The coffee smells good.' He rubbed his hands together and grinned. 'The restaurant is just down here.'

Nat led the way. After a substantial full cooked breakfast, Hattie felt better. Finn tucked in, but Nat only ate an egg and drank several cups of strong coffee. His eyes were roving all over the place, as were Finn's. There was no one that looked familiar or like they were watching the trio.

'Quite comfy those recliners,' Nat commented, 'so what's next?'

Finn was mopping up egg yolk with fried bread. 'God, one of the great perks of not race riding is being able to have a good blow out. Heaven!'

Nat raised his eyes heavenward and continued to sip his coffee.

'Everything OK?' Hattie lowered her voice, 'not seen anyone you recognise?'

'Nah, don't think so, so right let's get off and go to this Scalloway place. The sooner we find Sam then the sooner we can find out who is behind this nonsense and sort it out.'

The ferry docked and one by one the cars rumbled off. The little port reminded Hattie of others she'd been to but was much smaller. They headed off through Lerwick, an attractive little harbour town with grey stone buildings and a bustling, thriving air, towards Scalloway, following signs for the castle. As they left the port behind, Hattie was stuck by the clear, bright cool air and the grey green colours of the moorland they passed. Hardly any houses, just acres of moorland and heath. There were no trees either, but the scenery was bleak, atmospheric, spectacular and very beautiful. There were gunmetal grey clouds moving across the sky and Hattie shivered and turned up the heater. She was glad she'd bought her warmest jacket and her trusty Doc Martens.

Hattie read out the passages about Scalloway from the leaflets they'd picked up on the ferry.

'Well, Shetland is the home of the infamous Black Patie, Patrick Stewart,' she told them.

'What the Star Trek actor?' asked Nat grinning. 'You know the one with the fruity voice.'

Hattie grinned. 'Nah, the Earl of Orkney and Shetland. He appropriated lands and feuded with the lairds and was executed in 1615. Sounds like a thoroughly bad lot to me.'

Finn smiled but she noticed he kept looking in the mirror, watching for the big 4x4, she presumed. They seemed to be followed by cars, probably mostly locals she guessed. No four wheel drive vehicles with blue lights in sight, so far.

They drove around six miles and reached the opposite coastline of the Shetland mainland, dipping down into Scalloway. They could spot the imposing castle easily, looking out towards the sea. Scalloway was a smallish but picturesque place with a couple of streets and a handful of shops. The ruined stone castle dominated the handsome landscape. Seagulls shrieked overhead and the tang of the sea, mingled with the smell of fish, reached their nostrils. There was a compact harbour where some small boats bobbed around in the wintry ghost grey sea. It was a dull day; a thin drizzle was starting to fall, and it was bitterly cold. Finn pulled up his collar and Hattie grabbed a woolly hat from her pocket and some thick gloves. Hattie scanned the road, spotting a small all purpose shop which also doubled as a post office. She nodded in its direction.

'There's the place.' Finn was about to pull over.

'Listen, I think we need to be careful. If we are being followed, then we don't want to lead them straight to Sam. How about you drop me off to find Sam or at least pass a message onto him to ring you, Finn, and you two go and tour around. You said his nan works at the Post Office, didn't you? I'll join you in the coffee shop over there in about an hour?' Nat pointed at a building on the corner.

Finn nodded. 'Good thinking. Sam knows you, anyway, doesn't he?'

'Oh yes. I have ridden with him several times.' Finn pulled up, Nat put on a wool beanie and hopped out. He winked at Harriet.

'See you later. I'll ring you when I'm done.'

Hattie watched him as he made his way down the road.

'I suppose he's right. What shall we do?'

'Course he is. How about a tour of Scalloway Castle?'

They were both horribly tense, but they knew they had to protect Sam. It was going to be incredibly hard to concentrate on bloody sightseeing, she realised. Rather like spring cleaning, dusting and vacuuming inside whilst waiting in the path of a hurricane and certain devastation. Hattie scanned the faces and the traffic around her, realising that Finn was doing the same. It was unnerving to think that they were out there watching and waiting.

Scalloway Castle was an atmospheric tower house and they listened to the guide take them through the various antics of the Stewart family. It was bitingly cold and fascinating. However, neither were really taking any of it in. After about forty minutes they gave up and made their way back to the coffee shop on the corner where they were to meet Nat. They settled down with their cappuccinos, Finn craning his neck to look for Nat.

'So, what happen if we can't find Sam?'

Finn shrugged. 'God knows. I suppose we'll have to go back to the drawing board.' He took a sip of his drink. 'Anyway, here's Nat, so let's hope he has good news.'

Hattie felt obscurely disappointed when she realised that Nat was alone. She had expected that he would come in Sam, but that would be too easy, she supposed.

Nat sank down pulled off his hat and grinned.

'Well, that was trickier than I thought. The young girl was rather suspicious to say the least. She didn't confirm that Sam was there but said she would leave a message with Mrs McKay the owner. So, I left a message for Sam to contact Finn McCarthy. He will have your number, won't he?' Finn nodded. 'Yeah.'

Nat grinned. 'I reckon he is there, though.'

'How do you work that out?' Hattie was intrigued.

'Well, I spotted a blue Ariat jacket and a pair of muddy jodhpur boots in the hallway, so I think we're on the right lines.'

Standard stable wear, she supposed. Her heart lifted. Perhaps things were going to be alright after all.

'OK, I suppose we had better just wait.'

Finn looked at a sign at the rear of the coffee shop. 'They have rooms here. How about we book them and them and organise some dinner?'

Nat shrugged. 'Fab.'

It was going to be a long evening waiting for Sam to contact them. Hattie realised that he would be scared, anxious and very aware that whoever was behind the scam, might well be after him too. He would need to make sure that it wasn't a trick.

She shivered when she thought about the distorted voice and the underlying threat behind it. It was strange but there was something familiar about the words, not the voice, but the use of language that resonated somewhere with something in her brain. Still, hopefully they would speak to Sam very soon, find out what he knew, alert the authorities and all would be well. Soon the job would be done, and they could all get back to normality.

Chapter 23

Finn and Nat shared a twin bedded room whilst Hattie had her own room. The Bed and Breakfast was basic but thankfully clean. They had eaten a reasonable Italian meal and were settling down for bed. Finn looked at Nat and decided now would be a good time to clear the air.

'You know, Nat, I don't really buy your story about you taking drugs and having a cocaine habit. OK, so you may have had the odd fix but how would that give someone such a strong hand to blackmail you? It would simply be their word against yours, wouldn't it? Where would the physical proof come from after all this time?'

Nat suddenly looked incredibly weary. For a long time, he didn't speak.

'I could never fool you, could I? You're right there is more to it.'

Finn knew he had been right. He sat up expectantly.

'Well, whatever it is, I need to know. It might just help us find out who is behind all of this. Things are getting serious now, Nat. You have to tell me.'

Nat sighed. 'Alright. When I was first apprenticed, I was a stupid seventeen year old and I had a brush with the law. Whoever is behind this knows all about it and that's why I'm so desperately worried. I could lose everything and with the climate like it is at the moment, I would be utterly disgraced.' Nat looked completely ashen with worry. 'I'd lose Livvy, my job, everything, I'd be shunned…'

Finn shook his head. 'Don't you think you're overreacting? A few misdemeanors as a kid are not worth all this, surely? Let the blackmailer do their worst, face them out. That's what I'd do.'

Nat looked at him pityingly. 'It's easy for you to say. You're so upstanding, completely decent through and through. Everyone would believe you, but I'm not like that. You see I did do a bit of drugs, but I also had a relationship with a girl from the village. We went to a party and I drove her and another boy home. We'd had a bit to drink and I wanted to impress her and took a corner too fast and another car hit us.' He gulped. 'Me and the girl escaped with cuts and bruises but, but the lad was killed. I killed him...'

Finn took this in. All these years he had known Nat and yet he had never heard even a whisper about this. 'What? So, were you charged?'

Nat shook his head. 'No.' He sighed. 'What I'm about to tell you, you must not tell another living soul. I'm only telling you, so you understand. Do you promise?'

Finn took a deep breath. 'OK, I promise.'

He studied his friend's face and waited for him to tell his story.

'After the crash I got out of the car. It was in a remote place and I rang for an ambulance. The girl was unconscious. She had minor cuts but that was all. I left her and tried to revive Nick. He was in the back and took a lot of the impact. He was dead, Finn, stone dead, otherwise I would never have done it…'

'Done what?'

Nat's face was ashen. 'I moved him, so it looked like he was driving. I told the police and the doctor that I'd been in the back. I'm not proud of what I did but there was no sense messing up two lives instead of one. I didn't think I'd get away with it. Forensics and stuff were not as good as they are now, and the police and medics didn't question it. The lad had just passed his test and in the inquest, they put it down to driver error.' Nat shuddered. 'I know it was wrong, but I was starting to get rides, things were going well, and I knew I was over the limit and would be heading for a driving ban and prison sentence. I would never have coped with that. And he was dead, Finn, it was all over for him.'

Finn sat in silence taking this in. He felt anger at Nat's actions and sorrow for the boy and his family.

'I know it was wrong, call it self-preservation, selfishness, call it what you like. Anyway, the blackmailer says they know about the lad and they have witnesses to say that I was driving. They are threatening to go to the police and have the case reopened. Can you imagine what the press would make of it? I'd be crucified now I'm well known, and the boy's parents would have the whole thing raked up again. I would go to prison, Livvy would leave me and none of it will help bring the boy back. I've not been able to sleep since they have rung.' He suddenly looked exhausted. 'And I'm not just thinking about myself, I am thinking about the boy's family. God knows how they feel, but I've thought about that lad every day since it happened. I'd give anything to turn the clock back, but I can't.'

Finn shook his head. He was shocked. His mind sorted through the information they knew to date. Surely this would help them find out who the blackmailer was? 'So, the girl is the only other person who knows?'

'No, she'd had a load to drink, she was out of it and unconscious when I moved the lad. She had no idea, I'm sure if it!'

'What about the boy's family? Who was he?'

'He was a lad called Nick Drayton, a local boy. His family even apologised to me about the lad writing my car off, they didn't suspect a thing.'

'How did you know him?'

'He was a young lad from the village. He had just started at the stables. He was a sweet kid, who looked up to me and I was showing off in front of him too, I suppose.' Nat raked his hand through his head. His eyes were glistening with tears. 'God, it's actually a relief to talk about it. It's been eating away at me for all these years, but you do understand why I can't let this come out, don't you? I have too much to lose.'

Finn's mind was in overdrive. His emotions seesawed wildly from disgust to pity. But he had to work out what this meant. Surely this gave them some sort of clue about the blackmailer? All they had to do was narrow down who could have known about Nat.

'Right, so where were you when you first became a conditional?'

'I was at Cuthbertson's place in Walton first, then I moved to Cheltenham.'

He hadn't met Nat until later, but he'd forgotten his link with Walton. Surely that couldn't be a coincidence?

'So, who else would have known about the accident then?'

Nat frowned. 'The girl, the police, hospital staff, the doctor who was first on the scene…'

'Are any of these people still around, after all it was fifteen plus years ago.'

Nat shrugged. 'Well, the girl, the policeman would have retired I suppose, the doctor, hospital staff. God knows. I have racked my brains trying to find a link, believe me.'

'So, the girl would be a woman now and how old would she be?

'I'm thirty-three so she'd be a couple of years younger, early thirties, I suppose.'

'Was Teasdale around at that time or Jimmy West or Boothroyd?'

'Not that I remember, no.'

'Can you remember the girl's name?'

Nat shrugged. 'God, I haven't thought about her in years. I think she was Ellen or something…'

'Have you ever seen her since?'

Nat shook his head. 'No, definitely not.'

'Could it be her who's behind it?'

Nat shrugged. 'I doubt it. I would have thought that like me, she'd have wanted to forget the whole sorry incident and besides she was out of it. I moved away from Walton soon after and never saw her again.'

Finn nodded. Nat had committed a terrible crime. But he was right. He would certainly be pilloried by the press and it would affect his career. It was the way Nat did everything, he loved, lived and rode like each day was his last and it was no surprise that there were casualties along the way, there were always going to be. He was a risk taker and it was this single factor that made him the successful jockey he was. He just went for things regardless of the consequences, saw a gap, rode a line, stole girlfriends with aplomb.

Nat's anxieties certainly made a lot more sense to him now, but he was also conscious of the fact that his revelations had opened the case wide open. His mind sifted through the information with no real conclusions. Who would know about Nat and any misdemeanours his young conditionals might have committed? The time frames were very wide, too wide. Over fifteen years in fact. It had to be someone who was around then and now. Or maybe there were several people involved?

Nat was in a reflective mood. 'Listen, whilst we are truth telling, I wanted to say something, Finn. I'm sorry about Livvy, truly I am but if it's any consolation, she means the world to me and I'd be lost without her. And for the record I'm glad that we are now talking, at last.'

Finn nodded. 'So am I.'

‘So, you and Hattie, do you think there’s any future in it?’

‘What? Nah. She’s a great girl but no, she is a friend, that’s all and far too young. Have you noticed her healthy appetite? If I was race riding, it would be really annoying.’

Nat chuckled. ‘Yes. I have actually. Anyway, stop changing the subject. Are you sure about you being just friends? Seems to me you’re protesting too much. And you’re not race riding, so what’s the problem? You never could see what was in front of your bloody nose.’

‘Well, I never predicted Livvy running off with you, that was for sure.’

‘I’m sorry. We couldn’t help ourselves.’

‘I know.’ Finn realised he did know and understand, sort of. It was progress. He drifted off to sleep wondering about Nat’s revelations, Hattie and praying that Sam would make contact and that the identity of the blackmailer would be revealed once and for all.

They got a message the following morning as they ate breakfast.

‘Sam says to meet him in the empty fish warehouse on the coastal road at eleven.’ Finn glanced at his watch. ‘OK. Shall we walk, it’s not far.’

Nat had eaten an egg and was munching half a slice of toast. The bacon, mushrooms and the rest of the fried bread lay untouched. Finn didn’t miss the wasting, he realised, the endless watching and counting every mouthful.

Nat fiddled around with his 'phone and brought up a map of the area.

'I reckon it'll take about ten minutes. Look, I think we should walk

one by one with a gap of at least fifteen minute intervals to avoid being followed. Good idea?'

Hattie looked longingly at Nat's plate. 'OK. Good plan. If you're not having that bacon, do you mind if I do?'

Nat laughed. 'Be my guest!' He winked at Finn who grinned back. Nat's good spirits were restored, it seemed. He was beginning to enjoy having Nat around again, he realised.

'Right. Nat can go first, then me and you can join us and get there for just past eleven.'

Hattie frowned. 'Why do I have to go last?' she said in a small voice.

Finn shrugged.

Nat put his arm around Hattie's shoulders. 'Listen, it's in case we get into a mess then we know we can rely on you to sort it out. First rule of combat,' Nat tapped his head, 'is knowing how to deploy your personnel, and you are definitely brainier than me or Finn. See?'

Hattie pouted and then grinned like a little child.

'Oh, alright.'

Finn had been about to explain that he was just trying to keep her safe which would have made her feel very patronised, but realised that Nat had dealt with the potential glitch far more smoothly. He had always been able to do that, Finn thought enviously. He could charm the birds off the trees.

'OK, I'll leave in about an hour.' Nat was right to be cautious and hopefully their planning would pay off. He wondered what Sam would have to say. He felt a frisson of excitement and anticipation. Soon it would all be over.

Chapter 24

It was a grey day, made worse by the icy wind rolling in from the sea. The scenery was undoubtedly breath taking, a mixture of shades of pewter from the stone, the greenery and the soft purple and shimmering amethyst heathers. But it was the light that was so unusual, almost celestial and the lack of trees which meant that there was little shelter against the wind. Hattie took in the scenery as she strode off to meet Sam. Finn, then Nat had already left, and she decided that they were being gallant in asking her to follow them. Nat had been charming in stating that she should arrive last, because she was the brains of the operation, but she hadn't been fooled. She was now feeling anxious and annoyed. Supposing she missed all the drama? She pulled her collar and continued to stride out along the bay road. The small town quickly gave way to a bleak coastal road with very little traffic. Up ahead she spotted a low building, which was unkempt and partially derelict. This must be the place. She imagined a happy reunion with the young man she had seen being attacked at Wetherby. She was certain that he would fill in the gaps, come back with them to Walton and speak to the authorities, so that the blackmailer would be brought to justice. Everything would be solved.

She decided to send her brother, Will, a quick text just in case their plans were thwarted.

'In Shetland with Finn. Going to meet Sam Foster. Don't ask. Will text you later x'

At least if she didn't send a further text, he would know where to find her. Couldn't they track 'phone signals these days too? She pondered on Will's reaction. He'd be annoyed with her and surprised, she knew he would have certainly dissuaded her from coming on such a trip had she discussed it with him, which is why she hadn't.

The place appeared to be deserted. The building was low and long, sufficient to house several hundred crates of fish, she supposed. She walked up to the large doors and put her ear to the wood. Apart from the wind whipping up from the sea, the place was eerily silent. As she advanced towards the building, her heart began to thump alarmingly. There was no sign of life, no noise, no flicker of movement, nothing. She had expected to find Finn and Nat waiting for her. What the hell was going on? She wanted to ring Finn but decided that this might place him in jeopardy if he didn't have his 'phone switched to silent. As she turned the corner, she recoiled as she noticed a dark 4x4 with blacked out windows parked there. Shit, she was willing to bet that the bloody headlights would be blue. Quickly, she ran out onto the pathway that led to the coastal road and hoped her footsteps would be drowned out by the sound of the wind, seagulls and the hiss of the sea. She ran and ran until her chest was about to burst, searching for cover and found it amongst the coarse grasses of the sand dunes. She squatted down and peered at the warehouse. Her heart thundered in her ears as she realised that she might just have got away with it. There was no one following her and then elation turned to fear as she realised why. She suddenly felt her arms being pinned behind her, everything went black as a sharp smell entered her nostrils and a cloth was pressed over her mouth. Her last thought before she lost consciousness was that Nat's faith in her was completely misplaced.

Finn's head felt like it had been prised open with a fork. The pain was excruciating. He dimly remembered the violent rocking of a vehicle over uneven ground, the low murmurs of the voices of his captors, and being thrown somewhere cold, with the foul scent of decay and winter all around him. He tried to rub his head to ease the pain but quickly realised that his arms were tied, and his legs were numb with cold.

A humming noise emanated from across the room. He opened his eyes and was suddenly blinded by light. The humming became more urgent, so he opened his eyes to see Hattie, her auburn curls hanging over her pale face, her green eyes wide with fear. Her eyes were locked upon his, but though he tried to talk to her, his mouth was stuffed with something smooth and tight, digging into his flesh. He made out the shapes of Nat and Sam, similarly trussed up, lying on the floor.

They were in a small room, the walls were a dirty off white colour, poorly plastered, with a gas heater was standing in one corner. It was unlit. The temperature was below freezing, and he began to shiver involuntarily. He dozed again until the place was blazing with light which hurt his eyes. He could hear the footsteps of their captors walking up and down surveying them.

'Well, well, well. You played a good hand Mr McCarthy, Nat Wilson and Harriet.' The voice became angry. 'But I told you not to get involved Harriet and you wouldn't listen, would you? Why couldn't you have left it to Mr McCarthy, hey?'

The voice was familiar and all the more shocking for being so. Finn tried to rub his sore eyes but with his hands tied, he had to let them itch. Pavel had cracked him over the head, and he was feeling dizzy. He took in the scene and the faces came into focus. It couldn't be! He looked up to see Dr Pinkerton gazing at them and the blond stable lad, Pavel, pointing a gun at Hattie's head. Spud stood by the door, acting as look out. Finn could see the fear and shock in Harriet's eyes and her valiant attempt to look brave. At the same time, he recognised the metallic taste of blood in his mouth. He wriggled and stretched his arms and felt the knot that had been tied in the rope which bound them. His fingers felt for the end of the rope as he tried to visualise the knot. There was some play in it, and he wondered if he could work it loose enough to slip his hand out.

Dr Pinkerton sighed. 'Well, I'm sure you've worked it out by now, all of you. You wanted to know what the problem was with your conditionals, well, I am behind the problem. I have blackmailed a whole network of jockeys, Nat included, over the years.'

He paused to let this sink in, clearly enjoying the effect it was having. Hattie was staring at him in absolute horror. Dr Pinkerton looked supremely pleased with himself and Finn felt anger coursing through him. Nat looked sick.

'You see in my job, I find myself in a position of power over the waifs and strays that visit me with their ridiculous problems. Those lads are all registered with me, they come to me and confide their deepest darkest, grubby little secrets, things they would hate to be exposed and then I use it against them. All they had to do for me is a little favour to stop me telling the world, just stop the odd horse or two. Simple really. Then I put on my bets, an outsider comes through to win because two or three lads pull their horses and I make a load of money. Easy, really.'

Finn began to tug at the loose end with one hand and loop the rope back, so he could ease the knot. God, it was impossible. He glanced at Harriet's tearful face, tried to smile to reassure her and redoubled his efforts. He had to get them out of there.

Dr Pinkerton was striding about, deep in his own thoughts.

'Want to know how it started? Well, it was your old friend, Nat Wilson, that got me into it.' He viciously kicked the prone figure of Nat. 'You see, years ago he was involved in a car accident when a boy died. I was working as a junior doctor then and on call when they came in.' His voice vibrated with rage. 'There was a beautiful girl in the car with him. I later fell in love with her and married her. She was perfect except for the scars she still bears on her cheek to this day. You see, Nat was driving, and I know he moved the boy into the driver's seat to save his own skin. It was obvious from the injuries to the boy, but the coroner was an idiot and didn't want to look into the cause of death more deeply.'

He paused theatrically so they could absorb this information, rather like an actor.

'They say that vengeance is a dish best served cold and so it turned out. He was cleared of charges by the useless police, so I extracted my own revenge by blackmailing him to pull horses. He caused the death of an innocent young lad but also facial injuries to my beautiful wife and that I can never forgive. As you know I like to bet and before long I got a taste for it. As a GP in a racing town, I was in a position to know so many of those silly conditionals' secrets, and I then expanded my business by using those against them. I needed to involve Teasdale and the odd heavy,' he pointed at Pavel and Spud, 'to add some menace. It was all going so well, then the lads had to go and get a conscience, didn't they! Sam refused to co-operate, Connor and Harry both deliberately injured themselves, so they couldn't ride, and then a bloody ex-jockey with a social conscience is appointed as their mentor! Paddy worked out what was going on and was too close to Sam, so he had to be disposed of too.' He spat these last words out and kicked Finn's leg viciously.

He turned to Hattie. 'I told you to leave it and not get involved, Harriet but you wouldn't listen, would you? And now I'll have to leave you here. I have one last big race planned and then Honor and I will be far away by the time you're free. Not that she's involved, you understand, but she does like to spend money, loads of it.' Hattie whimpered. 'Don't worry, my dear. Your mum suspected you were in Shetland, apparently you mentioned it out of the blue, so before long they'll come looking for you, in a day or so but by then I'll be long gone…' He saluted his heavies, Spud and Pavel. 'We will all make an absolute fortune. You see the race I have selected is at Cheltenham. The winner will be an outsider ridden by an honourable amateur who no one would suspect. And they'd be right, because I have something on each of the other jockeys and they will do my bidding. With other jockeys being more obliging than Sam and Nat here, I shall clean up. And no one will ever find us. So, we'll take our leave and by the time you have escaped, we'll be long gone. Bonne chance!'

Finn had been manoeuvring himself into position near an empty Coke can, edging closer and closer. The effort of moving stealthily was excruciating especially as his head felt like it was filled with cotton wool. If he could just create a distraction, then he could maybe grab Pavel's ankle and trip him up. He had to do something rather than lie there all meek and mild. He had to give it a go. He edged nearer and nearer as Pinkerton droned on and on and with one deft movement lifted both his legs up and kicked the can behind him. It clattered noisily. Then all hell broke loose, Pavel pointed his gun at Finn, Nat launched himself in front of his friend as a shot rang out like a whip cracking into the dark skies.

Chapter 25

Hattie stirred. Pale yellow light was pouring through the crack in the ceiling. Her head ached, as if it had been shaken or kicked. Bit by bit appalling snatches of what happened arranged themselves into some sort of order, like pieces of a jigsaw puzzle. Finn, Nat and Sam. Where the hell were they? Hattie raised herself from the rough, dirt floor to see Finn's outline, his jacket and jeans beside her. There were two other figures slumped beside him. Sam and Nat. She remembered that she had come to find them, been given chloroform or something and had passed out. At first, she had been pleased to hear a familiar voice, that of her friend Dr. Pinkerton and then joy had turned to shock as he outlined his leading role in the blackmail. She felt utterly wretched about him. Then Finn had kicked a can and the noise caused Pavel to shoot at him, but Nat had got in the way. They were all bound tightly with rope, with duct tape stretched over their mouths. Sam had a trickle of blood coming from his head and appeared to be unconscious. Finn laid on his side, and then there was Nat, his thigh crimson red, his face pale. And it was bloody freezing, but she noticed that Pinkerton, Pavel and Spud had gone.

'Hmm.' Hattie tried to speak, and Finn opened his eyes. Hattie was amazed how relieved she felt, and it gave her renewed strength just to be able to see him. If she could creep towards Finn and position herself behind him then maybe he could use his fingers to untie her, then she could check on Nat and go and get help?

'Hmm.' Hattie wriggled her eyebrows by way of communication and began the awkward task of pushing her legs out flat in front of her and shuffling her bottom towards them. Her limbs felt stiff and her stomach growled with hunger. The effort was exhausting so she had to rest a little and then tried the same process all over again. Eventually, after what felt like an age, she was close to Finn's back and she had to shuffle backwards until she felt the reassuring pressure from his fingers. Finn had been dozing, his fingers felt horribly cold, but he started to feel around the knots and began to tug. His fingers brushed hers and she felt utter relief, he had clearly understood her plan. In time surely, they would be free and as the least injured, she would need to go for help. She felt slightly dizzy when she realised that their lives depended on her.

Bloody hurry up, Hattie tried to speak, but it was impossible. Finn appeared to give up and she gave his fingers a squeeze which revived him, and he started the process all over again. Just as despair washed over her, she resolved to wait for a few more minutes, as Finn continued to pull at the knot with fumbling fingers, when she felt the rope loosen and she was miraculously untied.

Quickly she undid the ropes which bound her feet, ripped the tape from her mouth and untied Finn and Sam.

'Thank God!' She hugged Finn.

'You OK?'

'Yeah apart from head. I feel a bit weird.' He rubbed his eyes and looked round him. Hattie guessed he was concussed judging by his confused expression. Several blows to the head from Pavel had done its job, she guessed.

'Listen, Nat's been shot. I think it looks worse than it is.' Finn frowned at this but didn't disagree. Nat held his hand to his thigh and groaned. There appeared to be heavy blood loss. Hattie looked at the red stain on his denim jeans and felt alarm course through her. God, this was serious. She took off her coat and folded it up to make a pillow for him. She gently lifted his head and placed it underneath.

'That bastard Pavel shot you,' she told him. He groaned in response. She looked around the bleak room to see what she could use to prevent further blood loss. There was a dusty cupboard in one corner, a dirty sink with running water and a few grimy tins of beans and soup. She searched in the cupboard found some rags and tied them around Nat's leg, tightly like a tourniquet. The blood flow seemed to ease. He shuddered in pain but managed to grin at her all the same. She searched around, found some damp matches, some cutlery and thankfully a tin opener. She fiddled with the gas heater and after three dead matches, the fourth lit up and the heater spluttered into light.

Hattie gave a little dance. 'Hurray! There's some tins and water.

Her eyes flicked over Sam. Sam! God, she needed to check him over. He looked younger than she remembered and was dressed in jeans and a warm coat. She gently slapped his face and his eyes flickered open.

'Sam, you're fine. You're with me, Nat and Finn. We came to find you. Nat's been shot, Finn is concussed but I'm fine and I'm going to get help.' He looked confused and groaned as he tried to stand. 'Where does it hurt?'

Sam gasped. 'God, my head and my ankle. I think it's broken.'

Gently Hattie lifted up the hem of his jeans and saw that the ankle was clearly swollen and red. She touched it and Sam leapt in pain.

'OK, OK. I'm sorry. You must have twisted and broken it when you fell.'

'You know all about Pinkerton and Teasdale blackmailing me and the others to fix races?'

'Yep. Listen, you all need medical attention. I'm going to go for help, so you'll be on your own for a bit. The heater is on, I'll leave water, some tins of beans and soup and I'll be back before you know it. Can you keep an eye on Nat? Is that OK?'

Sam's eyes widened but he nodded. 'How bad are they?' Sam glanced at the two older jockeys with concern.

'They're as tough as old boots the pair of them and mad like all you jockeys. Just try and keep them talking, keep them warm and give them some water. Don't worry.' Hattie lied. She had absolutely no idea how they were. Finn would certainly recover but Nat's injury might be something far worse. It might be a flesh wound, but would it bleed so much? She had no idea.

'What is this place, anyway?'

Sam looked around him. 'Well, it's not the barn I went to. It looks like a bothy. They must have moved us. These are dotted around Shetland for shelter, but they are never far from civilisation.'

'How far?'

Sam shrugged. 'Five or ten miles, maybe…'

Hattie grinned, feeling suddenly elated. She remembered that she had texted her brother, Will, so surely, he would send someone from the local force out to look for them? Then she remembered that she had mentioned the fish warehouse and they had been moved. Damn. Still, she should find someone who could help them? Suddenly, she thought of something. 'I suppose they took our 'phones?'

She searched in her pocket, Finn's and Sam's but it was clear that they had. Damn, Still, there wouldn't be any signal anyway.

Hattie looked at Nat's wound again, prodded it, saw him grimace and decided that she needed to go now. One glance outside told her it was still daylight, just, so she had to go, before it was too late. She reckoned that she'd have a couple of hours before darkness fell. She could do it. What was it Nat had said? She had the brains to sort everything out. She felt heartened by his words, even if he didn't really mean it. It would all soon be a distant memory they'd laugh about in the future. She hugged them all, told them she'd be back soon and stepped out into the cold with a renewed sense of purpose. She had to get help, find someone and then everything would be fine. Five or ten miles, Sam had said. She could do it. She was still reasonably fit, uninjured and three lives depended on her. No pressure then.

She took a few seconds to try to work out their location. There were precious few clues, just grey green hills as far as the eye could see and the distant sound of sheep. How the hell was she going to get help to Nat before he bled to death? On another day and in different circumstances Hattie thought she might like Shetland, the autumn view had a different colour palate to home, stone greys, blue-green grass, a clear-eyed ruggedness, which was very pleasing to the eye. There also seemed to be acres more sky than home, but how was that possible? God, she wished she'd taken more notice of that orienteering course she once went on at Uni, something about looking at which side the moss grew on trees and which way the grasses grew, which could give pointers about the direction. Was this right? She thought so, and it was downhill so all the better.

Hattie strode out, far quicker and more confidently than she felt, spurred on by images of Nat lying prostrate, bleeding and in need of urgent help which now seemed seared on the inside of her eyelids. On and on she went, in a kind of jog trot. To pass the time, she tried to entertain herself with songs. The Skye Boat song seemed appropriate, but she didn't really remember the words. The Proclaimers 'Five Hundred Miles' was a good one to march along to she found. She was just finishing her third rendition when she suddenly spotted a walled enclosure with a horse looking out over it. Hattie approached holding out her hand. The horse, a dapple grey was more of a pony, Highland if she was any judge. The old boy sniffed her hand and blew friendly, grassy breath over her face. She peered at his feet. He had been shod recently, so must be ridden, she reasoned.

'Are you up for a ride?' she asked him, 'because it'd really help if you were...'

If Hattie's throat was parched, then God knows how Nat was coping and riding somewhere would speed things up, surely. Besides, someone must ride and visit the horse so there had to be a house or a croft somewhere near, surely?

Hattie slipped her belt off and together with the laces from her Doc Martens, she fashioned makeshift reins to add to his halter, doubling the laces back over the horse's nose for greater control. The pony was quiet enough as she fiddled with the reins and scrambled up onto his back using the stonewall, after opening the gate first. At first, they walked and then images of the three males made her attempt to trot. It was uncomfortable though and she bounced up and down awkwardly.

'Come on boy,' she urged him into a canter, letting him have his head and trusting that he would lead her somewhere sensible. She clung onto his mane and tried to relax into the rhythm, realising that all Daisy's lessons had not been in vain. Eventually she slowed and could see a small town in the distance. She urged the pony on to the hill, but he stopped clear and she soon saw why. They were at the top of a hillside, with rocks leading down to a mini loch. Hell. They could go all the way around, but it looked like miles, or she could scramble down and swim across into what looked like a small harbour with boats about. It looked like Scalloway. Reluctantly she jumped off the horse, now named Angus in her mind and she took off the makeshift reins and replaced her boots. She patted him and let him put his head down to eat.

'See you fella, thanks,' she said. She knew he would make his way back home. She scrambled back into her Doc Martens. She blew Angus a kiss and then set off down the rocks, slithering and scrambling, falling twice, tired but resolute. She had to get help right away.

At the water's edge Hattie took off her jacket and boots. Right, here goes, she thought, feeling like she had to consciously recall the swims of her pentathlon, it was no longer automatic. But she was a strong swimmer and the distance was relatively short compared to what she was used to. Just do front crawl, she told herself and then you'll get there quickest.

She dived in, the cold taking her breath and then swam. A bystander would have recognised her professional technique, the alternate breathing, the discipline. Closer, she paused and looked up, treaded water and checked her direction. And then set off again. Nearer the harbour, she heard voices.

'Look out, it's a wee lassie…'

'Over here, we'll pull you up. '

Hands reached down to grasp hers as she reached a sort of jetty.

They hauled her up.

Hattie took in the faces, a white haired, bearded man, another younger man wearing wellies and fishing clothes.

Gasping she tried to speak.

'Well lassie, that was quite some swim,' said the older man. 'You look to be in a bit of a hurry.'

'Quick. My friends are in trouble,' she said, 'they need an ambulance, they're stuck in a barn back there and one of them has been shot.' She wondered if there would still be time to stop the race. 'And I need to ring the police.'

Chapter 26

Finn was coming up to the last fence in the Gold Cup. His horse, Honourable Man, took the last at a huge leap and he was steeling himself for the biggest win of his career in front of a record crowd at Cheltenham. In a split second, he anticipated punching the air in the winner's enclosure, accepting all the plaudits that were bound to come his way. He imagined Livvy's face lighting up, thrilled that she had stayed with Finn after all that nonsense with Nat. They could put all that behind them now. But fate had something else in store for him as, midway over the fence, a loose horse careered into Honourable Man's rear, appearing to come from nowhere. In horrible slow motion, he felt his horse twist under him, gallantly trying to scramble over the brush fence, but it was hopeless. He felt himself falling, heard the thunder of hooves all around him and the gasp of the crowd as he tried to curl up tightly into a ball. It suddenly went dark as he was hit over the back of his head by a flailing hoof.

Shards of light penetrated his sight, he was aware of a someone holding his hand, a faint medicinal aroma and realised that his whole body was bruised and painful. His mouth felt horribly dry, like he had spent the night on the tiles, but he was almost sure he hadn't been drinking. Something momentous had happened, he knew that, but he couldn't exactly remember what. He ought to feel glad, triumphant even. He felt incredibly woozy and different faces kept coming into focus. Dr Christopher Pinkerton and then that Polish stable lad, Pavel, but for the life he had no idea why. The pressure on his hand became firmer.

'Hey Finn. How are you feeling?'

He opened his eyes fully. He was lying in a high bed in a white room with strip lighting, there were several bunches of flowers on the side. An auburn haired girl was gazing at him. Hattie. A flashback suddenly came to him, of being in a stone barn, somewhere remote, of feeling terrified and panic stricken as someone glared at him and fired. My God, they had cracked the case and Nat had been shot!

Hattie grinned. 'You're in hospital, do you remember what happened? Well, we got them. Sam is fine, he'll be calling in later.'

'And Nat?'

Hattie bit her lip. 'He was shot in the thigh. I think they are operating, but he's stable, so try not to worry.'

Finn stared at her. 'Do they think he'll be OK?'

Hattie nodded. 'He's made of stern stuff and he's in good hands.'

Finn gazed at her, well aware that she was an awful liar and she hadn't exactly answered his question.

'Where am I? I mean we're not still in the Shetlands, surely?'

'No, you were all airlifted to Aberdeen. Do you remember? Teasdale, Pavel, Spud and Pinkerton are all locked up. Sam is in here too with a broken ankle, but he'll be fine. I've just been to see him, and he sends his best. He told me to tell you that you are the best coach ever!'

Finn suddenly remembered. 'God, it wasn't the drugs was it? It was race fixing and it was Dr Pinkerton who was the brains behind it!'

Hattie nodded. 'Yep. The conditionals and some other well known jockeys, Nat included, were all blackmailed to pull races. Sam has told the police everything and the gang are all in custody as we speak.'

Finn took this in. He felt huge relief and like he wanted to dance a jig, but he didn't think he could what with the pain.

'It was Pinkerton then who was behind it all…'

Hattie gave a weak smile. 'Yes. The good doctor turned out to be not so good after all. He knew all this stuff about the lads and used it to blackmail them. He was desperate to avenge Honor, you see. Something about a car accident which caused an injury to Honor's cheek. Then he blackmailed more and more jockeys demanding more and more money from them. He stupidly thought a lavish lifestyle might save his crumbling marriage.'

Finn nodded remembering that the doctor and his wife did not seem at all well suited.

'So, it was Teasdale and Pinkerton?'

'Yes. Mainly Pinkerton, actually. I think he even blackmailed Teasdale to play ball. Christopher knew about Gina being pregnant with his child, you see. Teasdale and Gina were having an affair.'

Finn noticed Hattie blinking back tears. It must be very hard to discover that a close family friend, someone who had been a confidante and supporter could turn out to be a master criminal. Finn suddenly felt incredibly tired. Then another fragment of memory came back to him.

'Who shot Nat? I know we were in the bothy and Pinkerton had us tied up and was explaining how he did everything and then I kicked a can, and someone fired…'

'Pavel, it was Pavel. He was a sort of hired thug. You were lucky though. Nat lunged in front of you and took a bullet in his thigh.'

Finn shrugged and felt ashamed. He had been so angry with Nat about Livvy and the car accident, had been churlish and grudging about forgiving him and the man literally took a bullet for him. God, supposing he never got to thank him?

'You'll let me know about Nat?'

Hattie nodded. 'Course.'

'And don't sugar the pill, just tell me.'

Hattie nodded gravely.

'So, how did you get out and get help?'

Hattie flushed. 'Well, I sort of found a Highland pony to ride then swam to shore. Some fishermen rescued me, and I was able to raise the alarm. I had managed to send a text to Will before going to the warehouse and he sent people out to try and find us. He's here now too, though he's angry with us for not telling him where we were going. Still all's well that ends well.'

Finn smiled at her understatement.

'He wouldn't have let you come if you told him, would he?'

'Oh no. Don't worry I can handle it.' Finn had no doubt about that. He looked at her in wonderment.

'Bloody hell. You went off on your own, then rode and swam all that way. You saved us, didn't you? We might have died otherwise.'

Hattie shrugged and looked embarrassed. 'You'd have done the same for me, you know you would.'

Finn shook his head admiringly. 'You are amazing! Remind me never to fall out with you, Harriet Lucas.'

'I hope you never will.' Hattie smiled. 'Hey, I knew my pentathlon skills would come in handy one day, after all those years of training.' She frowned as she watched him unsuccessfully trying to stifle a yawn. 'Now you get some rest. I'll come back later.'

Finn watched as she walked out of the ward. She went a few steps.

'We got them, Hattie, we got them!'

Hattie turned back and grinned. 'We did Finn, yes we did.'

'Thank you. You saved my life.'

Hattie smiled. 'It was nothing.' But Finn knew that it was most definitely something, an amazing, second chance at life. He just hoped that his friend, Nat, would be as lucky. Hattie had given him this opportunity and he had to grab it with both hands.

Epilogue

The crematorium was cold but jammed full of racing people, all determined to say goodbye to one of their own. Hattie and Finn sat together but Finn had been asked to do a reading and tell some racing anecdotes. As he stood at the lectern, he realised it was going to be hard to get the tone right, to temper the sombre occasion with some wit which highlighted the character of his friend. He disliked public speaking at the best of times, especially on such an occasion, when he knew he had to keep his own feelings in check and put on a good show for his friend.

Vince Hunt was in attendance and lots of his staff, Paddy's ex-wife Lisa, her children, assorted relatives, Sam, Harry and Connor and some people he assumed were journalists. The unmasking of Dr Christopher Pinkerton as the master blackmailer had attracted a lot of media attention and reignited the debate about the integrity of racing once again. Finn looked at the coffin, inhaled the scent of lilies from the numerous bouquets and steeled himself to begin.

'Paddy Owen was my friend and a brilliant jockey. The fact that there are so many people here today demonstrates the high esteem in which he was held…'

He saw Hattie smiling at him as he paused to survey the large crowd. 'He was a thoroughly decent man with strong family values and integrity. He loved racing and was committed to the highest standards of behaviour, which is why the manner of his death, is doubly hard to bear. But we must rise above this and remember Paddy for his superb, competitive riding, his sense of humour, his support and kindness to everyone. But it is especially his integrity that we should celebrate. To not do this is to let those who want to ruin and discredit our sport for personal gain, win and this cannot, must not happen. Otherwise, we will sully Paddy's memory.'

There was a murmur of approval which rippled along the rows of mourners. He looked at the rapt expression on Lisa's face and knew how much she appreciated his words, and this gave him the courage to continue for her and Paddy's sakes.

Christmas had been and gone for another year along with all its craziness, glitter and endless good cheer. Now everyone was bracing themselves for New Year's Eve, the resolutions, drunken promises and hope. Finn always liked the New Year, loved the new beginnings. He was pleased to be invited to the Lucas's annual New Year's Eve party but had felt slightly persona non grata, after everything that had happened in the last few weeks. After all, he and Hattie had uncovered a major betting scam. The final denouement had had huge repercussions for the Lucas family and Finn was not at all sure how he might be received. When close friends were involved, and loyalties tested, then it was hard to know how people might feel towards someone who had been instrumental in their downfall. He wasn't even sure how Hattie felt. Christopher Pinkerton had been a close family friend for years. She had been very quiet after everything came to a head and the whole case cracked open like some great piñata, flinging debris about rather than sweeties.

Finn found himself clutching a bottle of decent red wine, knocking tentatively on the Lucas's front door, avoiding the now bedraggled Christmas wreath, his collar pulled up against the cold, listening to the festive music and the hum of garbled conversations. Hattie came to the door, admitting him in a burst of light and warmth. She was wearing an eye catching tight black dress, high heels and her dark auburn hair was piled up on her head in a messy up do. She looked self-conscious, and utterly adorable.'

'Come in, come in. Everyone's here, even Tony Murphy. They are all dying to know how we cracked the case and I am struggling how to explain some parts of it.'

Finn kissed the cheek she proffered.

'Really?'

Hattie looked ill at ease. 'Well, I'm sure you can explain about the racing bits better than me.'

Finn took in her strained appearance.

'Are you alright?'

Hattie nodded. 'I do know it's all true, it's just that I still don't like it. Christopher was a sort of a hero for me and it's hard to take in, I suppose. I'm such a fool.'

Finn grinned. 'Look, I get it. All your illusions have been shattered. It will take some getting used to, that's all. You mustn't blame yourself either. Is Honor here too?'

'Yes'. She bit her lip. 'Turns out there were lots of tensions in the relationship anyway. She is shocked but coping. Nat is here and Livvy. He's in a wheelchair but doing fine. He's in good spirits actually.'

Finn grinned. He had visited Nat in hospital and had been kept up to date with his health. He was going to make a full recovery and he would be able to go back to riding. And with his good looks and charm, a position in TV presenting beckoned, so either way Nat Wilson would survive, and Finn was pleased. Nat still had a few more years riding and would be keen to get to the top once again. He owed Nat a great deal, the way he had leapt in front of Finn meant that Nat had actually saved his life. He had even run into Livvy a few times and had made his peace with her, which was real progress.'

'Come on then, let's face the music.'

Hattie nodded and entered the busy front room where all eyes swivelled towards them. It was time to reveal what had really happened. Mr Lucas turned off the Christmas compilation CD, just as Mariah Carey was just about to reveal all she wanted for Christmas. Finn looked at the assembled guests as Will trust a glass into his hands and raised his own.

'To Finn, Nat and Hattie. Now tell us how you bloody well did it?' His gaze held more than a little professional curiosity.

'So, it all started with the conditionals. Sam was beaten up after he'd won a race, then went missing, Connor was involved in a hit and run and then Paddy was killed. We thought that there was some drug dealing going on, but it was hard to find out the details.'

Will nodded. 'The police are currently making inquiries, I can't say much but it seems unrelated to the race fixing.'

Finn's money was on West and Boothroyd, but he knew better than to push it. Tony Murphy raised an eyebrow. Finn wondered if he'd be called upon to investigate the drug issues.

Hattie took up the story. 'We were worried about what had happened to the young jockeys. Paddy was suspicious about the race fixing and that was why Pavel pushed him off the Clock Tower stand at Doncaster. Pinkerton was on the scene and planted the epilepsy medication to cast doubt on the reason for Paddy's fall. I can confirm that Paddy did not have epilepsy and was murdered by Pavel at the behest of Pinkerton. He realised that something strange was going on and was going to share his concerns with Finn. Pavel got to him before he was able to do that.'

Honor paled. 'Christopher was involved in that? I knew he was a fool, I was suspicious about where he got his money from. I thought he'd just got lucky on the horses. I had no idea that he was blackmailing jockeys.'

Finn smiled. Even though their relationship had apparently been over for years, it must still be hard to find out about your partner's criminal activities, especially when carried on under your nose.

'Yes. Christopher and Teasdale were involved and used Pavel and Spud as heavies. We were still thinking that Sam was involved in drugs but then Nat came and spoke to me and told me that he was being blackmailed by someone and suddenly it looked like the same thing which was happening to Sam.'

Everyone turned to look at Nat who was flanked by Livvy.

'Yeah, I was being blackmailed for something that happened years ago. Something that I very much regret. You see, me and Honor were involved in a car accident in which a man died…'

Honor cut in before Nat could continue. 'But you were not driving, and you must not blame yourself,' she continued, 'it was a tragic accident.'

Nat gave her an uncertain smile. 'Anyway, Hattie worked out that Sam was in the Shetland and we all set off there to find him. Nothing would have happened if Finn hadn't been so dedicated to his job and conscientious in checking the welfare of his young charges. Anyway, we knew that something big was coming up and worked out that me and a few conditionals were booked to ride in a race at Cheltenham where Pinkerton had something on most of the jockeys except one who happened to be riding the outsider. That jockey, Alfie Dwyer, an amateur famed for being strait laced and trustworthy, would not be suspected, so it was the perfect race. We even nicknamed Dwyer, the Vicar. Pinkerton manipulated the jockeys to pull their mounts, so that the horse with the longest odds would win netting Pinkerton a fortune. He had a whole squad of associates who would put smallish amounts of money on the horse at roughly the same time to avoid suspicion. The horse who he planned to back, had odds of 35-1, so he would have netted a small fortune.'

Honor looked faint. 'But how did Christopher manage to blackmail all these people?'

Finn cleared his throat. 'I'm afraid that your husband used his position as their GP in the area to gain sensitive information from the conditionals and jockeys to blackmail them to pull races. This was the last race Christopher wanted to fix. He had been at it for a few years before, but things came to a head when Sam refused to be blackmailed and simply ran away. And Connor and Harry both avoided riding by injuring themselves after Sam disappeared. If it wasn't for Sam's bravery, then none of this would have come to light.'

All heads swivelled to the pale young man dressed in a check shirt in the corner.

'Yes. I hadn't been with Teasdale long before it became apparent that to keep my job, I would be required to comply with Teasdale's requests to pull horses. I didn't pull Saffron Sun, he won, and I was beaten up because of it. I knew Connor Moore and knew he had been asked to pull races too and we knew they were planning a big job. Connor threatened to tell the authorities and was run over by Teasdale to put the frighteners on him. I decided to get the hell out of there and lie low after that. Christopher Pinkerton was very threatening. I had tried to tell Paddy but didn't want him to be compromised. I asked him to keep the notes of my research and sent him postcards to hint at what was going on. When Paddy was killed by Pavel, Teasdale, and Pinkerton decided it was getting risky and they planned one last job.'

Mrs Lucas shook her head. 'What I don't get is why you didn't tell Finn here?'

'Because I barely knew him, and I thought the pair of them, Teasdale and Pinkerton would discredit me. Now, I know him, I realise, that I was wrong. I should have trusted him.'

Finn sighed. Things would have been so much easier if he had. He took up the story.'

'Hattie and I got Sam's postcards and realised that the notes referred to race fixing. But Pinkerton wanted to find Sam before they embarked on their last job. He thought Sam would ruin their plans. But Hattie worked out where Sam was, and it was a race to get to him before they did.'

Hattie wriggled her eyebrows. 'Yes, it was the visit to your mother's house that gave it away. She's Scottish isn't she and your sister mentioned that your grandmother lived in the Shetland Isles, so what better place to hide? But then Pinkerton tied us up in an old barn and we had to get out.'

Finn grinned. 'Hattie really came into her own escaping and raising the alarm.' She blushed.

Honor frowned. 'What information did Christopher use to blackmail the jockeys?'

Finn looked at both Sam, Harry Connor. GPs were in a unique position to acquire sensitive information and all the lads had been registered with him. Finn was not about to reveal any information. Sam had taken cocaine to boost his nerves when he had first ridden in races, Connor had confided his worries about his sexuality and Harry had betrayed his girlfriend and had an STD. All this information Christopher had used to manipulate and blackmail vulnerable young men who relied on their bosses to give them opportunities and support them. Teasdale had been called upon by Pinkerton to apply yet more pressure. The actual scam had been going on for several years, and there had been a pattern with established jockeys also being called on to pull horses from time to time. Pinkerton used the money to fund his lifestyle and as his relationship with Honor deteriorated, he became increasingly desperate to lavish money on her. So, the race fixing became more frequent. Of course, Finn wasn't going to reveal anyone's secrets, not even Nat's.

He shrugged. 'I guess we'll never know now, but it would have been deeply personal and enough to cause serious harm if it was disclosed.'

Tony seemed confused. 'So, what was Christopher Pinkerton's motive. Was it just greed?'

Finn looked at Honor pointedly. 'I think love and vengeance may have had something to do with it…'

Honor scowled. 'Not real love. Christopher was a domineering and controlling man. I was much younger when I first met him, and he was charming and handsome then. I was dazzled by him but once we married, he changed. He became aggressive and controlling, violent sometimes…' She shook her head angrily. 'God, what that man put me through. I was frightened of my own shadow. He tried to buy me, more so, as things grew worse between us. Of course, it never worked. He blamed Nat for being in the car when we had the accident that caused my scar.' Honor fingered the scar on the left side of her face. 'He was more bothered about it than ever I was. I think he thought it made me less perfect in his eyes and he hated Nat because of that…' Honor looked at Livvy. 'I didn't actually know what happened on that evening, we had a great time with lots of alcohol and Nick Drayton drove us home. There was a terrible accident and I was out of it for a while… Nat pulled me out, but it was too late for Nick.'

Whatever Honor did or did not know about that evening, it was clear that she had no intention of revealing it.

A voice broke in from the back. It was Vince Hunt. 'I can only apologise, I was taken in by Christopher and Teasdale. They said that I wasn't placing my horses carefully enough, that if I listened to them, I would double my winners.' He paused and ran his hands through his hair, looking distressed. 'Things were bad, you see, I needed more horses, I listened, even let Teasdale help me with the entries, but I knew nothing about any of this…'

Daisy patted his arm. 'It's OK, Dad, don't upset yourself. You've been cleared of any involvement, just take it easy…'

There was a silence as they contemplated just how much the respectable doctor had misled them all.

'Well, you've all done a marvellous job,' declared Mr Lucas. 'It's a pity that Nat was shot, but it could have been so much worse.'

Finn grinned at Nat. That was an understatement.

'Now I propose that we get this party started properly.'

'To Finn, Nat and Hattie!'

As the music was turned back on and the drink flowed, Finn chatted to Sam, Connor, Harry and Nat. All were doing fine now, on the surface at least, though he knew that it might take a little longer for the invisible wounds to heal.

'So, do you have any New Year's resolutions?' Finn asked Nat.

Nat nodded. 'To be a better person, to deserve your friendship and Livvy's love.' He paused. 'And to make some amends, have you heard that Nick Drayton's family have found that a mystery benefactor has paid off their mortgage for them? I suspect other windfalls may also come their way. So that's a start.'

Finn smiled. 'It is indeed.' He had made his peace with Nat for what he had done. Nat wasn't perfect by any stretch of imagination but on the positive side, he had literally taken a bullet which was intended for him, so that had to count for something.

'How about you?'

'Maybe one or two.' Nat winked and nodded over to where Hattie was standing, and Finn made his way towards her. Everyone assembled as midnight approached. He grasped her hand as the bells began to strike. He had accepted what had happened with Nat and Livvy and now he was ready to move on with his life. He was looking forward to the New Year, and he saw it as full of possibilities and hope. Finn had always liked the rituals, the resolutions, even singing Auld Lang Syne. As Hattie turned and smiled at him, his heart swelled. He couldn't think of anyone he would rather spend it with.

About Charlie De Luca

Charlie De Luca was brought up on a stud farm, where his father held a permit to train National Hunt horses, hence his lifelong passion for racing was borne. He reckons he visited most of the racecourses in England by the time he was ten. He has always loved horses but grew too tall to be a jockey. Charlie lives in rural Lincolnshire with his family and a variety of animals, including some ex-racehorses.

Charlie has written several racing thrillers which include: Rank Outsiders, The Gift Horse, Twelve in the Sixth and Making Allowances.

You can connect with Charlie via twitter; @charliedeluca8 or visit his website.
Charlie is more than happy to connect with readers, so please feel free to contact him directly using the CONTACT button on the website.
www.charliedeluca.co.uk

If you enjoyed this book, then please leave a review. It only needs to be a line or two, but it makes such a difference to authors.

Praise for Charlie De Luca.

'He is fast becoming my favourite author.'

'Enjoyable books which are really well plotted and keep you guessing.'

'Satisfying reads, great plots.'

Printed in Great Britain
by Amazon